THE WIDOWS' TEA CHALLENGE

THE WIDOWS' TEA CHALLENGE

A Novel

by

JOANNE STUART SLOAN

Regimen Books

THE WIDOWS' TEA CHALLENGE

Copyright © 2020

Regimen Books
an imprint of Vision Press

http://vision-press.com

vision.press.books@gmail.com

All rights reserved. No part of this publication may be reproduced, stored in a retrieval system, or transmitted in any form without the prior written permission of the publisher.

ISBN 978-1-885219-85-5

Printed in the United States of America

Dedication

I grew up with widows. They were family members, church members, neighbors, and friends.

I dedicate this book to my mother and other strong women, who influenced me as I became an adult and then as a writer of this novel.

Acknowledgments

This novel could not have been published without my dear husband. He has inspired me as well as challenged me. Every day David amazes me with his strong work ethic and the help he has provided to so many writers.
He is the best editor I know.

My daughter, Cheryl, and son, Christopher, have supported me with their interest in my initial idea and through the writing of it.

Contents

1	January: The Challenge	1
2	February: Genevieve	21
3	March: Verity	41
4	April: Mary Olivia	63
5	May: Chattie	83
6	June: Genevieve	107
7	July: Verity	123
8	August: Mary Olivia	147
9	September: Chattie	169
10	October: Genevieve	189
11	November: Verity	207
12	December: Mary Olivia	235
13	January: New Horizons	257
Appendix		271

The History of English & American Tea
How To Make a Perfect Cup of Tea
Dessert Recipes
Book Club Questions

THE WIDOWS' TEA CHALLENGE

"It's never too late to be what you might have been."
Mary Ann Evans

1
JANUARY

⁓

THE CHALLENGE

"When you stop having dreams and ideals — well, you might as well stop altogether."
American singer Marian Anderson (1897-1993)

Thankful to find a parking place directly in front of Tessie's Tea Room, Chattie glanced at her watch and realized she was seven minutes late.

Why didn't I arrive on time or even early? Genevieve Shipman is in charge of the Tea, and it WILL start exactly at 2 p.m.

Little did she know that this afternoon's Widows' Tea would begin a revolution in her life — and also in the lives of the three new friends she was about to make.

She dusted large snowflakes from her jacket and rushed into the Tea Room. The wallpaper was decorated with pictures of teapots and teacups. As she walked past a tiny gift shop, she read a quote above the door: "There are few hours in life more agreeable than the hour dedicated to the ceremony known as afternoon tea."

Agreeable. I like that word. Will the Tea today be agreeable? She looked around at the smiling faces of the people in the room. Mostly women. A few men were scattered here and there.

She couldn't help but think what an inviting place it was to enjoy tea and conversation.

She saw three women in a small reserved alcove sitting at a round table next to a large window. As she walked toward them, she remembered when she met Genevieve.

Several months before she retired as dean of students at the local community college, she had worked with Genevieve, who was volunteering as a tutor. She teamed her up with a young woman named Heather, who needed help with her language skills. Always punctual and well prepared, Genevieve spent much time with Heather. In turn, the student responded positively to her white-haired mentor who encouraged her to excel.

When Genevieve invited her to join the Tea, she was excited. She asked her, though, for time to think about it. After praying about the invitation, she called her friend a few days later, telling her she would be honored to be a member.

Genevieve stood up as soon as she saw Chattie and then pulled the extra chair out for her to sit next to her.

"Chattie Milano, I want you ... to meet Verity Harris and Mary Olivia McDuff." Genevieve sometimes spoke haltingly because she had suffered a stroke years earlier.

"It's wonderful to meet you two. I've seen you together at charity events. I'm looking forward to knowing both ... the three of you better." She leaned forward and quietly said: "I'm honored to be part of The Widows' Tea."

They all laughed but not loud enough to disturb anyone around them.

"The privilege is ours," Verity said, smiling broadly.

Mary Oliva chimed in, "Glad you've joined us."

Mary Olivia and Verity are apparently close friends but polar opposites, she thought, sizing both of them up quickly. Verity is slender and neatly dressed. Flawless brown complexion. High cheekbones. She may have a Native American in her past. Mary Olivia is overweight and casually dressed. Little makeup. Her freckles and red hair cry out a Scotch-Irish ancestry.

Chattie couldn't stop smiling.

When was the last time I smiled this much? She knew it was before Roberto's death.

She sniffed the scent of apple pie from the large candle on the gold candleholder. As she gazed out the window at the overcast skies, she saw two Eastern bluebirds fly from atop an angel birdbath that was fast filling up with snow.

Bluebirds were Roberto's favorite birds. They are now my favorite.

"You are here … at exactly the right time," said Genevieve. "Here comes our server."

A plump waitress walked to their table — as if on cue — with two baskets of scones. She poured tea from a blue willow teapot into four dainty matching cups.

"Today we are having Lady Grey tea," said Genevieve. "I hope you like it."

"It's great," Chattie said, sipping the hot tea.

"What kind of scones are these?" asked Mary Olivia.

"Lemon yogurt scones with lemon curd to spread on them," said the waitress, who hurried to another table.

"I have never eaten a lemon yogurt scone. To tell the truth, I've never heard of a lemon scone."

Mary Olivia spread lemon curd on her scone and took two bites.

Chattie now remembered the last time she had smiled so much. It was the day before Roberto's death. She was in the bakery to pick up a grocery list from him. Since they were alone, Roberto asked her to dance. They loved to dance, but they had never done so in the bakery. She reluctantly consented to a slow dance knowing that a customer might come in. They danced and laughed for about ten minutes. After she left, she was smiling for a long time. Little did she know it would be their last dance.

"Well," Verity asked Mary Olivia. "What's your verdict?"

"Indescribable. But I'll try to describe the taste in one word: scrumptious."

The other three women ate a few bites of their scones and immediately agreed with Mary Olivia.

Chattie was sure she had made the right decision to join this group. She hoped to build a close relationship with her new friends. And she desired — and needed — the relaxed atmosphere the monthly Tea would provide.

The four continued to sip their tea and munch on their scones while chatting about large snowfalls of past years when everything came to a stop in Breeze Hill, Alabama.

"The snow is coming down fast," said Genevieve, "but we should be ... finished before the roads get bad."

Turning to Chattie, she said, "Tell us a little bit about yourself. Haven't you been a widow about a year?"

"A year next month. A difficult year. Of course, you three know better than I do about adjusting to widowhood."

"It certainly isn't easy," said Genevieve. "Now we want to hear about you."

"What do you want to know?" asked Chattie.

"Anything you want to tell us," Verity replied, patting Chattie on the arm. "By the way, you look so young. Not one gray streak in your brown hair."

"Thank you. If I look younger than 57, it must be genes. When my paternal grandmother died at 82, her face was as smooth as a baby's.

"My father was Dutch. My maiden name is Van den Berg, meaning 'of the mountains.' Of course, Holland has no mountains. My mother's maiden name was Johnson. English, of course. I lost both of them 10 years ago.

"My older brother and I had an idyllic childhood living at several national parks where my father served as a park ranger. When it was time for me to go to college, my parents retired to our family's farm in northwest Alabama. After getting a degree in business, I worked as assistant registrar at Breeze Hill Community College for many years and then as registrar. Five years ago I became dean of students. I retired when Roberto died."

Chattie sipped tea and wondered if she were talking too much. She could get carried away sometimes. She had to tell them, though, about her two boys.

"Oh, I can't forget the most important people in my life.

My twin sons. Antonio and Mario are freshmen at the University. They've been my rocks and have spent much time with me this last year. I'm so blessed."

"Italian names?" asked Mary Olivia.

"Yes. Roberto named the boys after his two grandfathers in Italy."

"Continuing family names is a good tradition," said Genevieve. "Are your twins identical?"

"No, fraternal twins. They are close but possess opposite personalities. Antonio is extroverted and athletic. Mario likes to read and study.

"Well, if you're like most people, you want to know about *my* name. Though my name is Chattie, I'm not quite as loquacious as my name suggests."

"Is it your real name?" asked Mary Olivia. "It's a bit unusual."

"I agree. I guess I shouldn't apologize about my name, but most people seem curious about it."

"I understand, believe me," said Verity, nodding. "Wait until you hear the names in my family."

"My mother had twin spinster sisters named Bertha Charlotte and Charlotte Bertha. You're probably thinking how odd to give twins the same names except for reversing the first and middle names. Well, my grandmother liked both names, so my grandfather convinced her to use both names. They went, though, by their nicknames Bertie and Chattie. Aunt Bertie — Bertha Charlotte — was quiet and introspective. She died last year. Aunt Chattie — Charlotte Bertha — is loquacious. She lives in a nursing home in Wichita, Kansas. At 92, she has several church friends who watch after her.

"It's obvious my mother named me after the talkative one. I talk regularly to Aunt Chattie on the phone, and, I can assure you, she can still hold a lively conversation."

The women smiled.

"Aunt Chattie does have many life experiences to share. Both of my aunts were missionary nurses in Brazil for over 30 years."

"What role models," Verity nodded.

"Yes. I was fortunate to grow up with their inspiring stories. I have letters they sent my mother. I treasure them."

The women grew quiet for a few minutes.

"Back to my name. I remember vividly in elementary school two of my playmates teasing me, 'Chattie's such a chatty. Chattie's such a chatty.' From that moment on I decided to talk only when necessary."

"Schoolmates can be cruel," said Mary Olivia. "I know from personal experience that chubby red-heads are often picked on."

"You understand then how I felt. It wasn't until I married Roberto that I came out of my shell and started talking more and being true to myself — and not to my name."

"Your husband had a stellar reputation as a businessman in the community," said Genevieve.

"I appreciate what you said. He was an extraordinary husband, father, and person. And I can't forget, chef."

Smiling, she stopped talking and sipped her tea and thought about how she had talked too much.

How rejuvenating. Finally after eleven months I'm having fun

— *and talking about Roberto without crying.*

Chattie watched as a tiny 60-something woman approached their table.

"Welcome to the Tea Room. I'm Tessie, the owner," she smiled. "How are the scones?"

"Perfect," said Genevieve.

"Could I get a recipe for them?" asked Verity. "I've never eaten lemon ones, and they're delicious."

"We have a cookbook called *Tessie's Tea Room Recipes* at our gift shop with all of our recipes."

"Good. I'm buying it before I leave."

"Enjoy your stay. Please let me know if I can be of any more help," Tessie said before going to the next table.

Slowly munching on a scone, Chattie relished each morsel. She wanted to appreciate every moment of this time with her new friends. And she looked forward to knowing more about them. How did they get their names? She had never known women named Genevieve or Verity. And there probably was a story behind Mary Olivia's beautiful name.

"I'm giving Pru the recipe book as soon as I return home," said Verity. "Maybe she'll try the scones soon."

Who is Pru?

"The tea is what we needed today with the weather so cold," said Genevieve, pulling her sweater closer around her slender body.

Chattie's mind wandered again to Roberto. Socializing. That was his thing. *He would like my being here today.*

Genevieve lightly tapped her teaspoon on the table. It was the slightest of noise, but it brought Chattie back to the present.

"It has been our custom, Chattie, to have our January meeting in a tea room. And the oldest member ... leads the first meeting of the year. Of course, I qualify. I didn't ten years ago when I formed the group. Albertine Kent did. Can you believe ... she was 85 and led us six more years? What a woman! And Estella and Priscilla. All fascinating women." Genevieve stopped to drink some water. "Since you are new to the club, I want to share a little about our history. But before I go any further ... let me apologize for my speech. I had a stroke years ago ... and have to pause during my talking and rest or drink water or tea. Sometimes I forget where I am."

"Understandable," replied Chattie. "I haven't had a stroke and often can't find my reading glasses."

"Another thing. I usually refer to you three as girls. Hope you don't mind."

How endearing.

"Now to our history. I had a tough year after my Shipman died. After a time of grieving, I started back playing bridge on Thursday afternoons with the same friends I had played with for years. I was the only widow, and ... after playing a few more times with them, I decided I needed women who were 'in my same shoes.' Women I could relate to ... and learn from and enjoy the company of." Genevieve paused to drink some tea. "Also, I had to begin my new life as a widow, and I sure didn't want to feel isolated. Alone. What better way ... than to have friends who had gone through similar experiences." She waited a few moments to get her breath.

"I had always enjoyed my daily tea time, so I ran an ad in

the local paper:

"Christian widows interested in tea and conversation contact Genevieve Shipman at P.O. Box 100, Breeze Hill, Alabama."

"In the next four days Albertine Kent, Estella Rogers, and Priscilla Wright wrote me. I heard from several others, but the first three ... were the ones I felt should join me to start the Tea. I chose the right women because they came faithfully until their deaths.

"Albertine wanted to be called Bert. After her retirement from the bank, she worked at the local funeral home. What stories she told. Although we often didn't care to hear them over tea." After a short pause and a deep breath, Genevieve continued. "I remember her telling us about a 90-year-old woman who stipulated she wanted to be buried in a go-go dress."

"My word!" interrupted Chattie, "a woman her age."

"Bert said the woman's children were embarrassed, but they complied with her wishes. One thing that bothered Bert was when the deceased person's wishes were not followed." Genevieve stopped and sipped more tea before continuing. "Once a woman wanted to be buried next to her third husband, but her children buried her next to strangers."

"Why would anyone want to work at a funeral home?" asked Chattie. "No way I could."

"Bert considered it a ministry. She greeted and consoled relatives and friends. She didn't embalm, of course. Although she did fix some of the women's hair when a beautician wasn't available.

I am glad she didn't have to embalm.

"Care to guess where she died?" asked Genevieve, looking around at the three women.

"At the funeral home, of course," said Mary Olivia. "I'm cheating. I replaced her."

"Sorry, girls," said Genevieve. "Senior moment."

"How did she die?" asked Chattie.

"I can answer that also," said Mary Olivia. "She had a massive heart attack trying to separate two feuding brothers arguing over their mother's piano."

"A sad story," said Verity, shaking her head.

"Now to Estella who shortened her name to Stella," continued Genevieve.

"A superb cook and full-time homemaker, she was the most nervous person I have ever known. She would jump at the least noise. ... During one Tea she broke one of my blue porcelain teacups. Shipman gave me them for an anniversary gift.

"Her marriage had been difficult. She confided to us that her husband Thornton had been extremely jealous and often accused her of infidelities. Poppycock. Of all people, she was a loyal person." Genevieve took a deep breath. "Thorn — we shortened his name because we thought it fit him — even accused her of running around when she was at her weekly beauty shop appointment." She paused a moment. "None of us had known Thorn, but we believed Stella when she said her bad case of nerves was due to Thorn's verbal abuse. By the way, Stella didn't mind our calling him Thorn. I believe after his death she experienced a freedom she had never known."

"How did she die?" asked Chattie.

"Again, I can answer that. Peacefully in her sleep. Appropriate, I thought, since she had endured so much from that rascal Thorn. "What a welcome replacement you were, Verity."

"Now for the last founding member," said Genevieve. "Priscilla Deborah Rebecca Wright. Her husband Edmund called her Doll, and it stuck."

"Beautiful names," said Verity.

"Yes. But Priscilla adored her nickname Doll. We lost her last fall — a week before Thanksgiving — to pancreatic cancer. She lived only two months after the cancer was found. She was a retired fourth-grade schoolteacher. Doll lived life to the fullest. She volunteered as a storyteller at schools and libraries for over 20 years. ... She epitomized to me what a widow can do with her life."

How can I ever measure up to Doll?

"We didn't know Doll's age until her death. She would never divulge it to anyone because she said it was a 'woman's prerogative' not to discuss her age. Her obituary stated she was 84 — five years older than any of us thought.

"She was known for her hats and was buried in her favorite white one. And we all wore hats to her funeral at First Methodist."

"'Elegant' described Doll," said Mary Olivia. "She met her husband at Mackinaw Island in Michigan at that beautiful hotel."

"They went back up there for their wedding," continued Genevieve. "She was buried in a wedding dress. Hers had faded, but years before her death ... she had one made to look like the original.

"Another tidbit about Doll which I found interesting was

she started wearing hats to draw attention away from Edmund." Genevieve looked at the snowfall. "Where was I?"

"Doll started wearing hats to draw attention away from Edmund," repeated Mary Olivia.

"Oh, yes. He was a charming, handsome man … except for a large wart near his right ear. She thought wearing a hat softened people's responses to his wart."

"I've never heard that wart story," said Mary Olivia. "I wonder how many more tidbits you have."

"More than I could ever tell. Many I wouldn't dare divulge." Genevieve stopped for a few minutes.

Genevieve must be remembering those stories she wouldn't tell or couldn't.

"By the way, I forgot to mention to you," said Genevieve, leaning toward Chattie so she wouldn't be heard by other patrons: "The Widows' Tea has another slogan: 'What is said at the Widows' Tea stays at the Widows' Tea.'"

"I'm mum, and thanks for the fascinating history of the Tea."

"Now for our meetings. After our January meeting we always meet at the home of the hostess. I have our schedules for this year." Genevieve gave each woman one. "Look them over and tell me if you have any conflicts with your months. As you can see, I'm down for February; Verity, you're down for March; Mary Olivia, you're April; Chattie, May; etc.

"We meet the second Tuesday of the month from 2 to 4 p.m. The hostess may serve any type of tea and dessert she desires. We meet at our homes, but the hostess is not confined to her dining room. She can have the Tea on her porch, patio, anywhere. She also decides if the Tea should be formal or casual and selects the dishes and napkins. We do *like* to be surprised. That's always fun."

By May I should be ready to be a hostess and do something special. Then by September surely I....

Chattie's thinking was diverted again to Genevieve's speaking.

"Girls, at this time we usually continue to socialize among ourselves, but I would like ... to propose something new — and exciting — for us to consider this year.

"First, I have a bookmark for each of you. I hope the quotation on it will set the tone for our entire year."

Genevieve reached into her purse and took out four bookmarks and gave one to each woman and kept one for herself.

Chattie looked at Verity and Mary Olivia.

We all must be thinking the same thing. What's coming next?

"This is one of my favorite sayings. It's by George Eliot, a Victorian novelist. Her real name was Mary Ann Evans. ... She wrote many novels, including *Silas Marner*. You probably remember it from high school."

"I loved to read, but I hated that book in tenth-grade English," reflected Mary Olivia. "I never finished it."

Genevieve ignored Mary Olivia's remarks.

"After reading this quote, you'll probably agree with me that it is inspiring."

Genevieve read more slowly than she usually did: "It's never too late to be what you might have been."

"Let me read it again: 'It's never too late to be what you

might have been.' Let's think about what this statement means."

The women remained quiet, considering the quote.

Verity broke the silence. "It pretty well means what it says. Whatever our age it's never too late to be what we might have wanted to be. One of us may have had a dream years ago to go on a safari to Kenya or to raise orchids or to volunteer helping abused children, but never got to fulfill the dream."

"I could not have stated it better," said Genevieve. She lightly clapped her hands.

"Girls, this is my challenge. I want you — us — to do something we have always wanted to do. Stretch ourselves — find something that moves us."

My first meeting of the Tea, and I'm given a challenge to stretch myself. What a year to join. What have I always wanted to do? I've gone to Paris and Venice with my romantic husband … met the Pope at the Vatican.

"You may be thinking you don't have the courage or strength or time to pursue something you have wanted to do. Our lives are short. We all saw our husbands die too young." Genevieve rested a few minutes and then spoke slowly but boldly: "Imagine this year is going to be the last year of your life. Is there something you have wanted to do but have not stepped out of your comfort zone and gone for it?"

"I'm reminded of a verse Papa made us children memorize," said Verity. "It was Proverbs 16:3: 'Commit to the Lord whatever you do, and your plans will succeed.' I'll have to rely on that verse when I take up my challenge," Verity nodded.

"Great verse for whatever we attempt in life," added Genevieve.

"My son James and grandson Blake," said Mary Olivia, "have moved back home with me since the death of my daughter-in-law Adriana last year. Together they both had a good income, but James couldn't make it on his own as a social worker. Also, Eric is living at home. He's trying to find himself. All he thinks about is fencing. Now how's that going to get him a good job? He needs to go back to college. You see. I have my hands full. What's our Tea about anyway? I thought it was a time to relax, chat, and enjoy ourselves."

"The Tea is not changing," said Genevieve, taking a dogmatic tone. "As usual, we will be socializing and enjoying good conversation. I'm talking about what we are going to be doing the *rest* of the month — the time we are not spending two hours at the Tea."

"But I need to simplify my life," said Mary Olivia, throwing up her hands dramatically. "Now I have more to do."

"You can *still* simplify your life," emphasized Genevieve. "In fact, this challenge will help you simplify — focus — on something you really want to do.

"I know this is not going to be easy for any of us. But I know we are all up to it. We have health problems and obligations, but we are strong women. I understand obstacles." She stopped a moment and stared out the window. "My stroke 12 years ago slowed me down, but with God's help, I refused to give up."

"I admire your tenacity," Chattie said.

"You are kind, but I am one of many who keep on going despite adversities. People older than I are skydiving, running marathons, delivering babies. Remember Grandma Moses. She didn't start painting until she was in her 70s, and at almost 80 she sold her first painting. ... She lived to be 101, painting 25 pictures the last year of her life.

"Girls, we must realize that the way we live our lives influences women around us."

"Isn't that statement a bit feminist?" asked Chattie.

"Definitely," said Mary Olivia.

"We must be a positive role model to other women, but also for the next generation," said Genevieve, "including our own families."

"Years ago I had a friend," said Chattie, "who on her 50th birthday made a list of 50 things she wanted to do before she died. She called it her life list. I only remember two of them — travel to Iceland and write a sonnet. I thought she was on to a novel idea. She must have led an amazing life."

Mary Olivia sighed. "And I bet she's *still* working on her list."

"She probably is. But what a sense of adventure," said Verity, nodding her affirmation. "That's what my life needs — more adventure."

My Roberto approached each day as an adventure. Dancing with me in our bakery was his last one.

"Why can't we all have a sense of adventure this year?" asked Genevieve. "All I have been trying to say is for us to choose one dream we have always had. It may be a hobby — or even more than one — we want to pursue. Or we may have deep unfulfilled ... passions we have not allowed ourselves to think about. Our dreams may result in complete life changes for us. I'm getting excited just thinking about the year ahead. I hope you girls are."

Genevieve paused before saying, "O.K., girls, let's go for it. Let's see what we can accomplish this year."

"You sound like a cheerleader," said Verity. "But I can't imagine you jumping up and down with pom poms."

"I never told you, but I was a cheerleader a hundred years ago."

"We're certainly seeing a different side of you," said Mary Olivia.

"Seriously, girls, we must encourage and bolster one another. Only real friends can do that, you know."

"You're right about that," said Verity.

Mary Olivia asked the waitress to bring them more tea.

"If Papa were in good health, he would love this challenge," Verity said enthusiastically. "He often quotes Philippians 4:13 when the apostle Paul says, 'I can do all things through Christ who strengthens me.' Papa always wanted his four children and all of God's children to live life to the fullest."

"Roberto definitely would want me to consider any latent dreams I have. He loved spontaneity. He would want me to embrace this challenge."

"I'll try … try my best … to give this challenge serious thought," said Mary Olivia. "Please forgive my negativity today. I've been stressed out lately. I'll try being more positive next month."

"I appreciate your honesty," said Genevieve. "Life must be hectic for you now."

The women sipped their tea and talked among themselves

until Genevieve tapped her spoon lightly on the table.

"I know we need to get home soon. But before we go, I have a questionnaire for each of you," she said, handing the sheets to the three women. "These ten statements may be helpful as you study and ponder my challenge — our challenge.

"Remember next month. My home. I'm planning a surprise."

"Another challenge?" Mary Olivia asked, stuffing the questionnaire into her purse. "One is going to be enough for me."

"Oh, no," Genevieve laughed. "Something fun."

Chattie wondered about Genevieve's surprise. She didn't seem the fun type, but she had an old Southern charm. It was hard to describe, but she knew it when she saw it.

The four women walked to the gift shop and waited while Verity bought a cookbook. Chattie read the quote above the door again. She agreed with Henry James, the author. Her first Tea was an agreeable time.

After saying their good-byes, Chattie walked Genevieve to her car. They waved to Mary Olivia and Verity as they drove off together.

꩜

Chattie sat in her car until she saw Genevieve safely pull away.

The snow was falling hard, but she knew she couldn't wait until she got home to read her questionnaire. She took it from her purse and read:

Do you have a hunger within you that has gone unmet?

Do you fear/not fear getting out of your comfort zone?

Are you prepared to face defeat until you reach your final

goal?

    Are you willing to invest time working toward your dream?
    Would your dream give your life meaning?
    Is it something that could benefit others?
    Do you believe you can achieve your dream?
    Take time to be alone to listen to longings of years ago.
    Name several things that you have dreamed of doing.
    What would God have you to do?
    Choose one (or more) of them as your goal for the year.

"It's never too late to be what you might have been." Chattie continued to mull over the quote as she slowly drove home through the oak-lined streets of Breeze Hill. As she watched the large snowflakes fall, she reflected upon the afternoon. She smiled as she experienced an inexplicable anticipation for the months ahead.

I don't know what I'll do, but I'm ready for a new passion — definitely not a man — but an invigorating pursuit.

2

FEBRUARY

GENEVIEVE

"I dread no more the first white in my hair,
Or even age itself, the easy shoe,
The cane, the wrinkled hands, the special chair:
Time, doing this to me, may alter too
My anguish, into something I can bear."
> from *"Time, That Renews the Tissues of This Frame"*
> American poet Edna St. Vincent Millay (1892-1950)

Genevieve awoke as usual at seven o'clock. A demanding morning awaited her. She had been too busy the day before to prepare for the Tea, and everything had to be perfect. She dressed in her favorite purple dress, put on her makeup, and brushed her hair. Grabbing an outdoor jacket, four red balloons, and her cane, she walked outside.

After tying the balloons to her mailbox, she watched as a cool breeze bounced them around. She looked up at the gray clouds and hoped it wouldn't rain.

Even if it does, my spirits won't be dampened one bit.

With much help from her cane, she slowly climbed the sloping driveway to her house. Her back ached.

Why did I carry that large box of food into the Community Soup Kitchen last week? Someone would have helped me if only I had asked. Next time I will accept the kindness of friends or strangers.

Today is no day for complaining about my back. I am excited about the day ahead. And I have every reason to be.

As she rested with a cup of coffee, Genevieve jotted down a list of chores to be done before the Tea: Dust. Vacuum. Decorate. Bake. She stopped. Her back ached. She couldn't prepare for the Tea alone. She had no choice but to call Hannah, her loyal friend and part-time housekeeper.

Hannah never finished high school and never had married. She lived in the old historic area, now a run-down part of town.

As usual, Hannah immediately came to her rescue, as she had done for the last five years. After cleaning the house, she helped Genevieve decorate the dining room and then bake.

As Genevieve rinsed out a red teapot, she thought about the challenge she had given the girls a month ago. In fact, she had experienced second thoughts about her challenge many times during the month.

Did I ask too much of them? Did my idea cause too much stress for any of them? What can I expect today? Opposition? Enthusiasm? Apathy? Is it too much to hope that one of them already has a plan in action?

At 1:30 the doorbell rang. She set the teapot down and headed for the foyer. When she opened the door, she saw a smiling Chattie.

"Come in," Genevieve said, greeting her with a hug.

Chattie appears to be happy. Maybe I didn't disrupt her life too much.

"Your house is beautiful. And the colonial style looks grand."

"Thank you, dear. Shipman and I were grateful to have it. It's too large for me now, but I'm not ready to give it up yet. And I am blessed to have friends help me when I need them."

"I was determined to be early today after I arrived late last month for my first Tea. May I help?"

"Yes. Absolutely. You are an angel coming when I need you.... First, though, how are *you* doing? Hasn't it been about a year since you lost Roberto?"

"A year today. But please don't tell Verity and Mary Olivia today is the anniversary. I might fall apart. And I don't want to do that. I got my crying over this morning. I want to enjoy myself this afternoon. Roberto would want me to."

"Not a word from me. I am good at keeping secrets."

I want to tell Chattie how much I admire her courage and grace. But I might embarrass her, or worse, make her cry.

"I did something today that helped me deal with this first anniversary. I wrote Roberto a letter and poured out my feelings, telling him how much I miss him."

"Writing is great therapy," Genevieve said. She hung up Chattie's red jacket and scarf in the coat closet.

"Are you planning to write him a letter each year?"

"I think so. I should have a lot to tell him next year."

"I imagine you will. Let's go into the kitchen. I'm putting you to work."

Maybe I can get Chattie's mind off her grief even if only for a while. I know what she is going through.

From the spacious foyer, they stepped into a tastefully decorated dining room. Red camellias floated in a round crystal bowl in the center of a round cherry table. Two glass candleholders held long red taper candles. Red streamers with red balloons hung overhead from a glass chandelier. Crystal dessert plates with matching cups and saucers on red placemats and red heart-shaped napkin rings holding white linen napkins completed the setting.

"What beautiful decorations!" exclaimed Chattie, walking around the table. "Is your table an antique?"

"Yes. Shipman inherited his parents' and grandparents' furniture. We had a furniture store and could have had any new furniture we wanted.... Ironic, isn't it? But we both treasured our antiques because they were from our family."

"I can't wait to have our Tea in here. Everything looks so festive … so perfect."

"Nothing is ever perfect," commented Genevieve, leading Chattie into the kitchen.

"I knew you enjoyed tea, but I didn't realize how much until now," said Chattie as she entered the kitchen. "Teapots and teacups everywhere. I've never seen a wallpaper border of red, white, and blue teapots and teacups. Simply charming."

"Thank you. I've never thought about the combination of colors before. I do enjoy my kitchen."

Chattie looked around at the lighted oak cabinets with glass doors and glass shelves highlighting several matching teapot and sugar and creamer sets. On the granite countertop was a large red tea tray holding a red teapot with a matching sugar and creamer set.

"Shipman gave me a teapot set each Christmas and birthday for years. I have quite a collection. If — when — I leave this old house, I'll be sure to give you and the other girls one of my teapots."

"I would treasure it. How generous you are."

Hannah entered the room.

"Chattie Milano, I want you to meet my friend and trusted helper, Hannah Doolittle."

"My pleasure, Miss Chattie," said Hannah, extending her good left hand but not hiding her shriveled right one.

"Nice to meet you," replied Chattie, shaking her hand, "but please call me Chattie."

"It's time we got busy," said Genevieve. "With one good hand, Hannah works better than someone with two good ones."

"She brags on me too much. I appreciate Miss Genevieve for hiring me. God knows I need the money, and she needs the help. And by the way, if you wonder — everyone does — a birth defect caused my ugly hand."

"It doesn't seem to stop you," said Chattie.

She helped them spread red frosting on heart-shaped sugar cookies and dipped strawberries in melted white chocolate and placed them on waxed paper. They then arranged the cookies and cooled strawberries on crystal platters.

At 1:55 the women breathed sighs of relief.

"If I do say so myself," said Hannah, "I think we done a good job."

"Thanks go to you, Hannah, for all of your work and to

you, Chattie, for arriving when we needed you."

At 2:02 Genevieve welcomed Mary Olivia and Verity at the front door.

"What a charming door," said Mary Olivia. "Only you, Genevieve, would think of putting up a Valentine wreath."

"It's a special day, girls."

"Our Tea is always a special time," replied Verity, "and no one entertains better than you."

Genevieve smiled.

If only they knew what this day means to me.

After Verity and Mary Olivia greeted Chattie, the four widows gathered at the dining room table.

"Thank you, Genevieve, for surrounding us with such style," said Mary Olivia. "You can't imagine how uplifting this is to me. You should see my house now. The boys can make such a mess."

Hannah entered with the red teapot and poured each woman Earl Grey tea. She then brought in the cookies and strawberries. Soon the women were eating and drinking.

"Mary Olivia," said Chattie, putting down her teacup, "Have you ever thought about calling a family meeting to discuss how your family can pitch in and help?"

"No. But a good idea. Pointers, anyone?"

"Be up front and honest with the children," said Genevieve. "Insist that you need their help."

"Ask for volunteers for different jobs," added Chattie. "If no one volunteers, delegate."

"You'll probably find," said Verity, "they'll be willing to help you if you only ask."

"Thanks. I sure need all the help I can get. I'm too independent for my own good."

"What sweet, juicy strawberries these are," said Verity. She reached for another one. "I must tell Sister about them. Maybe Papa would like them. It's difficult for Pru to find something to cook that he'll eat."

"Is Rev. Isaiah not any better?" asked Genevieve.

"No. In fact, Papa's declining. The doctor says it's only a matter of months."

"Never give up," said Chattie. "God's still in the miracle business."

"I believe that, but Papa's heart is giving out. He's so weak. He talks about joining Mama. And he doesn't have the love of life that he's always had. I pray next month he'll be well enough for you to visit with him."

"I hope so," said Mary Olivia.

"Girls," Genevieve said, "I can't wait much longer to ask about the challenge I gave you last month. Has anyone chosen something you want to do?"

The three looked at each other.

Please one of you speak up. I knew I was asking too much of them.

"I'm 99% sure I've found something I want to do," said a smiling Chattie. "I believe it would please Roberto as well as honor his memory. I'm researching the subject now."

"Great start," said Genevieve. She was relieved that at least one of the girls had a challenge in mind.

"What is it?" asked Verity.

"I can't tell you now. I've got to do more research."

"Next month I plan to announce details about my first important endeavor," said Mary Olivia.

"First?" asked Verity.

I am shocked. Mary Olivia is the last of the girls I would have guessed to sign on to my challenge.

"Yes. I've been thinking since last month about what I might be interested in doing. Riding a burro down the Grand Canyon, traveling across the Sahara Desert on a camel, going on the Iditarod, climbing...."

"Hold up. Iditarod? What is that?" interrupted Verity. "I do declare, Mary Olivia, I've known you for years, but I've never seen this side of you."

"It must be teaching history for 30 years. I studied vicariously about many places and never had the opportunity and especially the money to go to any of them."

"The Iditarod ... you must tell us what that is," said Verity.

"Well, the Iditarod is the famous sled dog race from Anchorage to Nome, Alaska. It's an annual re-enactment of the freight route to Nome and commemorates the part that sled dogs played in the settlement of Alaska."

"You're going dog sledding?" asked a puzzled Verity.

"Probably not. But it does fascinate me."

Turning to Verity, Genevieve asked if she had anything to report.

"I have my hands full. My two sisters and I are doing all we can to make Papa comfortable. He has to come first. I'll continue playing the piano for the church, of course. But I have hopes of pursuing something different than being a pianist and giving piano lessons. I have a dream of long ago — something I promised Mama I would do. I definitely will need assistance some time in the future. It most likely will be a grueling undertaking."

What in the world does Verity have in mind? A grueling undertaking. It sounds like an arduous task.

"Don't forget we are here to help each other," Genevieve said.

"I won't forget. I promise."

"You've created suspense for sure," said Mary Olivia. "Sounds to me your challenge isn't going to be boring."

Verity shook her head. "Exhausting. Backbreaking. Tiring. But not boring."

"Your description has worn me out," said Mary Olivia. "I'm getting more tea."

"I hope you girls are hungry. More food is on the way."

Hannah promptly brought out a cake with a few candles. They all watched as Genevieve's eyes lit up.

"I am throwing myself a birthday party. Not a surprise for me, but one for you. I want you to share my 77th birthday with me."

"My word! How could I have helped you in the kitchen and not had a clue about a birthday party?" asked Chattie.

Genevieve grinned. "I always could keep a secret."

"But if we had known, we would have brought gifts," said Mary Olivia.

"I didn't want gifts. I don't need any more *things*."

Hannah lit the candles that were arranged to form the number 77. "Now, Miss Genevieve, make a wish and blow out the candles."

"Hold on, Hannah. Let me say a few words."

She paused to collect her thoughts.

"Thank you for your friendship, love, and support. As long as I live, I hope to make new friends such as you," she said, pointing to Chattie. "Younger friends. Of course, you three are all younger. Which is good. You girls keep me young."

"Are you ever going to blow the candles out?" Hannah asked. "Your cake may burn up."

The women smiled.

Genevieve closed her eyes tightly, drew in a deep breath, and blew all the candles out.

Her friends clapped, and so did Genevieve.

"Did you make a wish?" asked Hannah.

Genevieve nodded and then smiled broadly.

Hannah loudly began singing "Happy Birthday." She sang out of tune, but Genevieve knew her heart was in it. The rest joined in. Then Hannah led them in clapping again.

"Thank you. Thank you," Genevieve said, standing and bowing from the waist with a big smile on her face. "Hannah, we need ice cream to eat with the cake."

She returned to the kitchen and brought out vanilla ice cream to go with the three-layered Italian Cream Cake. She placed pieces of cake with ice cream on the plates and gave them to each woman beginning with Genevieve.

"Delectable," Genevieve said. She took her time to slowly eat each bite of the cake. She giggled as she looked at her friends. "Pardon me, but I am enjoying my birthday."

Each woman smiled.

I love our Tea because these are my real friends. So many of my so-called friends over the years have been interested in only my name, my money, and philanthropy.

"Did Hannah bake the cake?" asked Mary Olivia. "It's delicious."

"No. I made it myself. My favorite cake was my gift to myself."

"What a great idea — giving yourself one of your favorite things," said Chattie.

"When you get my age, you give yourself permission to do what makes you happy. You all have something to look forward to in your old age."

The women laughed.

The girls seem to be having fun at my birthday party. That makes me so happy.

"I want you girls to see an early birthday gift I also gave myself. Hannah, please bring in my surprise."

In a few minutes Hannah came in cuddling a Persian cat and handed her to Genevieve.

"Girls, meet Laptop."

"She's gorgeous," said Mary Olivia. "What inquisitive eyes. She's looking us over."

"How in the world did you come up with her name?" asked Chattie.

"Well, she jumped on my laptop the first day she was here, so I thought it would be a fitting name.

"Except for Chattie, you all know I lost my beloved Midnight the day after Christmas. Her death was difficult since she had been with me for 15 years." Genevieve paused to drink some water. "Fortunately, last month Hannah read a news story about several neglected cats brought to our local animal shelter. She and I immediately went there and found Laptop."

"What a mess she was before the vet got a hold of her. We nursed her back to health," said Hannah. "Her eye is almost healed now.

"She stays in Miss Genevieve's office and sleeps in her basket."

"She's ready for a nap. Hannah, take Laptop back to my office."

"Only after I feed her and love on her," said Hannah, leaving the room smiling.

"I think Laptop is getting some much deserved attention," said Mary Olivia.

Chattie looked at Genevieve. "She's not the only one who gets attention. With such a clear complexion and few wrinkles, you sure don't look 77. You must have some beauty secrets you could share with us."

"I don't think so. Well, maybe, if I think awhile, I can come up with a few do's and don'ts."

After finishing her cake, she spoke slowly, thinking through each point: "Never get out in the sun without a hat and sunscreen. Every morning and night use a cleanser and moisturizer. I highly recommend putting petroleum jelly all over your face and neck at least once a week. And, uh, my last tip would be to drink six or more glasses of water daily."

"Vaseline. Never thought about using it," said Mary Olivia. "Maybe it's not too late for me to try some."

"Genevieve," said Chattie, "last month I explained about

my name. Can you tell us how you got your name? I've never known another woman named Genevieve."

"It's a family name. I was named after my maternal great-grandmother, who was named after Saint Genevieve, the patron saint of Paris. My father always called me Gen. After he died, I wanted to be called Genevieve. I've always liked my name."

"A precious story," said Verity. "This is my first time to hear it."

"My dear mother was an invalid for many years. She died when I was twelve. My father and his widowed mother, my Grandma Lottie, raised me.

"I always wanted my father to be proud of me. Daddy was a man with strong principled convictions. He was protective of me. When I got to know Shipman, I sensed he had those same traits. And I was right."

∾

"What a birthday! Your being here to celebrate it with me has made me so happy," said Genevieve, leading the girls to the den.

Everyone but Genevieve chose a chair and chatted about how much they enjoyed her party and how full they were.

"Now it is time for me to tell you about my pursuit," said Genevieve, taking a deep breath. "After all, I gave you the challenge. It seems fitting I should be the first to share a dream I've had for at least a decade."

"I've known you so long," said Mary Olivia. "With all your volunteer work, I can't imagine how you would have time to do anything else."

"I will curtail my volunteering," Genevieve said, finally sitting down. "At least, for a while. I may stay on a few charity boards." She paused before saying, "but writing a novel takes a lot of time."

"A novel?" asked Verity.. "I never would have guessed. Not that you couldn't ... can't ... write a novel. I'm shocked."

"Me, too," said Mary Olivia. "I know you're a voracious reader, but I never thought of you as a writer."

"That was exactly my problem. I didn't think of myself as a writer. Until, that is, the first day of this year. I was on the verandah early in the morning thinking about my goals for the year. All of a sudden it came to me: 'Genevieve, you're turning 77 this year. You've been dreaming about writing your novel for years. Now write it.' I decided right then and there I was going to fulfill my dream. I prayed, asking God to give me time, energy, and enthusiasm for the project."

"You've inspired me," said Chattie, "with your commitment and passion. I want to have that same attitude toward my project."

"What type of novel are you writing?" asked Mary Olivia.

"A romance. I hope you girls will like it — that is, once it is finished."

"Can you tell us about it?" asked Verity.

"A little bit. Successful authors recommend not talking about a story until you get it down on paper. And I have only about 40 typed pages now."

"That's a lot," said Chattie. "You only started last month."

"You're right. I've had a dream for at least ten years to write a historical romance. For years I have immersed myself in reading them. At the same time, I wrote down notes. Pieces of dialogue. Descriptions of places. Like Emily Dickinson, I scribbled on the back of envelopes and grocery lists. I even wrote on napkins. You probably didn't see me, but I jotted down a note at our Tea last month."

Genevieve sipped tea as she tried to collect her thoughts. "Now where was I?"

"Jotted down a note at our Tea last…."

"Thanks, Verity."

"Since I made a commitment to write, I have written some every day. I usually write early in the morning, but sometime I write all day."

"Now we know why Laptop's camped out in your office," observed Mary Olivia.

"What's your romance about?" asked Verity.

"It's set in World War II and is about the human heart in conflict. A romance about a man and woman in love. He gets killed in the war. She marries another man and finally grows to love him."

"Your description has me hooked," said Verity..

"I read something recently," said Chattie, "that resonated with me: 'If we don't say it, it won't be said.' I guess that could refer to speaking or writing. Do you feel that way about your writing?"

"'If we don't say it, it won't be said,'" Genevieve said thoughtfully. "That quote states in some ways my reason for writing."

"I'm writing that sentence down and giving it to Pru," said Verity. She turned to Chattie. "My sister collects quotes."

"Enough about my novel-in-progress. Let's talk about something else."

"I've got an idea. We're having a Valentine's Party, which is all about love," said Chattie. "Why don't we describe how we met our husbands?"

Chattie keeps our conversation moving. A delightful girl.

The girls remained quiet for a minute as if they were trying to remember.

"I'll start," said Chattie. "I met Roberto at a bakery where he was a pastry chef. He had a degree in culinary arts and planned to open his own bakery. He came from a long line of Italian bakers. His Aunt Boo — I've never known her real name — and my mother knew each other. They invited me to the bakery one day and introduced us. What girl could resist such a handsome, courteous man! It was love at first sight. One more personal thing — I've never told anyone this: We exchanged locks of hair during our courtship. I have both of them intertwined in a locket."

"What a romantic you are," said Mary Olivia. "I wish I were."

"Shipman was a romantic also." said Genevieve. "A tender, quiet, unassuming man. Let me stop now and explain why I called L.T. his last name — Shipman. Years ago it was not unusual for women to call their husbands by their last names. In fact, my friend Jennie Outlaw calls her husband Outlaw."

"Outlaw?" asked Verity. "I've never heard that name around here."

"Jennie is a childhood friend who moved out West and married Jessie Outlaw. I always thought it was a fitting name for someone living there."

Genevieve stopped. "Where was I in my romance?"

"You were saying that you thought Outlaw was a fitting name for someone living out West."

"Thanks, Verity.

"L.T. liked my calling him Shipman. He never liked L.T. and disliked more his real name — Lochlear Tobias. By the way, my mother always called my father Boswell. Young people, such as my granddaughter Jessica, think it's a strange practice. It is a dying custom.

"Now back to romance. It was because of a hat that I married Shipman."

"A hat?" asked Chattie.

"I'll explain. After a trip to Europe with his parents, Shipman returned home. We had known each other as kids. He fell in love with me, he said, when standing outside of a millinery shop, he watched me try on a green felt hat." Genevieve drank some water. "He came into the shop, and we renewed our friendship. It was a whirlwind romance. After only a few dates, we married."

Shipman loved me so much. How I wish I had told him and showed him how much I loved him. Not just respected him. But loved him deeply.

"In the early 80s I was teaching history in high school," said Mary Olivia. "I met Liam at a dance in the small town. We dated six months before we married. I was drawn to him because he was Irish and I was Scottish."

"Verity, what's your story?" asked Chattie.

"I went to Chicago to stay with my mother's spinster

cousin. I found a job as a pianist at a large church and during the day taught private piano lessons. After two years I met Micah Harris when he inquired about taking lessons.

"I gave him two lessons. Then when we started dating, he stopped them. Obviously, they were a means to meet me because one of Sarah's friends told him I was staying with her. I fell deeply in love with him at first sight. I never told him, though. What a charmer he was. A tall handsome man with smooth almond skin. I was 39 when I married Micah. It was wonderful to be loved."

Verity is a reserved person. But today she's opening up. Maybe the spontaneity of my birthday party has brought out her emotions.

"Nothing can be compared to being loved. By the way, did you quiz your husbands before you consented to marry them?" asked Genevieve.

The women looked at one other as if to try to comprehend the question.

"I assumed you didn't, but Doll did. I'm sure, Chattie, you remember her from my Tea history last month."

Chattie nodded. "I won't forget Doll. Who could?"

"When Edmund asked her to marry him, she hesitated. She told him she couldn't consider his proposal until she had answers to some questions. Her questions included 'What is your IQ? What kind of grades did you make in school? Any diabetes in your family?' Doll was scared to death of diabetes. 'Have you ever lost a job? Do you enjoy your work? Do you take vacations?' The only question he had a problem with was 'What diseases killed your grandparents?' He told her he would research that one. After asking him around 25 questions, she told us he passed. She thought him brilliant. Enough about Doll.

"Our sharing about the way we met was apropos to end our Valentine's Party — and my birthday party. Before you go, though, I have some news. Genevieve Boswell-Shipman will be my official name now. Hope you don't think I'm being silly, but I want my maiden name included on my books to honor my father and Grandma Lottie."

"You're being modern — trendy — taking on a hyphenated name," Chattie said.

Chattie is trying to encourage me. But being trendy might increase my book sales.

Before Genevieve could reply to Chattie, Verity spoke up.

"I must get back to Papa. I would appreciate your prayers for him and for our family. By the way, I'm hosting next month, but Pru will be making our dessert."

"We're in for a treat then. And we will pray for your family. But before you girls go," Genevieve said, walking into the doorway and slightly raising her voice: "Hannah, bring in their flowers, please."

Always on cue, Hannah brought in two red camellias for each of them.

"My word! I've never had a camellia," said Chattie.

"State flower of Alabama. Float flowers in a clear shallow bowl of water. Change the water each day. The flowers will cheer you up for at least two days."

Each woman thanked Genevieve and hugged her before leaving.

Genevieve watched the girls walk down the hill and get in

their cars. She blew kisses to them until they were out of sight.

What an afternoon of fun. I'm glad I told the girls about my novel. Knowing I have three people to be accountable to should make me get some serious writing done. But it won't be easy with my aching back.

3
March

~

VERITY

"You gain strength, courage, and confidence by every experience in which you really stop to look fear in the face.... You must do the thing you think you cannot do."
U.S. First Lady Eleanor Roosevelt (1884-1962)

Verity entered the kitchen just as she heard a knock at the back door.

It was Mary Olivia.

Verity's oldest sister, Prudence, stopped washing dishes and dried her hands on her apron. She hugged Mary Olivia and said, "It's always good to see my oldest friend."

Mercy, Verity's other sister, joined them and embraced Mary Olivia. Both Mercy and Prudence were spinsters.

Verity was as glad to see Mary Olivia as her sisters were. She now understood why Pru and Mary Olivia had been such good friends over the years. Since she had returned from Chicago three years ago, she and Mary Olivia had become close.

How grateful I am that Mary Olivia suggested to Genevieve

and Doll that I join the Tea. I remember Mary Olivia coming to see me after Stella's funeral. She wanted so much for me to be a part of the monthly Tea. I didn't hesitate at all when I agreed to attend the next Tea.

"Why did you come to the back door, M.O.," asked Mercy.

"I knew Prudence would be in the kitchen," said Mary Olivia. "If I had a beautiful kitchen with red cabinets and a red table, I might enjoy doing kitchen chores."

"I like my red kitchen too." Prudence smiled from the kitchen sink, where she had returned to washing dishes.

"You came in because you like our red kitchen?" Mercy asked.

"Yes and no. The *numero uno* reason was I smelled tea cakes and hoped I could raid your *rojo* cookie jar."

Mary Oliva walked over and embraced Verity.

Mercy broke into a loud laugh. "You and your Spanish outbursts."

I am glad that Mercy can find humor in the smallest happenings.

"M.O., you're smart. You know Pru makes the best tea cakes in the whole country."

"I agree."

"You can give Mary Olivia one tea cake," announced Prudence as she watched Mercy reach for another.

Prudence straightened herself to her full height of five feet, ten inches and said, "Mary Olivia, I've been reminiscing about our friendship. We've known each other for as long as I can remember. Why, both of our grandfathers farmed next to each other. We read *Heidi* and *Jane Eyre* under Grandpapa's apple trees."

"I remember well. Those were great times having you and your family as neighbors."

"Yummy," said Mary Olivia, slowly eating her teacake. "You're the best cook I know. I'd plead for another one, but my waistline doesn't need it."

"Thanks has to go to Great-Grandmama Ida's recipe," said Prudence. "I've used the same recipe for decades — always including a secret ingredient that's been passed down."

"That word *secret* again. Verity, we heard that word several times last month. I wonder if we'll hear it again today."

Secret. I don't like to hear or think about that word. I'm reminded too much of my own secret.

"I don't know, but I do know that Genevieve didn't seem herself last month. Laid back. Affectionate. And fun."

"I like Miss Genevieve," said Mercy. "She's a nice lady. Are you gossiping about her behind her back? You know what Papa says about gossip."

"Of course not. I love Genevieve. Her birthday brought out a different Genevieve. One who was more transparent than reserved. It was refreshing to see her enjoy herself."

"Mercy, get me our glass platter to put these tea cakes on," Prudence said.

Pru always knows when to come to the rescue.

Mercy quickly gave the platter to her sister.

"I thought if I came early I could help," said Mary Olivia. "I know you're busy with Rev. Isaiah."

"That's thoughtful of you," said Prudence, "but I think we have everything under control."

"Verity, take Mary Olivia into the parlor. You two relax. Mercy and I are setting up everything for the Tea."

"And I'm also waiting for our other two guests," said Mercy.

"Good," said Prudence.

⚬

"I'm sorry I started that about Genevieve," said Mary Olivia, as she and Verity entered the parlor.

"Think nothing of it. We both know Mercy means well. She was being protective of Genevieve."

"I agree that she was not her usual self last month. It's probably because she's finally writing the novel she's dreamed about for years. She acts more vibrant and alive."

"It most likely is her novel," agreed Verity.

Will a passion change me? I can't deal with one now. Papa sick and my ever present secret I've lived with for three years. In January Genevieve said she started the Tea to join with women "in her shoes." Oh, if only she knew about me.

Mary Olivia walked around in the parlor. "I never tire of this room and the family pictures of you girls and your brother, Temperance, as children."

"Those were happy times. My favorite ones are of Mama and Papa when they were young. When I step into this room, I feel a link to my family's past that is increasingly important to me. The parlor is decorated much the way it was decades ago. The Victorian sofa and chairs and mahogany end tables were part of my childhood. Pru and Mercy have always followed Papa's wish not to make changes."

"I'm glad. I like the familiar. Maybe it's because I've had so many changes in my life the last several years."

Mary Olivia looked at the family Bible resting on a book holder. "I see that your Bible is opened to the book of Isaiah."

"Pru read this week that Florence Nightingale revered Isaiah as a writer more than she did Shakespeare. And she also read that Harriet Tubman loved Isaiah 16:3, so the Bible is opened on that verse. You know how we all benefit from Pru's research."

"She inspires me to study more. No wonder Tubman loved this verse, 'Hide the fugitives, do not betray the refugees.'"

An antique oak library table contained a diverse collection of books. *Having Our Say: The Delaney Sisters' First 100 Years* sat next to a stack of Dickens' novels, *The Complete Works of Shakespeare*, and *Their Eyes Were Watching God*.

"Who's reading the Zora Neale Hurston novel?" asked Mary Olivia, picking up the book and reading the first page.

"I finished it last week. Can you believe I never had read it? And Hurston an Alabama writer. She was such a pioneer in writing African-American novels. It's so unlike what I expected."

"I read it many years ago. It's a memorable story. I had to read it slowly to get through the dialect."

"Not me. I soaked in every word."

"Janie is a strong widow," observed Mary Olivia, returning the book to the table.

"She certainly is. She's widowed three times. After her second husband dies, the town expects her to stay in mourning. But she decides to finally live her life her way. I liked that about her. Although she's a wealthy widow, she still operates her store. She has plenty of suitors but doesn't like any of them."

"No wonder. They're only after her money. Remember one day, while the entire town is away, a stranger named Tea Cake stops by the store and ends up joking with her. He teaches her to have fun."

"I love his name. And to think we're talking about a fictional character named Tea Cake, and we're serving tea cakes today," said Verity, laughing. "Purely coincidental."

"But so funny."

"Tea Cake continues to visit Janie and take her out. He finally tells her he loves her. They leave town, get married, and Janie starts a different life."

"And a sad one. Tea Cake dies tragically when Janie kills him in self-defense. Being bitten by a mad dog would make anyone crazy."

"Janie is a survivor. I love what she says at the end of the book about the two things we have to do for ourselves. It's my favorite quote from the novel."

Picking up the book and finding the selection, Verity read: "They got tuh go tuh God, and they got tuh find out about livin' fuh theyselves."

"What wisdom," said Mary Olivia. "Appropriate words for everyone, including widows. Aren't we finding out about living for ourselves this year?"

"Yes. But I hope we're going to God first and then finding out about living for ourselves."

A knock at the door interrupted their conversation. Mercy soon showed Genevieve into the parlor and quickly rushed out when she heard another knock.

Hurrying back to the parlor, Mercy said, "I'm introducing

Chattie to Pru before bringing her in here. I assume, Verity, that's fine with you."

"Sure, you're a gracious and efficient hostess."

Turning to Genevieve, who was comfortably seated on the sofa, Verity asked how she was doing.

"Except for being older," she joked, "I'm fine."

"I sure hope you grow old for many years and invite me to every one of your birthday parties. I had so much fun last month."

"So did I," said Mary Olivia, "and I think the birthday girl did also."

"I sure did."

"And how exciting to find out about your novel," said Verity. "You must tell us today how your writing is going."

"I will."

Before I got to know Genevieve, really know her for the decent person she is, I thought she would be unapproachable. High society. Sometimes I'm wrong about people. I sure was about her — and Micah.

Mercy appeared at the door with Chattie in tow. "Sorry for the delay, but Pru took Chattie out to her garden. I have to get right back to work."

"Prudence certainly has a flourishing herb garden," Chattie said, smiling broadly. "She insisted I take cuttings of lavender, lemon balm, and orange mint home with me. She didn't have to beg me to take them. I appreciated the offer."

"She loves to give away her plants," said Verity.

As they chatted about the herbs, Mercy reappeared. "Sister says for me to tell you she's gone upstairs to check on Papa.

She wants us to join her. Follow me. We want Chattie to meet Papa."

"Everyone ready?" asked Verity.

"If you can make sure," said Genevieve, "I don't fall down the stairs."

The four women climbed the winding stairs behind Mercy. Verity and Chattie helped Genevieve maneuver each step. Mary Olivia brought up the rear. They stopped midway up for Genevieve to rest.

At the top of the stairs, they followed Mercy down the hall to Rev. Isaiah's bedroom. Verity quietly pointed out pictures of her grandparents and her great-grandparents displayed on the walls.

In the bedroom, Prudence had propped up pillows behind her frail but smiling father.

His Bible lay on the nightstand next to his bed. A glass of water stood next to a Victorian lamp along with a picture of his wife.

"Papa, do you feel like talking?" asked Verity. "My Tea friends are here to see you. Our newest member, Chattie, wants to meet you."

"My pleasure," Rev. Isaiah whispered. He slowly reached out his hand to Chattie.

As she took his large age-weathered hand, tears welled up in her eyes.

Chattie knows Papa's not long for this earth.

"A joy to meet you, Rev. Isaiah. You have a special family."

"Thank you," he whispered, taking his hand away and pointing to the water.

Prudence slowly brought the glass up to his lips, and he took a few sips.

Chattie stepped back from the bed while Mary Olivia went forward to kiss him on his forehead. They all could hear her say, "I love you."

Then Genevieve went to his bedside. She took his hand, gently patted it, and said, "God bless you."

He mumbled "God bless you" and smiled and then closed his eyes.

"Papa needs his rest now," said Verity. "Let's go downstairs."

"Everything is ready for your Tea," said Prudence. "Mercy and I will sit with Papa."

When the four women entered the kitchen, Chattie stopped to read aloud words on the refrigerator written on a 5 x 7 pink index card in large letters: "OPPROBRIOUS: DISGRACEFUL; SHAMEFUL."

"I learned a new word," said Chattie.

I don't like that word.

"Placing words on the refrigerator makes them visible to everyone," said Mary Olivia. "I may try it for my boys and myself."

"Pru is posting a word a week. With Papa ill she sometimes keeps the same word up for two weeks. 'Disconsolate.' 'Ethereal.' 'Satiate.' We never know what word will be next," said Verity. "She started with one a day, but we couldn't memorize them fast enough. She gave up on us and kept the word and meaning up a week. Also, she collects inspiring quotes. She posts a favorite one each week along with our word to learn. This week's quote is by Ralph Waldo Emerson: 'Go oft to the house of thy friend, for weeds choke the unused path.'"

"Great quote. Prudence probably won't get Alzheimer's because she's using her brain cells," said Genevieve. "And you and Mercy won't because you two are learning not only from Prudence but from your own activities."

I need Genevieve's encouragement.

Genevieve, Mary Olivia, and Chattie followed Verity through the kitchen to the wrap-around porch and sat down at a round table covered by a red tablecloth. An antique glass vase containing two white irises served as the centerpiece. A depression-era platter covered with Saran Wrap overflowed with large tea cakes. A white teapot filled with hot decaffeinated tea sat next to the dessert. A small glass bowl held sugar cubes. White cups, saucers, and plates completed the setting.

"A gorgeous table and a perfect view," said Genevieve. "The redbud tree next to the porch is simply stunning with its pink blossoms. And that forsythia still has some yellow blooms."

"Look ... look everyone ... at the mockingbird in the quince bush," said Mary Olivia. "And next to the bush a robin looking for worms. When I see my first robin, I know spring is here."

I appreciate my time with the girls. I know they're being chipper and upbeat for me today. The Tea is my monthly treat. As Papa worsens, our time together is even more precious.

After Verity offered thanks for her friends and for the food, she uncovered the tea cakes and poured the tea.

"I do enjoy our porch," she said, passing around the tea cakes. "This is an old house. It needs repairs, including painting, but we love it. Maybe because it's full of so many memories. It's our constant prayer one day Temp will come home and help us repair it."

"'Hope springs eternal.' It may be a cliché, but hope is something we all have to cling to," said Mary Olivia.

"I'll have to pass on the tea cakes," said Chattie. "I should have said something earlier. I've given up desserts for Lent. But I'm drinking plenty of tea."

"I believe in observing Lent even though I am not Catholic or Eastern Orthodox," said Verity. "Other Protestants observe Lent. I wish more Baptists would. Our family does. One year Mercy gave up chewing gum, one of her favorite treats. Another year Pru gave up baking. We nearly starved." Verity laughed. She became serious before adding, "This year I'm trying my best to give up worrying."

"These are undoubtedly the best tea cakes I've ever eaten," said Genevieve. "Not too sweet. Perfect." She finished a second one. "Sorry, Chattie."

"Think nothing of it. I'm not hungry. I've gone a week without sweets and don't crave them at all — that is, so far."

"No one makes tea cakes any more," said Mary Olivia.

"Pru is the only one I know who does. She stays in that kitchen, it seems, for hours each day. I'm glad she enjoys cooking. She says it's her therapy."

While eating and drinking, the friends talked about spring coming early.

Reaching for another tea cake, Genevieve asked, "Would you and your sisters please consider our helping you by sitting with Rev. Isaiah?"

"What a kind offer," answered Verity. "Although we take turns sitting with Papa, we each have our chores. Pru does the shopping and cooking. Mercy cleans the house and washes clothes. I take care of all the household business such as paying bills. I also play hymns on the piano for Papa. Of course, that's not work. It's my therapy. Your offer would be a great help to us. I'll have to ask my sisters, but I'm sure they'll agree."

"Fine," said Genevieve. "Then I propose that beginning next week we sit three hours from 1 to 4 p.m. I'll come on Mondays, Chattie on Wednesdays, and Mary Olivia on Thursdays if that is convenient for you two."

Mary Olivia and Chattie nodded their agreement.

Thank you, God, for their thoughtfulness. We could use some help but not from anyone. It has to be close friends whom we can trust with Papa.

"Have you heard from Temp lately?" asked Mary Olivia.

"He was here on New Year's Day for our usual good luck meal of black-eyed peas, collard greens, and cornbread. Then he stopped by for Valentine's Day. Mercy gave him his usual box of candy — the same Whitman's Sampler Assorted Chocolates he loves.

"Our brother is a recluse," Verity said, looking at Chattie. "Temperance — Temp — lives two miles outside of town in a ramshackle cabin. He walks to town each day going right by our house, but he visits us only on 12 holidays. He chose these days many years ago. He turns up at our house unkempt, unshaven, filthy, often disoriented, and always hungry."

"My word!" declared Chattie. "How sad for all of you — and especially for him."

"The good news for Temp is that he always leaves clean and his stomach full after eating one of Pru's good meals.

"Soon he'll stop by for St. Patrick's Day. Pru will treat us to corned beef and cabbage. On Easter Sunday he arrives early before church to get dressed up for our noon meal. This year he'll stay with Papa while we go to church. Then we'll eat Pru's Easter feast. Mercy gives him his usual chocolate bunny when he leaves."

Chattie wiped away a tear.

She sincerely cares about people.

"We see him twice in May. On Mother's Day Pru cooks a delicious Sunday meal. She always remembers Mama by making her favorite dessert — strawberry shortcake. Then on Memorial Day Papa tells Temp again about one of our cousins who was killed in Vietnam. A few weeks later we see him on Father's Day. I don't think Papa's any happier than when Temp brings him his usual present: an animal he's whittled, usually a duck or a bear."

"Temperance is multi-talented," said Mary Olivia. "When he was married, he had his own painting business. He painted my house. Best painter I ever had. And, don't forget, Verity, he's also a good cook."

"That he is. He was — is — smart. On the 4th of July we have a picnic, and Mercy gives him fireworks to take home. She chooses sparklers because they're safer than firecrackers. He won't stop by again until Labor Day. By then, he's so dirty, and his beard is long. Mercy cries so much she can hardly run his bath water. She has his clean clothes ready — the ones he left to be washed the last time he came by. Pru always has cornbread, field peas, and potatoes packed for him to take.

"On Columbus Day he wants to know all about the explorer. Pru relates with her usual preciseness about his four voyages to North America and answers Temp's questions. If she doesn't know the answers, they do research on the Internet, which is fascinating to Temp, who has never owned a computer. While Pru is our computer expert, the librarian in her prefers to consult old-fashioned sources such as books."

"Good for her," said Genevieve. "Give me a book any day."

"You have an amazing sister," said Chattie.

"Yes. Pru has a photographic memory and shares what she's learned with all of us."

"Temp enjoys Thanksgiving. Mercy and I decorate the house with turkeys, cornucopias, pilgrims, and pumpkins. After he bathes, he goes around to each little figure, examining it while Pru finishes dinner. He eats so much that he takes a nap after dinner. Then he leaves with leftovers of turkey and his favorite sweet potato pie that Pru saves for him.

"He always spends the night on Christmas Eve. That's a special time for us. I play several Christmas carols. His favorite is 'Away in a Manger.' Pru reads the Christmas story from the second chapter of Luke. Then Mercy gets out a Christmas collection of short stories. She and Temp always want to hear Truman Capote's 'A Christmas Memory.' Pru and I take turns reading it aloud. We love it also."

"I've never read 'A Christmas Memory' although I saw the movie," said Chattie. "I may read it this Christmas."

"On Christmas morning Temp is up before everyone. His gift to us is always the same — a package of three handkerchiefs for each of us. Mercy says he knows we need them to catch our tears. We give him warm clothes and a new blanket each year.

After a large Christmas dinner and a little rest, Temp is off with his gifts and Pru's homemade fudge.

"Father has always blamed Eleanor for his behavior change. After she jilted him, he never was the same. He walks daily into town going by her house — her former house, that is. She and her boyfriend married a few weeks after she divorced Temp. She moved from the house long ago, but he never understood. He still thinks she lives there. Sometimes he goes right up to the house and shouts, 'Eleanor. Eleanor.' The elderly owners know his story and never come out. We've tried to talk to him, but we never get through to him," said Verity, shaking her head.

"As sisters, you three have gone beyond the call of duty," stated Mary Olivia. "Temperance will come around one day."

"I pray daily he will. Papa might have grandchildren if only Eleanor had stayed with Temp. But Papa has many descendants — spiritual ones."

"I hope to meet Temp one day," said Chattie. "Could you tell us how you got your names?"

"I knew you'd be asking that question," said Verity, smiling. "Mary Olivia and Genevieve will have to endure the story again."

"Fine with me," said Genevieve. "I can listen to a good tale more than once."

Verity gave the dictionary meaning of each of their names. "'Temperance' means self-control, moderate in action, speech, habits, and in the use of alcoholic drinks. 'Prudence' means wise thought and good judgment. 'Verity' means truth. 'Mercy' means showing compassion, kindness, forgiveness. I think Papa picked out these names intentionally because he wanted us to display complete integrity in our lives.

"I was so proud of my name growing up. Classmates at school asked me, 'What does your name mean?' I'd proudly say 'Truth,' pausing a moment before saying the word."

"Your names represent you well," said Mary Olivia. "With the exception of Temperance, you all live up to your names."

Oh, my precious friend, if you only knew everything about me. How ironic my name is. One day I hope to live up to it.

"Mercy never dated. She likes to tease Pru saying: 'Who would want to marry you? You're too smart for anyone.' She laughs, but Pru, always the serious one, never laughs.

"Unlike Mercy, Pru dated. In fact, she was engaged after college to a young man named Percy Jemison, but her beloved Percy died in a fire the day before they were to be married. She never dated again and never mentioned his name. Sometimes, though, when I see a far-off look in her eyes, I know she's thinking about him."

"I understand so well," said Genevieve, "how difficult the memories are to Prudence."

What an interesting observation for Genevieve to make.

"Pru's beloved Percy was named after the great African-American scientist Percy Julian who developed a drug for glaucoma in 1935. Pru's Percy was born in 1939. He was quite a lot older than my sister. By the way, Pru is 64. Temp is 62. Mercy and I were born years later. Mercy is 53, and I am 50."

"Thanks for the explanation," Chattie said. "You know how curious I am."

"Chattie, the more you get to know Pru, you'll find she's formal, extremely intelligent, a good decision maker. She lives up to her name. She disapproves highly of Mercy and me shortening hers and Temp's names.

"I love my sisters dearly, but at times I get perturbed at them. Pru has always lived at home. She worked 30 years at the public library. Mercy has always lived and worked at home helping Mama and Papa. Being spinsters has made them set in their ways. And they can be downright eccentric."

"But so witty and fun," added Mary Olivia.

"True. Now why don't we change the conversation to another topic. I've waited long enough to ask our writer about her novel." Turning to Genevieve, Verity asked, "How's your novel going?"

"Slowly but surely. This last week I stayed in the library for hours learning about the World War II era. Everything in a novel has to be historically correct. How the characters dress. Hairdos. Makeup. I remember my Grandma Lottie telling me some things about the period, but I had to do a lot more research." Genevieve paused for a few seconds. "I learned that the movie *Gone With the Wind* in 1939 inspired a new look for women's hairstyles. The hair was pulled back and held in a woven net called a snood. What many people don't know about the 1940s was how glamorous the period was. False eyelashes. Bright red lipstick. Penciled eyebrows. Curled hair."

"And don't forget the snood," added Chattie. "I never knew what that hairstyle was called."

"I can't imagine writing a novel," said Verity. "I could never write anything. How long will it take you to finish it?"

"I have no idea. Right now I have only eighty pages."

"That's double what you had last month," added Chattie.

"You're right. I have a lot more to write, but I do have a momentum going. How's your pursuit, Chattie?"

"I'm spending hours each day not only researching my subject but also working diligently at it. Next month I'll share what has become my passion."

"I can't wait to hear about it. How about you, Mary Olivia? Anything to report?"

"Yes. And I'm ecstatic about it."

"Wonderful," smiled Genevieve. "I like your enthusiasm."

"Girls, you may be surprised," Mary Olivia said, pausing for a couple of seconds, and then blurting out: "I'm going to a monastery next month for a weekend retreat."

"Monastery!" exclaimed Verity. "Monastery. I've never heard you even mention going to a monastery. How did this come about?"

"I've been praying about what I should be doing at this juncture in my life ever since Genevieve presented us with the challenge in January. I don't want to go down the Grand Canyon on a mule right now," she laughed. "Last month I said I might want to travel to some of the places I've read about or taught about in my history classes. But I believe God may have other plans for me.

"When I read on Genevieve's questionnaire: 'Take time to be alone to listen to longings of long ago,' it was that sentence that kept coming back to me again and again. Then the question — 'What would God have you to do?' — showed me I needed guidance. I knew I had to leave home. I researched monasteries last week and found one right here in Alabama that had a cancellation in April. A whole weekend alone without stress and distraction. I'll be able to think. I'll get an inspiration from God. What better place than a monastery to hear the voice of God. I'll be listening."

God can speak to us anywhere. But I'm sure he'll speak to Mary Olivia at a monastery. He'll have to speak to me here.

"I'm looking forward to seeing you girls at my house next month for the Tea. I'll be leaving for the monastery a few days afterwards."

I can't pursue a mission I promised Mama I would do as long as Papa is ill. But one day I will with the help of my friends.

"More tea?" asked Verity.

The women nodded.

As they sipped their tea, they talked about the monastery visit until Chattie stood up.

"I must go. I have work to do. I'll pick up my plant cuttings from Prudence. Thanks to you and your sisters for the splendid Tea," she said, hugging Verity. "See you next month."

"Anyone have any idea what she might be doing?" inquired Mary Olivia as she watched Chattie leave.

"I don't have a clue, but I believe whatever Chattie does," said Genevieve, slowly rising from her chair, "will be a project she undertakes with much passion."

After seeing Genevieve off, Verity walked Mary Olivia to her car. "I'm happy about your trip to the monastery," she said, embracing her friend. "You need some time alone."

"I do. Losing Liam was difficult, but Adriana's sudden death last year from an aneurysm was hard on all of us. Watching James and Blake mourn was heart-wrenching. Blake is adjusting better than James. He's strong for Blake, but he's still in deep grief."

"Prayer is the answer," said Verity.

"I agree. Prayer together with some needed solitude. When I return from the monastery, maybe I can be more helpful to them," she said, getting in her car.

Verity waved as her friend drove away.

∞

Taking the dishes back to the kitchen, Verity was surprised to find Prudence and Mercy sitting at the table.

"Papa's asleep," said Prudence, "so we're having a cup of tea."

"And a tea cake," added her sister.

"The girls want to help us beginning next week by sitting with Papa."

"How kind," said Mercy. "Maybe then I can get some cleaning done."

"Those three would be the only ones I would trust with Papa," said Prudence.

"I have some more news, and it's about Mary Olivia." She sat down with her sisters. "You'll never guess where she's going next month."

"Where? Don't keep us in suspense," pleaded Mercy.

"Brace yourselves," Verity said, pausing a few seconds to proceed. "She's going to a monastery for a weekend retreat."

"That's great," Prudence said. "Why not? Her husband was a Catholic."

"Come on, Pru," said Mercy. "M.O. at a monastery. It's hard for me to imagine her leaving her family and friends to go to a quiet monastery."

"Mary Olivia is searching for a deeper spiritual life. Remember, I've known her longer than either of you."

"I agree with you. But time will tell," said Verity.

Mercy and Prudence went upstairs to check on their father.

Verity placed the dishes in the sink. In a pensive mood, she sat down at the table.

Interesting things are happening. Mary Olivia is going to a monastery to seek her calling. Chattie has found hers. Genevieve is working hard on hers. I can't pursue mine yet. And I have a shameful secret, or an opprobrious one, as Pru would say, that I live with every day.

4

APRIL

~

MARY OLIVIA

"Hope is the thing with feathers
That perches in the soul."
American poet Emily Dickinson (1830-1886)

Mary Olivia stood at her living room window listening to the rain drip from the eaves of her house.

She remembered the first spring rain last month. She was feeding the horses when it started sprinkling. She stayed outside even when the rain turned into a downpour. The horses ran around in the pasture. They must have felt as alive and refreshed as she had.

Watching the grass turn green and ponds fill up with water was a favorite part of her childhood growing up on her family's farm. After the Tea she planned to go for a long walk to praise God for the rain and ponder her monastery visit.

Looking down the winding road amidst the green rolling hills, she spotted Chattie's P.T. Cruiser slowly turning up the circular driveway in front of her house. She watched as Chattie maneuvered her umbrella out of the car along with her purse and a vase of flowers.

As soon as Chattie reached the door, Mary Olivia opened it and took her umbrella.

"Thanks." Chattie hugged her and handed her a bouquet of flowers.

THANKS. BEAUTIFUL, Mary Olivia wrote in large black letters on a white legal pad.

Chattie looked at her quizzically.

Mary Olivia quickly took a slip of paper out of her pocket and handed it to her friend.

Chattie read the note aloud: "Yesterday morning I committed myself to a vow of silence. I'll be going to a monastery in three days. Today I need your support as I remain silent."

"Wholeheartedly. These days of silence will prepare you well for the monastery.

"Your Victorian house is charming. And the location is picturesque — picture postcard perfect."

THANKS, Mary Olivia wrote again.

"I thought Gerber daisies would be fitting for an April Tea."

Mary Olivia motioned for Chattie to follow her to the dining room table. Indicating with her hands for her to stay there, Mary Olivia went to the kitchen sink and filled the vase with water.

She stopped at the fridge to read — "Taciturn: inclined to not talking; by nature silent." After last month's Tea, she decided to follow Prudence's practice of putting words on her fridge. She thought it a good idea for her boys — and herself. Blake was taking the vocabulary study seriously, writing down the word and meaning in a notebook. James and Eric had never mentioned the words. Maybe they hadn't noticed them.

Hearing Chattie approach the kitchen, Mary Olivia quickly walked to the dining room. She didn't want Chattie to see her messy kitchen.

She set the arrangement in the middle of the rectangular table.

Now the table is complete for the Tea.

"What a mood you've set with the background music. Who's the composer?"

Mary Olivia had anticipated that question. She reached in her pocket for a note.

Chattie read aloud: "DEBUSSEY: 'REVERIE' and 'CLAIR DE LUNE.'

"Debussey. Sure. I can rarely match a composer to his music.

"I anticipate a distinctive Tea today," Chattie said. "A change in routine is good for us. This is only my fourth Tea, but what has impressed me thus far is that each has been unique."

Mary Olivia smiled and nodded again. Then she thought about what had made the Teas different this year.

It's Genevieve's challenge and Chattie's presence. Genevieve's challenge is stretching us. And we all needed Chattie to bring out our emotions and feelings. In the past, our Tea has been surface-level. Chit-chat. Not that we haven't cared for each other and been there for each other. But this year we are digging deeper. At least I am.

Mary Olivia hoped the girls would benefit from today's Tea. She had learned much about silence the last 24 hours.

More aware of her surroundings, she had heard and seen things — sometimes for the first time. This morning the singing of birds awakened her. She went outside and watched as a hawk took off from a tree and then marveled at its flight. The hawk reminded her of a passage in the Bible, so she went inside and searched for it, finding it in Job 39:26, "Is it by your wisdom that the hawk soars ...?"

"What a book collection," said Chattie, noticing a library with bookshelves filled with books. "Do you mind if I look?"

Mary Olivia walked to the library and motioned Chattie to join her.

"I've heard it said that books tell much about a person."

Mary Olivia nodded and smiled.

"You're truly a bibliophile. But how do you dust all of them?"

That's a good question. I'm not writing anything down because I rarely dust.

"I've never seen so many books in a home. Biographies. Sandburg's *Lincoln*. Plutarch's *Lives*. Boswell's *Life of Samuel Johnson*. Christian classics. C.S. Lewis. *Mere Christianity*. *Confessions of Augustine*. Classic novels. Charles Dickens. Jane Austen. Short story collections. Flannery O'Connor. O. Henry. Poetry collections. Emily Dickinson. Elizabeth Barrett Browning. Robert Frost. You have an eclectic taste, but I don't see any contemporary fiction."

Mary Olivia nodded.

I don't have much interest in current fiction. Real people's lives and ideas fascinate me. Last night I read the 11th century long poem, The Song of Roland. Would a psychologist say I read to avoid something — maybe dusting?

Mary Olivia knew she needed to clean her house. A stack of magazines and newspapers along with DVDs were piled high in the den. Wall-to-wall furniture filled the house. Even after the boys and she had worked for hours straightening up, the house still looked untidy.

I hadn't noticed the house being so cluttered until I stopped talking.

They heard a knock at the door. Mary Olivia walked to open it while Chattie continued to scan the bookshelves.

Mary Olivia took Genevieve's umbrella and motioned her to come in.

"I can't remember a Tea when it rained so much," Genevieve said. "We need the rain, but it sure is making my arthritis act up."

"I'm sorry about your arthritis," said Chattie, greeting her friend and leading her to the sofa.

"It's all about getting old." Genevieve slowly sat down. She smiled. "Actually, it's all about my genes. I've had arthritis as long as I can remember. It's in the Boswell family genes."

"Is wit also in your family genes?"

"You are the clever one," said Genevieve, smiling broadly. "I guess I did get my wit from Grandma Lottie."

Mary Olivia embraced Genevieve before handing her a note. She watched as Genevieve read it.

"A silent hostess. First time for everything. Our Tea will be different, but I do like surprises."

Mary Olivia nodded. She saw Verity arrive.

"I'm sorry I'm late. I had to wait for Pru to relieve me sitting with Papa."

Mary Olivia hugged Verity and gave her a note.

"Bless you," dear friend," she said after reading it. "Of course, I will support your vow of silence."

"Was Prudence at the public ibrary?" asked Genevieve.

"Yes, her weekly visit." Verity sat on the sofa. "You know Pru — a life-long student. As a former librarian, she can't stay away. No telling what she was studying. We'll know when she shares her stories. Last week it was Marco Polo's 17-year stay with Kublai Khan. The week before it was King Edward VIII's abdication in 1936 to marry American divorcee Wallis Simpson. Pru told us every juicy detail — history she calls it — which is correct, about Edward's two mistresses before he met Wallis. The Bubonic Plague. The Irish Potato Famine. We never know what stories we'll hear during our dinner conversations. Although sometimes we wish she would wait until after dinner."

Prudence and I grew up sharing a love of history. I enjoy hearing about her research

"What a fascinating sister," said Chattie. "By the way, what word and quote has she selected this week?"

"As usual, she posted new ones on the fridge Sunday afternoon. The word is 'munificent,' which means extremely generous. And the quote. Let me get it right. It's short. 'Rest and you rust.' It's from the actress Helen Hayes."

"Even I can remember that quote. 'Rest and you rust.' And I agree with it," Genevieve smiled. "No one in our group will ever rust."

Mary Olivia motioned them into the adjoining dining

room.

Verity walked to the window, and the others followed. Three chestnut horses grazed in the pasture nearby.

"I never tire of seeing your beautiful horses. They must have heard me. They're looking straight at us. Are they as curious about us as we are about them?"

Mary Olivia smiled and wrote, MAYBE.

"Watching your horses brings back memories. Grandpapa Williams had horses named Jacob and Esau that pulled his plow. Grandpapa was a minister like Papa. So Grandpapa named them Jacob and Esau. The Biblical brothers didn't get along. Neither did the horses."

"Beyond the fence about 500 yards from here," Verity said, pointing out the place to Chattie, "was Grandpapa's place complete with a rambling farmhouse that was torn down years ago. I've often told Mary Olivia, I'm sure, too many times: 'What if Papa hadn't sold the farm and house? We would still live next door to each other.' But Mama was a city girl. Papa loved her so much he agreed to move to town. I'll admit we had a happy family life in town. But what wonderful early childhood memories I have. And then after we moved, what a treat when Mary Olivia's family invited us out to visit."

Mary Olivia nodded in agreement.

Verity's mind is on the past now that Rev. Isaiah is dying.

Mary Olivia walked to the table and gestured them to sit down. She pulled out a chair for Genevieve and then sat down beside her. Chattie and Verity joined them.

"Noritake china," said Genevieve. "Elegant."

"And exquisite white linen napkins," said Chattie. "We

must be having a formal Tea today."

Mary Olivia nodded.

Thunder and lightning crashed, and almost immediately the electricity went out.

"Oh, no," said Genevieve.

Mary Olivia had already left the table to get some matches. She returned and lit the four candles on the table.

She wrote, NOW WE CAN SEE.

The friends looked around the table.

I know they are wondering how the Tea will progress. I think everything will go fine. In fact, I like it.

The storm subsided, but it was still raining.

A small framed quotation was placed next to their plates along with a note saying it was a gift for them.

"How precious. May we read our quotes aloud?" asked Verity.

Mary Olivia nodded.

Great. Just what I wanted them to do.

"'Silence is more musical than any song.' Christina Rossetti," read Verity, leaning closer to the light of the candle. "Isn't she one of your favorite poets?"

Mary Olivia nodded.

"'The religious need silence to hear God speak to them.' Mother Teresa," read Chattie. "You chose the right one for me. Mother Teresa is one of my heroines."

"My quote is a clever one," said Genevieve. "'My personal hobbies are reading, listening to music, and silence.' Dame Edith Sitwell, a British poet who lived from 1887-1964."

Mary Olivia pointed to Verity and wrote, PLEASE PRAY.

"Lord, thank you for this special time together. Guide Mary Olivia as she withdraws to pray and listen to Your counsel. I ask that You reveal to her and to us what You would have us to do with our lives each day. In the name of Jesus. Amen."

Mary Olivia wrote, THANK YOU and TEA MENU: BANANA NUT BREAD AND LEMON GREEN TEA and then lifted her pad in front of her so they could read the words. Next she carried a white teapot around the table, methodically picking up each cup and saucer and pouring tea into each cup. After sitting down, she poured her own tea and passed a plate of sliced banana nut bread to each woman. They ate and drank in silence.

They seem reflective.

"Delicious bread and so moist," said Genevieve. "Did you make it?"

Mary Olivia nodded.

"I seldom drink green tea," added Genevieve. "But this isn't bad. I know it's healthy, but, of course, I prefer Earl Grey."

Mary Olivia smiled. She glanced at Chattie and Verity, who were also amused.

"What a tranquil mood you've provided for us with the indoor fountain on your buffet," Verity said. "The sound of water calms me. Especially in this storm."

ME TOO, wrote Mary Olivia.

"I've enjoyed my visits with Rev. Isaiah," Chattie said, looking at Verity.

"Your staying with Papa has helped us get some needed rest and also catch up on our chores. Can you believe one day I found Mercy washing the walls of our parlor?"

"Probably a good change for her," said Genevieve. "We will continue coming our usual days if that's all right with you and your sisters."

"It's fine with us. Please remember what a blessing you are," Verity said.

Chattie asked Genevieve about the progress of her novel.

"Whoever thinks the writing life is glamorous should spend a day with me. I find writing hard work...although it's rewarding. My problem has been making time to write. I decided after our Tea last month that to write I had to get away and do nothing else but write." She stopped to get her breath and drink a sip of tea. "I caught a train from Birmingham to New Orleans and wrote all the way there and then rode a train back writing all the way back. I took the train to New Orleans twice."

"How glamorous to write on a train," said Chattie. "My word! I'm sorry I used that word, but I think it would be glam.... I mean fun. Out of the routine."

"It certainly was not glamorous, but it did work for me. I would have preferred to write on a freighter as Alex Haley did; but, of course, that's impossible since I'm not in the Coast Guard as Haley was.

"I not only wrote but watched people — their gestures, mannerisms, speech. I incorporated some of those observations into my novel."

THANKS FOR TELLING US ABOUT YOUR NOVEL, wrote Mary Olivia, pouring more tea.

"Did I ever tell you what we four called ourselves as kids?" asked Verity.

"I don't believe so," said Genevieve.

"Well, our paternal grandmother was Indian — Crow. When we were young, we all had Indian names. Temp was Speaks Few Words, Mercy was Talks Too Much, Pru was Studies Too Much, and I was Thinks Too Much."

"How creative," Chattie commented.

"Lately while sitting up with Papa I've been thinking back on our childhood. Oops. I was Thinks Too Much."

Mary Olivia smiled, and the other women laughed.

"Can you believe it was Temp who gave us our names? It's always been mysterious to me that he understood our personalities so well to give us the names he did.

"Maybe Temp will come out of his self-imposed exile one day," continued Verity. "Then, hopefully, we can convince him to get a medical and psychiatric checkup."

"Do everything you can to encourage him to have a checkup," said Genevieve. "My Shipman died of a stroke. He procrastinated going to the doctor. A visit might have saved his life."

Genevieve's a caring person, but she hasn't expressed her feelings openly until this year. I wish I could open up more. Maybe after my monastery stay.

"I have two questions to ask each of you," said Chattie. "I hope you don't mind. How did your husband die? How did you react to his death?"

Chattie has us discussing things we've never talked about at our Tea. She's grieving and wants to know how we grieved. She's doing a reality check. She wants to know if she's grieving correctly. There's no right way. At least I didn't grieve the conventional way. I often feel guilty.

"Widows react to the deaths of their husbands in different ways," answered Genevieve. "Some widows are angry at their husbands for dying. Others feel as if they were the first to ever experience a loss and grieve for a long time. I knew a widow who grieved for 25 years until her death."

"Often widows get solace by going to the cemetery to visit their husbands' graves. Doll went to the cemetery every day for three months. I went to Shipman's grave only a few times the first months. I felt his presence with me at home." Genevieve paused a moment. "Now I go to his grave on our wedding anniversary and the annual Decoration Day at the cemetery. I don't know exactly how widows are supposed to act. I do think the grieving process continues until a widow experiences emotional and spiritual wellness."

Emotional and spiritual wellness. Then I'm still in the grieving process. I forgive Liam and then catch myself remembering his infidelities and get angry again.

"I've never heard grief expressed that way," said Chattie. "You've helped me."

"I have observed many widows over the years. Insight comes with age, you know.

"Shipman had a massive stroke with no prior warning. This month. On April 1 — April Fool's Day of all days."

POET T.S. ELIOT WROTE IN "THE WASTELAND" — "APRIL IS THE CRUELEST MONTH," Mary Olivia wrote quickly on her pad and held it up for them to read.

"That particular April was certainly a cruel one for me. I was in shock, but I didn't realize it at first because after the funeral I continued my usual volunteer activities. I worked at the library's weekly book sale, took groceries to the Vietnam Vet's group home, and read to children twice a week at an elementary school. I thought if I stayed busy enough I wouldn't think about my loss." Genevieve took a deep breath and drank some water.

"Where was I?"

"If I stayed busy enough I wouldn't think about my loss," said Verity.

"Then one day — a few weeks after Shipman's death — it hit me. I was reading or trying to read a book on grieving. I read the first page over probably 10 times. I then threw the book across the room. I remember saying aloud, 'I can't even concentrate on one page.' I broke down and sobbed and sobbed. Then the doorbell rang. It was my Aunt Harriet. When she saw I was crying, she marched in and started in on me: 'Get hold of yourself.' I told her I had for a few weeks, but I couldn't any more. I had to grieve. How thankful I was when she quickly left after insisting I face reality. What did she know about losing a husband? She had been married to Uncle Neeley for 60 years and had not quit bossing him around.

"Back to my breakdown. I stayed at home for two weeks. I kept the house dark and the shades drawn. I even joined a grief support group for a few months.

"Then I went back to my volunteer activities, and one day at the library I read a book on the history of tea. That book sparked a vision of starting this group. One of the best things I ever did."

AMEN, wrote Mary Olivia.

"What a moving story," said Chattie. "My losing Roberto

was also unexpected. You probably remember the details — since it was reported in the paper — of his accident. A hit and run. He was out jogging in the rain, and a car hit him. The police never found the person and said the driver may have never known he or she hit Roberto. Another jogger saw a car but couldn't remember anything about it, not even its color. I've accepted the fact that we'll never know who the driver was."

"Your husband's death was shocking," said Genevieve. "We prayed for your family at our church. Of course, so many in our town knew Roberto because of Roberto's Italian Bakery and his civic activities."

"Your prayers helped me get through the terrible ordeal. We think things will go on every day as they did the day before. I never dreamed Roberto wouldn't live to see his grandchildren." Chattie accepted a tissue Mary Olivia handed her. "I always expected us to grow old together," she said, dabbing the tears around her eyes. "I couldn't comprehend he was gone."

"I remember the feeling," said Genevieve.

Liam and I had such a different relationship. How wonderful it would have been if we had found the happiness that Chattie and Roberto had.

"When the policeman left after giving me the news of Roberto's death, I walked out into the rain dumbfounded. I didn't want to come in. How could I endure his death? How could I be a widow at 57? After getting drenched, I came in and called the boys' school. They came home immediately, but it was difficult to tell them about their father. We were such a close-knit family.

"By the way, if you ever wondered why I sold the bakery,

it was because the boys had no interest in baking; and I needed their help if I kept it. I decided to sell it after another baker approached me. I agreed to let him use the same name replacing Roberto with Giovanni."

"I'm glad you told us about the bakery. Giovanni is doing a great job, but everyone misses Roberto," said Genevieve. "It would be impossible to replace his friendliness and charisma."

"I know. During the week of the funeral, I went through the motions of doing what I had to do to remain strong for the boys and Roberto's family, many of whom came from Italy. When everyone left, I went to bed. It was a week before I realized I had worn my nightgown turned wrong side out. I didn't leave home for six weeks. Much of that time I stayed in bed. No words could express my sorrow, so I didn't want to talk to anyone. All I could think of was Roberto. How would I ever go on without him?

"I had no appetite and ate little. I lost several pounds. I couldn't sleep. I heard every noise at night. Police sirens. Train whistles. Early morning traffic. When I did sleep, I would suddenly wake up aching so much for Roberto I would physically hurt. I now know I was in shock all that time."

"That is not unusual, dear," said Genevieve.

"One day I experienced what I consider an epiphany. I vividly remember that morning. The sun shone unusually bright in my bedroom window. I jumped out of bed and ran to the window as if to embrace the sunshine. I spoke to Roberto as if he were in the room: 'You know I miss you intensely, but you don't want me to continue living like a recluse. You had an infectious love of life and taught me to appreciate each day. You want me to wear my nicest dress and do something I enjoy.' So I did. I went to a new coffee shop and ordered a cappuccino and biscotti and then browsed at a nearby boutique. I returned home and watched *It Happened One Night*, one of my favorite old movies."

What poignant stories! I've been missing out not listening — really listening to people. I think many times at our Teas when the girls talked I was daydreaming. Today I've made a conscious effort to listen. It hasn't been difficult since I can't talk.

"I'm glad you shared your experience," said Genevieve. "It helps us to know you better and what you have gone through this last year."

"I do apologize for talking so long," said Chattie.

She's living up to her name.

"Verity, how did you cope?" asked Genevieve.

"I'm sorry. I can't. It's too painful," Verity said, shaking her head. She removed her handkerchief from her pocket and wept.

Genevieve patted Verity on the shoulder. "Now, now. With your caretaking duties this is much too difficult a time for you to remember the past."

Mary Olivia pointed to Verity and then back to herself.

"Do you want me to tell about your experience?" asked Verity.

She nodded.

"I remember well Mary Olivia telling me about that terrible night. She was up late reading…"

Mary Olivia spelled out MADAME BOVARY BY GUSTAVE FLAUBERT.

Interesting choice of a novel. I was reading about an adulteress.

Verity continued, "...*Madame Bovary* while Liam attended a sales convention. The phone rang. She answered, expecting it to be Liam. Instead, it was the police saying Liam had suffered a heart attack in his hotel room. Do I have it right?"

Mary Olivia nodded.

Except he was with another woman. A young woman.

"Mary Olivia went immediately to the Atlanta hospital to be with him. He died before she arrived."

"My word!" exclaimed Chattie.

"I was in Chicago recovering from another miscarriage," Verity explained, "and couldn't attend the funeral. But Pru and Mercy kept me informed. I know Liam's death was devastating to Mary Olivia and the boys. Eric was still at home. I'm sure he helped her with her loneliness."

Mary Olivia gave a slight nod. BUT NOT WITH THE UNEXPECTED DEBT LIAM LEFT ME, she quickly wrote.

"I'm sorry," said Verity, shaking her head. "That must be painful for you to think about."

NO. Mary Olivia wrote again quickly, IT'S HEALING TO SHARE MY PAIN. *At least some of it.*

The women remained silent a few moments.

They're probably feeling sorry for me. I don't want pity. I needed to get rid of some emotional baggage. If I could talk, I would go into more detail. That rascal. But I must rid myself of those feelings. I still feel too much bitterness toward him. I must remember Liam's good qualities and put his infidelities and weaknesses behind me. I'm praying my monastery stay will help me heal.

"Next month I'll be no silent host," said Chattie, emphasizing the word 'silent.'

Mary Olivia put her hand over her mouth, trying to keep herself from laughing or blurting a word. The other women laughed.

"I didn't mean to be funny, but laughter is good for us. I'll try again," said Chattie, speaking as properly as she could. "For our May Tea I'm inviting you girls to a Garden Tea. I'll be showing off my new garden."

"Garden party? You are *gardening*?" asked Genevieve.

"Passionately," answered Chattie, pronouncing the word slowly, the enthusiasm emanating from her voice.

"I admit I am surprised. I knew you were doing research, but gardening never came to my mind," said Genevieve. "What fun it will be to see your garden."

"I can't begin to tell you what a challenge I took on. Next month I look forward to getting input as to whether I've pulled it off. It's difficult to be objective about your own work."

"I know it will be grand," said Verity.

"I do have a request," said Chattie. "I want each of you to wear a garden hat. A simple straw will be fine."

"I only have church hats," said Verity. "It should be fun shopping for a garden one."

"Occasionally I wear hats to church, but I have never owned a garden one. I may recruit Hannah to help me shop for one."

The electricity came back on.

"Just in time for us to leave," said Verity, smiling.

Mary Olivia handed each of them a typed note.

Chattie read hers aloud: "Thank you for coming to my Silent Tea."

"I believe I can speak for all of us," said Genevieve. "We would not have missed it. Who doesn't like change? We girls surely are experiencing it this year."

The women gathered their framed quotations.

Mary Olivia handed them another slip of paper.

"Please pray for me this weekend," Verity read aloud, "that I will be receptive to God's guidance."

The three women hugged Mary Olivia and assured her of their prayers.

"Pru and Mercy will also be praying," said Verity.

Mary Olivia quickly wrote, THANK YOU.

"I can't wait to hear about your experiences. See you next month—when you can talk. And don't forget your hats," said Chattie.

Verity and Genevieve followed Chattie out the door.

Mary Olivia gazed out the window and watched them drive away. Then she grabbed a jacket and headed out the door to walk and think.

Garden party. That should be fun.

I think the girls enjoyed our Silent Tea. I'm ready to go to the monastery to seek God's guidance and direction about my future. And my past. Should I tell the boys that before Liam's death I was planning to ask him for a divorce? Should I tell them the details of his death?

5

MAY

∽

CHATTIE

"The night is given us to take breath, to pray, to drink deep at the fountain of power. The day, to use the strength which has been given us, to go forth to work with it till the evening."
Pioneering Nurse Florence Nightingale (1820-1910)

Catching a glimpse of herself in her bedroom mirror, Chattie adjusted her hat and smiled.

She had gone to several shops the last month looking for the right hat. It had to look like a garden party hat. Finally she found it — a beige straw with a blue silk hydrangea.

She continued to look in the mirror.

The perfect hat for a spring Tea.

Stepping out onto the screened-in porch, she said aloud while throwing her hands up into the air and twirling around, "What a beautiful day for my first Tea!"

She thought of one of Roberto's favorite expressions: "Bask in the Moment."

That was exactly what she was doing. Basking in the moment. She was feeling great anticipation and pleasure about her first Tea. "Bask in the moment," she said aloud.

Talking aloud helps me not to feel alone. Perhaps it's my way of coping with Roberto's death. I've also started talking to my plants, which I've read is supposed to be good for them. I know it's good for me.

After taking a deep breath of the fresh air, Chattie walked around the green metal table, making sure the glass vase containing the blue hydrangea blooms was exactly in the middle of the round table. Wanting the flowers to be fresh, she had cut them after noon.

She never tired of hydrangeas.

They look so fragile and delicate; yet their blooms stay beautiful for weeks on end. A perfect analogy to a strong woman. Oh, we can appear to be fragile, but we are made of steel. My word! What thoughts are racing through my mind this morning. I must write them down in my gardening journal. Gardening has toughened me up, but it also has softened me. I'm more in awe of beauty. Not only in the garden but the clouds in the sky and the paintings on my walls. I feel a new awakening, something inward my thoughts cannot express.

"Gardening has made me philosophical," she said aloud. Sitting down on a cushioned chair at the table, she looked out into her garden and smiled.

Rising early, she had been looking forward to this day, when she would host the tea, ever since the last week in January when she decided to pursue gardening. She remembered it vividly.

∽

The morning after the January Tea she awoke with Genevieve's challenge on her mind. She couldn't stop thinking about it. She read the questionnaire over and over.

For about two weeks she pondered what to do. Finally, she focused on her childhood memories of flowers. Both her mother and maternal grandmother, avid gardeners, had belonged to a monthly garden club. She remembered their luxuriant flowers — roses, gardenias, irises, hydrangeas, petunias, azaleas, day lilies.

She couldn't stop thinking of flowers.

One morning while praying, she cried out to God: "Do You want me to take up gardening?" She didn't hear an audible voice, but an inner voice gave her the answer. She later called it an epiphany. She knew at that moment what she was to do.

Knowing that Roberto loved flowers was another confirmation for her that gardening should be her exploration. Outside his bakery, he had large concrete planters that held flowers in perpetual bloom. He enjoyed choosing the right plants for each season: pansies for winter, tulips for spring, petunias for summer, and mums for fall. Roberto thought the flowers drew many people into his bakery. Once they saw the beautiful flowers and then tasted his breads and pastries many became regular customers.

In February she watched television gardening shows about landscape design and what plants grew best in the shade and sun. She bought garden books, scoured magazines for articles on plants, and sent off for numerous catalogs. At the public library she checked out gardening books and read them from cover to cover. On cold days she stayed propped up in bed for hours immersed in research. The more she studied the more she realized she had an enormous task ahead of her.

One day she awoke feeling overwhelmed. Crying for the first time in a long time, it didn't take her long to come to a conclusion: she required some expert help in the form of a part-time gardener. But where could she find help? In the newspaper want ads section she found a labor company advertising landscape workers. She decided against going that route. She had to hire someone who came highly recommended. A widow had to be careful. She had to find a trustworthy, hardworking man who knew all about gardening — and someone who wouldn't take advantage of her being a widow. Fortunately, one day browsing at a garden center, she talked to a friend who recommended a retired county agricultural extension agent.

It was the first day of March that Theodore Root agreed to be Chattie's gardener. She had spoken to him only briefly on the phone, but she detected an eagerness on his part to help her. She wasn't wrong when he showed up at her house ready to work. What she was wrong about was his looks. She had imagined him a strong burly man. When she greeted him at the door, she met a sun-tanned attractive man of average height and build. They sat down in her den, and immediately he wanted to talk business. He offered to work for $16 an hour. That wage sounded steep to her, but she had no choice. She needed him, and if he didn't work out, well, she would cross that bridge later. Her instincts told her, though, he would be a good worker.

"I would appreciate it if you would come up with a garden design soon," he said.

"In two days, I'll have one."

It didn't take her long to sketch one since she had spent much time thinking about it. When he returned, studied it, and made suggestions, they soon agreed on an overall design. A large fountain would be set up in the middle of the large garden, and it would be surrounded by raised beds of flowers. She asked for his input about the flowers she had in mind. Theo knew exactly what flowers to plant and when to plant them.

She was ready to begin gardening.

The next day Theo called a retired friend who owned a sod cutter. The man came immediately and removed sod from the side yard to make room for the sun garden.

Theo calculated and measured for what seemed a long time to Chattie, but finally he found the center point of the garden. They decided it was the perfect place for a fountain. The two of them shopped for a concrete fountain and found one she liked — a three-tiered one with an angel on top.

After the fountain was delivered, Chattie could hardly wait until Theo hooked it up. She made a big deal about flipping the switch controlling it.

"Ready, set, go," she shouted, as she turned on the fountain. She was not disappointed — the sound of the water immediately soothed her.

The next week Theo arranged for three loads of topsoil to be delivered. A garden center brought out peat moss and fertilizer as well as stone pebbles for the walking paths that would wind around the garden. A brick company delivered red landscaping blocks to be used to enclose the raised flower beds and also be a border for the garden paths.

Theo got to work immediately making the raised beds and

the garden paths. The planting beds took much preparation. On late afternoons and on Saturdays Antonio and Mario helped Chattie spread dirt and compost. The boys never complained about being away from their friends or studies because they saw what a difference the garden was making in her life.

After 50 azaleas were delivered, she and the boys spent several afternoons helping Theo plant them in shady areas at the edge of the woods and around the house. Next, she had 20 hydrangeas delivered. Theo and the boys planted them in semi-shaded places around the house and near the woods.

"Wow!" Chattie exclaimed. "I love the azaleas and the hydrangeas. They would be enough for me."

"Hold on," said Theo. "We have many beds to fill. Fortunately for you, my late wife and I gardened for decades. I have many perennials — lilies, irises, mums, asters, cannas." He stopped to think. "And daisies and gladioluses. I will dig up some of the plants and transplant them here."

"I don't know what to say. You're being so gracious and saving me lots of money."

"It's my pleasure. I have so many."

They planted colorful bedding plants for summer blooms — marigolds, begonias, periwinkles, and zinnias.

Remembering how much she liked her grandmother's moon garden, she asked Theo to help her choose white-blooming flowers. At late dusk after they set them out, she walked out into the garden. To her delight the white flowers were the only ones she could see.

Theo helped her choose 10 Knock Out Rose bushes. After he set them out, she bought a book on growing roses. She was determined to have beautiful ones.

Roberto had planted a small herb garden years ago, but since his death she had neglected it. To her surprise, when she weeded it, she found basil, oregano, and rosemary thriving. At the March Tea when Prudence gave her cuttings of lemon balm, lavender, and orange mint, she knew she had taken up the right challenge. It was as if Prudence was validating what she was doing, even though Prudence had no idea Chattie had started gardening that month.

Chattie loved every moment in her garden even when she crawled into bed at night aching all over. She especially liked setting out plants and getting her hands dirty. She knew she had found her calling.

Although she appreciated others helping her in the garden, Chattie enjoyed working alone. Some days she would be so intent on working that she forgot all about the time until it was almost dark. The boys would phone and leave her a message, "Mom, where are you? Are you still in the garden? Call us."

∞

Chattie heard a car drive up and watched as Verity walked toward the back porch.

I'm glad Verity is here. It seems I've been reliving my gardening experiences for hours.

"Can you believe I'm the first to arrive?" she asked, embracing Chattie. "Pru insisted I come on. She's working a crossword puzzle while Papa takes his afternoon nap."

"You're a welcome surprise. And I absolutely love your straw hat."

"It's fancy for me. You know how plain I usually dress."

"The green chiffon bow on your hat goes well with your green dress. We may lose you in the garden today with your green."

"You're witty today. You sound happy."

"I am. Happy — and tired."

"No wonder." Verity looked out at the garden. "It looks great. I can't wait to see everything you've done. Here comes Mary Olivia. She should have lots to tell us about her weekend at the monastery."

Before Mary Olivia could reach them, she started apologizing for her hat. "I know I lack color, but the only hat I had was this crushable straw I took to the monastery. It proved to be a good travel hat."

"It looks comfortable," said Verity, nodding her approval.

"Here's Genevieve. Doesn't she look stylish?" asked Chattie.

With her cane, Genevieve walked to the porch and sat down. "It's my arthritis again," she announced. "All the rain we've had."

"Your fancy hat should cheer you up," said Mary Olivia. It was a large brimmed crocheted straw with red silk roses all around the crown.

"It does. I — that is, Hannah and I — had fun shopping for it. I tried on every hat I saw. When I found this one, I knew my search was over." After resting a few minutes, she added, "Roses, of course, are my favorite flowers."

They sat awhile chatting about shopping for hats.

"Are you three ready for me to lead you down the garden path?" asked Chattie, smiling broadly.

"Lead on," said Genevieve. "I'll follow. Slowly but enthusiastically."

What a trooper you are. You continually inspire me.

Chattie began the tour by pointing out the azaleas and hydrangeas all around the yard.

"The hydrangeas are breathtaking," said Genevieve. "Both the blues and pinks."

Then they lingered at a bed of summer bloomers.

"Marigolds, begonias, periwinkles — old favorites," said Mary Olivia.

"Next is a bed of cutting flowers. The zinnias and cosmos are small plants now, but I've been told they'll grow fast and make great cut flowers."

Then the girls marveled at beds of perennials — day lilies, calla lilies, irises, chrysanthemums, gladioluses, cannas.

"Of course, all aren't in bloom yet, but that's fine. I want blooms for all seasons."

"I don't believe you'll ever have to worry," said Verity.

Walking along the garden path, Chattie continually heard exclamations of surprise over the garden. "Your ooh's and aah's are so affirming and welcome."

"We're the fortunate ones. We get to appreciate the beauty without having to do the work," Genevieve said with a smile.

"Now for the herb garden. I can thank Prudence for these — lemon balm, orange mint, and lavender," said Chattie, pointing out the plants to Verity.

"She'll be pleased when I tell her how the plants have proliferated." Verity bent down to smell them. "All three of these herbs add great fragrance to your garden."

"Last, but not least, I want you to see my moon garden."

"What's a moon garden?" asked Mary Olivia.

"What do these flowers have in common?" asked Chattie when they arrived at the moon garden.

"White flowers," said Mary Olivia.

"Petunias, dianthus, irises, daisies. And a flower called a moonflower. All have white flowers. They can be seen at night during a full moon. In fact, they're the only flowers that stand out."

"What a garden!" exclaimed Genevieve, turning toward the porch and taking a deep breath. "I am proud of how you embraced my challenge. I am tired and ready for the Tea, but I would not have missed the tour. I predict your garden will be part of Breeze Hill's garden tour soon."

"I've never thought of that," said Chattie, helping Genevieve make her way to the porch.

Hmmm ... maybe in a few years. What fun that would be.

Sitting down at the table on the porch, Chattie said, "Please forgive my informality, but I poured our hot white tea in a decanter so it would stay warm while we toured the garden."

"Perfect," said Genevieve. "Did you ever see so many flowers at a table? Placemats. Cups. Dessert plates. All with pictures of flowers on them."

"They're all from my favorite consignment shop." Chattie poured the tea and passed around cream cheese tarts topped with strawberries.

"Let's each say a silent prayer before we eat," said Chattie, bowing her head.

After several minutes Genevieve said, "I thanked God for your garden. I also prayed He would give you energy for all the back-breaking work involved in maintaining your garden."

"I appreciate your prayer. Gardening is demanding."

"These tarts are luscious," said Verity, after picking up another one. We rarely have them at our teas."

"I haven't drunk white tea before," said Genevieve. "I like it. It's different — and surprisingly good. Light and slightly sweet."

"It's a healthy tea with many antioxidants," said Chattie.

The girls are eating and drinking as if they were starving. I think I may have lingered too long in the garden.

"I know your favorite flower," Verity said, slowly eating her second tart. "Blue hydrangea centerpiece. Blue hydrangeas on your porch and in your yard. And who could overlook the pretty blue silk hydrangea on your hat?"

"No competition. I enjoy all flowers, but hydrangeas are my favorite. I have twenty plants now, but I'll have more next year when I propagate them."

"Hydrangeas have gorgeous blooms," said Genevieve, "but I never grew them. My Shipman disliked them. He thought after they bloomed their mophead faded blooms were ugly."

"Did the hail storm last month damage any of your flowers?" asked Verity.

Verity is purposely changing the subject. She knows how much I love hydrangeas and doesn't want Genevieve's story ruining my fun.

"Not as much as I feared. I'll never forget the night of the storm. I lay in bed listening to the hail pounding on the roof. I knew it probably meant my plants were beaten down. I was right. The next day I cried when I saw them. Fortunately, after a few days of sunshine, most perked up and put on new leaves. Of course, I had to replace some."

"You couldn't tell today that you ever had a hail storm," said Genevieve.

"I'm thankful for that. I started a gardener's journal last month. I wrote about the effects of the hailstorm. I've also recorded when I planted flowers and when they bloomed."

"Are you also writing about your aching muscles?" asked Genevieve. "You must have them after all this work."

Verity and Mary Olivia laughed.

"No," said Chattie, smiling, "but I've had my share of aches. And I expect more pain because gardening is time intensive."

Are you willing to invest time working toward your dream? *What an appropriate question Genevieve included in her questionnaire in January. I've thought of this question over and over as I've spent countless hours gardening.*

"You know my favorite flower. And Genevieve's also. Do you two have favorites?" asked Chattie, looking at Verity and then at Mary Olivia.

"Petunias are the first flowers I remember. As a kid I liked to say the name — pe-tun-ia. My grandmother had the old-fashioned lavender petunias."

"Shasta daisies," Mary Olivia said quickly. "Mother grew a huge cutting bed of them."

Whew! That's over with. I had to find out what the girls' fa-

vorite flowers are to prepare for my September surprise.

"Genevieve, are you eating enough?" Verity asked. "Haven't you lost weight?"

"I have lost some. Sometimes I do forget to eat, but today I am making up for it."

Genevieve picked up another tart. The girls quietly sipped their tea while Genevieve ate. When she finished, she looked out at the garden. "What a treasure you have shown us today. You truly have the gift of gardening."

"I agree," said Verity. "How did you accomplish this spectacle in three months?"

"Working almost non-stop every day. But I will confess. I didn't do it alone. Antonio and Mario helped me on weekends. And…."

"And what?" asked Mary Olivia — who had been quiet until now.

"I found a retired man who's been my mentor. I believe — I know — God sent him to me. He was here yesterday weeding and…."

"What's his name?" asked Mary Olivia. "And is he married?"

"His name is Theodore Root. He goes by Theo. And, no, he's not married. He's a widower."

"Oh-h-h, a widower," said Mary Olivia.

Chattie blushed.

I wouldn't have this beautiful garden without him.

"Root," Genevieve mused. "A famous name."

"Famous?" inquired Chattie.

I'm glad Genevieve changed the conversation to names. I felt my face getting red.

"Certainly. Elihu Root was a U.S. senator and a secretary of state early in the last century," stated Mary Olivia.

"That's right. I read a story about Elihu not long ago," said Genevieve. "His father was a mathematician and his brother also. Can you believe their nicknames were Cube and Square?"

"Square Root and Cube Root. That's funny. I didn't know that," said Mary Oliva. "And I'm the former history teacher."

"Where do you learn all this trivia?" Chattie asked, looking at Genevieve.

"An advantage of being old. A lifetime of reading and listening. You know a lot if you can remember it."

The women laughed.

"Now back to names. Theo Root's name goes along with his vocation. Like Dr. Bone, who is an orthopedist.

"And Mr. Lamb, who owns a sheep farm. But sometimes names like my Hannah's last name — Doolittle — are exactly opposite of the person. She is the best worker I know."

"I've never thought about the connection of names to people's jobs or personalities," said Verity. "Mercy would love this conversation. She reads the newspaper's obituaries every morning for names. When she finds an odd name, we hear about it whether we want to or not. What sisters I have. One collects words to improve our vocabulary, quotes to inspire us, and stories to inform and entertain us. The other one reads obituaries for unusual names."

"Your sisters are simply delightful," said Genevieve. "And speaking of delightful, our Silent Tea last month with our Silent hostess was fantastic."

"Should I remain silent about that compliment?" asked a smiling Mary Olivia. "It was a completely different experience for me than it was for you since I had the pleasure of listening and appreciating your conversations."

"And we enjoyed the serenity and the formality of your serving the tea," said Verity. "And the background music and the calming flow of water from the fountain made it a unique experience. One I'll remember for a long time."

"I'm thankful it was memorable for all of us," said Mary Olivia. "Even the loss of electricity."

"Yes," said Genevieve. "It was our first Candlelight Tea."

"Since you couldn't speak last month," said Chattie, "I didn't get to ask you how you got your name or rather two names. Genevieve and Verity probably know."

"Mary Olivia McGregor McDuff is an unusual name. A girl of Scottish ancestry marries a man of Irish ancestry."

"It is a mouthful," said Genevieve. "But an interesting name."

"Mary is a family name, my mother's and grandmother's names. People are usually surprised how I got the name Olivia. My mother often read Shakespeare. While pregnant with me, she was reading *Twelfth Night* and liked the character Olivia. So I was named after her. By the way, my two sisters — both of whom live on the West coast — were also named for Shakespearean characters. Juliet, of course, was named after the main character in *Romeo and Juliet*; and Rosalind was named after a character in *As You Like It*."

"I've never known anyone named after a Shakespearean character," said Chattie.

"Neither have I except for my sisters and me. I love my two names. Until I married, everyone called me Mary Olivia. But Liam insisted on calling me Livvie from the first day we met. After Liam died, I asked everyone to call me Mary Olivia again. Of course, it's fine with me that Mercy calls me M.O."

"What we learn at our Tea!" said Chattie. "But now we want to hear about your experiences at the monastery."

"Thought you would never ask. But, first, I have to clear up something from last month's meeting. I wrote on my pad that Liam left me in debt. Due to my vow of silence, I couldn't elaborate. I was, of course, shocked when I discovered I was in debt. How could I allow that to happen? I'm a reasonably intelligent woman. How did he ever keep his spending from me? I now know I was too busy — being a wife, mother, and teacher — to pay attention to finances I thought he could handle. Unfortunately, he couldn't. He left me a huge credit card debt. None of the money spent was for his family."

"I'm sorry," said Verity, shaking her head.

They sipped tea in silence until Mary Olivia was ready to speak.

"Now for my monastery weekend. But first. Here I go again. I must tell you about two experiences I had before I left for the monastery."

"Are you keeping us in suspense for some reason?" asked Verity.

"No. I've been around Genevieve too long. I love stories. These are good ones. Not as good as hers, but decent."

"The day after our Silent Tea I was at a dollar store buying shampoo for my trip when the cashier asked how I was. I showed her my card — I'M TAKING A VOW OF SILENCE. The clerk shouted to the manager at the back of the store, 'I've got a woman here who can talk but won't. Strange, isn't it?' The manager shouted back, 'Leave her alone. She's probably going through menopause. It's a rough time. I remember I should have been silent, but instead I nagged and fussed all the time with my husband.' I shook my head. 'No,' the clerk shouted. 'She's shaking her head.' As I walked out the door, I heard the clerk shout, 'She probably stutters. My first husband stuttered. He never would talk to me.' Needless to say, I had a good laugh in my car."

"How funny," said Chattie, laughing as the others joined in.

"And now for an inspiring story. The same day I was at the grocery store paying for a tangelo. The cashier asked me if it tasted more like a grapefruit or a tangerine. When I showed her my card, the young woman stared at it but didn't say anything. But before I left, she said, 'I admire what you're doing. I may have a day of silence soon.'"

"Great stories," said Genevieve. "From a good storyteller."

"Thanks. Now for my monastery weekend. I went with an expectant attitude and wasn't disappointed. It was unbelievable. It's difficult for me to put the visit into words because it was hard to take in everything. What an overwhelming spiritual and emotional experience! I was in awe of everything. The natural beauty of the setting. The hospitality of the monks. The silence and solitude. And especially communing with God in that calm atmosphere.

"I felt free because of no commitments. With my sons and

grandson living with me, I have little time for myself. So you can understand how my spirit was nourished. I had an opportunity to slow down, rest, reflect, and get a new perspective on life.

"I was reminded again and again of simplicity. My room was plainly furnished. A twin bed with one sheet, a blanket, and a pillow. A small desk and chair. A cross on the wall. All I needed.

"I've always risen an hour before sunrise. In my room I knelt by my bed and prayed and then studied the Bible. Then I went outside and marveled at the sunrise and walked the grounds trying to take in all the beauty. Large oaks. Dogwoods in blossom. Azaleas in bloom all over the campus.

"I hope I'm making sense. I'm trying to recapture some of my thoughts and feelings."

"You are. Did you go to Mass?" asked Chattie.

"Oh, yes. In addition to Mass, I learned about the Liturgy of the Hours — four prayers throughout the day — morning prayers, midday prayers, evening prayers or vespers and night prayers or compline. Going to prayers was optional, but I wanted to. It was a spiritual experience watching the monks gather to pray, and I needed the prayer time myself. In fact, I spent much of my time praying. Especially listening to God."

"Tell us more about listening," interrupted Genevieve. "I don't listen enough to God."

"Well, I stilled myself by quoting Psalm 46:10: 'Be still and know that I am God.' Then I listened. Sure, I had to fight off distracting thoughts that often came. I'm still learning to be silent and listen to God."

"When I think about silence," said Verity, "I think of the prophet Elijah. Remember when he fled from Jezebel and hid in a cave in the wilderness. The word of the Lord told him to stand on the mountain to wait for the Lord to pass by. A great wind came, but the Lord wasn't in the wind; then an earthquake came, but the Lord wasn't in the earthquake; and then a fire came, and the Lord wasn't in the fire. But then a sound of sheer silence. God was in the silence. Like Elijah, you're finding God in the silence."

"You're right, Verity. I went to one seminar on silence that a monk taught. Of course, monks have a lot of time to be silent. But we do also. We need to give up distractions we substitute for spiritual pursuits. I'm talking about myself. I watch too much news and aimlessly surf the Internet. My time could better be spent in Bible study, prayer, and silence."

"I spend too much time reading garden books and contemporary romances," interjected Chattie.

"We all have our diversions," said Verity. "Some good and some a waste of time."

"I agree. From my retreat. I carried away two verses that impacted my life. The first verse was the words of Jesus in Matthew 11:28, 'Come to me, all who labor and are heavy laden, and I will give you rest.' The other one was Psalm 62:5 — 'Find rest, O my soul, in God alone.' I felt the weekend was the beginning of spiritual rest for me."

"Did God guide you to pursue a dream?" Genevieve asked. "You did go for direction and guidance."

"Yes. God has led me to simplify my life. That's my first challenge. I'm still praying about pursuing a life-changing dream. But first, simplicity.

"Most importantly, I want to simplify my inner life. Get back to basics. I've done some soul searching the last couple of months. God had not left me. I had left God. I don't mean I didn't believe. I had strayed away for too many years. Now I'm coming home."

The women were quiet until Verity began singing the chorus of a hymn:

> I've wandered far away from God, Now I'm coming home;
> The paths of sin too long I've trod, Lord, I'm coming home.
> Coming home, coming home, Nevermore to roam,
> Open wide thine arms of love, Lord, I'm coming home.

I feel a reverent awe filling the room. The Holy Spirit.

"Amen. That hymn expresses my feelings," said Mary Olivia. "May I look for nothing and find nothing except You and only You. May the things of this world mean nothing to me, because You, Jesus, are everything to me."

"Beautiful," said Verity, retrieving a Kleenex from her pocket and wiping tears running down her face.

"I wish I could claim it. It's a quote from St. Therese of Lisieux, a nineteenth-century Carmelite nun who lived only 24 years but still influences many people today. I love the words. I heard a monk recite them at the seminar. Praise the Lord for my trip to the monastery!

Mary Olivia did have a life-changing weekend. Maybe one day I can get away to that monastery.

"I want to grow spiritually, but I don't want to neglect my physical, mental, and emotional health," Mary Olivia continued.

"Healthy food, an exercise regimen, and more sleep are some goals for my physical health."

"Physical and spiritual health can't be separated," said Verity. "After all, Paul says in 1 Corinthians 6:19 and 20: 'Do you not know that your body is a temple of the Holy Spirit…. Therefore honor God with your body.'"

"Important verse," said Mary Olivia. "As for improving my mental and spiritual health, I want to read my Bible daily as well as Christian classics to keep my mind filled with positive thoughts. As Paul said in Philippians 4:8, 'Whatever is true, whatever is noble, whatever is right, whatever is pure, whatever is lovely, whatever is admirable — if anything is excellent or praiseworthy — think about such things.'

"I pray my life will become less stressful as I simplify it. My emotional health should improve as I grow spiritually. I want to be a better listener and confidante to my sons and grandson and more patient and loving toward them.

"Before I can be the person I was meant to be, I have to simplify my surroundings. In other words, I need to simplify my life beginning with my home. Last month I am sure you wondered how an old Victorian house with such potential isn't charming. You would never say so, but it's true. My house is cluttered, but now I'm determined to do something about it."

I did see stacks and stacks of books and magazines and wall-to-wall furniture. Mary Olivia is not a housekeeper.

"Genevieve, you said in January we're here to help each

other."

"That is exactly what I said. And I meant it."

"Well, I need help to sort through all my years of clutter. Any volunteers."

"I will," said Chattie. "I enjoy organizing. Besides, I need a break from gardening. I don't want my passion to become an obsession."

"I'm sorry I can't help," said Verity. "We've moved Papa's bed downstairs to the parlor. We appreciate everything you've done to help us the last few months. We're entering the last phase of Papa's life. Hospice is taking over tomorrow. Papa doesn't like to see us heartbroken, but he's ready to join Mama."

"I will never forget," said Genevieve, "Rev. Isaiah's eyes lighting up when I read to him from Thomas a Kempis' *Imitation of Christ*."

"He appreciated all of you for reading to him from his favorite books."

"You know what Rev. Isaiah means to me," said Mary Olivia. "I've known him all my life. Our Lord Jesus will greet him with open arms and tell him, 'Well done, devoted servant.' I praise the Lord for your father."

"I wish I could help, but I'm exhausted," Genevieve said, drinking a glass of water and getting her breath. "I have been too busy these last several weeks."

"Working on your novel, I bet," said Verity. "Maybe you need to put it away for awhile."

"Probably," said Genevieve. "A good night's sleep is what I need."

"Chattie, can you come next Tuesday to help me declutter?"

"I'll be there with all the organizational skills I can muster."

"Don't forget. My house next month," said Genevieve.

"Are you sure you're going to be able...?" asked Chattie.

"Of course. I have my loyal Hannah to help. I have never missed my month of hosting, and I don't plan to start now," Genevieve said, rising wearily. "I had a great time. See you next month," she said, as Verity also rose to leave.

Chattie accompanied the two to the door and watched Verity walk Genevieve to her car.

I admire Genevieve's tenacity and Verity's devotion.

Chattie found Mary Olivia walking in the garden.

"Gardening has brought me closer to God. And it has brought me a new awareness about life itself."

"Your garden is a peaceful place where you can pray and enjoy God's creation. I sense a tranquility here I experienced at the monastery gardens," said Mary Olivia, hugging Chattie good-bye.

"See you next Tuesday," she said, waving to Mary Olivia.

Walking to the garden bench, Chattie sat down and thought about the afternoon with her friends.

I'm thankful Mary Olivia has found a serenity and peace. And Verity seems at peace with Rev. Isaiah's dying. But I'm worried about Genevieve. She is exhausted. Maybe next month she'll be rested. But that's not likely if she's working non-stop on her novel.

6

JUNE

~

GENEVIEVE

"When you get into a tight place and everything goes against you, till it seems as though you could not hold on a minute longer, never give up then, for that is just the place and time that the tide will turn."

American author Harriett Beecher Stowe (1811-1896)

I'm coming!" shouted Genevieve as she peered out her bedroom window at Verity and Mary Olivia ringing the doorbell.

"Is it already 2 o'clock?"

Genevieve quickly put on a simple black dress, brushed through her tousled hair, and put on some red lipstick.

"Where is my face powder? It must be here somewhere. Forget the powder. Back to my hair. Another brushing may help. No. I can't do a thing with it. That's what happens when I miss my weekly hair appointment. First time I've done that in ages.

"I'm coming," she said. She felt a broken fingernail.

"I usually keep my nails filed neatly but no time now," she

said as she walked to the door.

What will they think about punctual Genevieve being late?

"Are you all right?" asked Mary Olivia when Genevieve opened the door. "Thought I heard someone talking."

"Oh, it's just me. I often talk to myself. By the way, health professionals now say talking to yourself is good. Come on in," she said, embracing them. "Let's go into the den. I'll sit here in this comfortable rocker and feel rested soon. We can visit until Chattie arrives."

After choosing her favorite Queen Anne chair, Mary Olivia picked up a magazine from the coffee table. A layer of dust lay around the outline of where the magazine had been.

I'm so embarrassed. I can't believe that much dust could be in my house. With Hannah's mother moving in with her, she hasn't been able to polish the furniture lately.

"Sorry about the dust. I have been overwhelmed since our meeting last month."

"Anything we can do to help?" asked Verity in a calming voice.

"Oh, no. No. I'll be fine."

No wonder they're concerned about me. I've never been at a Tea without makeup and every hair in place. And I never wear a black dress. Why did I put this one on? It must have been the first dress I saw. I always wear colorful dresses. And now the dust.

"How is Rev. Isaiah doing?" asked Genevieve. She was concerned about Verity's father but also wanted to not talk about her dusty house.

"He's extremely weak. We're grateful for Hospice. And for the chaplain. Rev. Stillwater is compassionate and, above all, an attentive listener. Good thing. Mercy takes him aside often to talk to him. He listens to her and then consoles her in his gentle voice. She's taking Papa's dying hard, but Rev. Stillwater's quiet and caring demeanor is helping her and us."

"His name does sound reassuring," said Genevieve.

It makes me think of the 23rd Psalm: 'He leadeth me beside the still waters.' I must repeat that verse often this week.

"I think so too. His name is Jonathan Edwards Stillwater. His parents named him after Jonathan Edwards because of their high regard for the Puritan minister. Papa admires the works of Edwards. Don't you think it's fitting that Rev. Stillwater is with us?"

"I'm sure God sent this particular chaplain to you," said Mary Olivia.

"You are fortunate to have Rev. Stillwater. It's difficult to give up your father," said Genevieve. "I remember well."

"What's that terrible smell?" Mary Olivia asked, sniffing.

"I have little sense of smell. Shipman always said I couldn't smell anything."

"Well, it's a strong odor. I think it's coming from your kitchen. If you don't mind, I'll look around."

"Go right ahead."

Let's see. What page was I on this morning? I must get my mind off the proofing of my manuscript, but it's difficult. Did I need to change the spelling of one character's name? Was it...?

The doorbell rang.

"While you play Nancy Drew solving the mystery odor, I'll greet Chattie," said Verity. She winked at Mary Olivia as they left the room together.

Genevieve saw the wink but decided to ignore it.

If today's Tea continues in the way it has started, I'll be a poor hostess.

Soon Verity and Chattie joined Genevieve. Chattie handed her a vase of red roses.

"Roses. How beautiful! How did you know roses are my favorite flowers?"

"You told us last...."

Mary Olivia walked into the den holding a paper towel full of rotten potatoes. "Genevieve, I'm sorry to interrupt — and snoop, although you gave me permission. I roamed around in your kitchen rifling through the garbage, looking in the refrigerator and pantry, peering under the sink. I finally went back to the pantry and found these culprits. Did you know you had five rotten potatoes in your vegetable bin?"

"No. But I'm not surprised. My! They do smell rotten. If I can smell them, then it must be terrible for you. I'm sorry, girls."

I don't have time to keep up with potatoes. I haven't been in my kitchen except for an occasional cup of tea. I've been too busy doing a line-by-line proofing of my novel.

"You don't seem yourself today," said Mary Olivia. "Are you working night and day on that novel of yours?"

"I am a bit preoccupied with it."

Rotten potatoes. Why did I have the Tea here today? But I'm the one who made the schedules this year. And I would never think of asking one of the girls to host during my designated month. Never.

"If you'll let me," said Mary Olivia, "I'll be glad to take

these potatoes out to your garbage can."

"I would appreciate that. We all would, I'm sure."

"By the way, where's Hannah?" asked Chattie, after Mary Olivia left the room.

"She's taking care of her mother, who has moved in with her."

"Is her mother ill?" asked Verity. "With Papa's prolonged sickness, I have developed an empathy for caregivers. You can't imagine how difficult it is."

"It must be terribly hard, but no one has been better as caregivers than you and your sisters. Hannah's mother is not physically ill, but at 84 she's reached the age where she forgets to take her medicine and eat. Hannah says she's in the first stage of Alzheimer's." Genevieve stopped a few moments. "Hannah keeps an upper chin about it. Her mother is still able to help a little with housework and cooking."

"Why didn't you let us know?" asked Chattie. "We could have helped...."

"Everything is fine. Hannah made our dessert and delivered it last night."

I sure didn't have time to bake. I don't even know what she prepared.

"Girls, please go out to the verandah and visit," said Genevieve, rising wearily. "I will get the tea and dessert from the kitchen."

I had no time to clean. I thought the verandah would be the best place for the Tea. It took only a few minutes to wipe down the table and chairs and sweep the tiled floor.

Walking by her office, Genevieve saw Laptop sleeping. She

closed the door to the cluttered room. As she started toward the kitchen, she met Mary Olivia.

"Thanks for ridding me — us — of those horrid potatoes. The girls are on the verandah. I'll only be a few minutes."

I'm not giving Mary Olivia a chance to say another word. I'm hurrying to the kitchen. Now where was I in the manuscript? I was correcting the spelling of Kristin's name. Or had I finished that and moved on to the next page? Oh, well, I better get my mind back on making the tea.

Genevieve brought some water to a boil, rinsed the teapot with hot water, threw Earl Grey tea bags into it, poured hot water into the pot, and replaced the top of the teapot. After grabbing Hannah's wrapped dessert from the refrigerator, she carefully picked up the teapot and slowly made her way to the verandah.

"We're celebrating summer with yellow paper plates and paper napkins," Genevieve said, after placing Tea items on the table. "Also, I have yellow and white china tea cups to match."

I have always used cloth napkins with my china tea cups. I hope I'm not disappointing them.

"This looks terrific," said Chattie. "And your yellow and white teapot completes the beautiful setting."

"Now for our dessert. I'm going to be as surprised as you are." Genevieve lifted the foil from the basket and removed a large plastic container of sandwiches.

"What a surprise. No wonder Hannah told me to refrigerate the food," she said, removing cucumber sandwiches. "My favorite, and how dainty. We haven't had sandwiches all year." She arranged them on a plate. "And here's another container and a note from Hannah.

"'Cucumber sandwiches. Gingerbread. Warm up dessert in microwave. Love, Hannah.'

"She always knows how to take care of me. How thoughtful. Soon I will have more energy.

At least with Hannah's sandwiches and gingerbread, things are going better. I must relax — if only for a little while.

"Chattie, would you please pour the tea and pass the sandwiches while I warm up the gingerbread?" asked Genevieve as she started for the kitchen.

She soon returned with warm gingerbread, a spray can of whipped cream, a knife, and four forks. She cut the gingerbread, placed a piece on each plate, and sprayed whipped cream on top. She then relaxed in her chair.

The three women waited for Genevieve to eat.

"Would you like us to eat dessert now?" asked Verity.

"Please."

I am so tired. While working on my novel, I've had to change my daily habits. No more getting up at the same time. No more lunch at noon and dinner at 6. No bedtime at 9. Sometimes I forget to eat. And I am behind on my sleep.

"Genevieve?" asked Verity. "You're going to eat, aren't you?"

"Oh, yes." She picked up a sandwich. "Sorry, girls, I was daydreaming."

No need for me to tell them my mind was elsewhere. I must pull myself together and enjoy this tea.

"How tasty," said Genevieve, after taking her first bite of sandwich. "This is how I like my cucumber sandwiches. Butter and cream cheese. Bless you, Hannah."

She watched as the women ate.

"I don't think you three have to say anything. I can tell by your expressions that you love Hannah's food."

They nodded and continued eating and drinking.

"I want to apologize for making such a deal about the potatoes," said Mary Olivia. "I was downright histrionic. And to think last month I told you that the monastery visit changed..."

"We are all human. Think nothing of it," interrupted Genevieve. "I am relieved you found those rotten potatoes. You spared Hannah the smell and the cleaning up. And now I must apologize. We didn't bless our food. Let's bow our heads and pray silently."

Raising her head slowly to make sure no one was still praying, Verity asked Chattie, "What's blooming in your garden?"

"It's amazing what a difference a month makes. Every plant blooming last month is bigger and has more blooms. I'm deadheading the zinnias and marigolds, and they're getting fuller. Cannas and summer mums are blooming."

"Is Theo still helping you?" asked Genevieve.

Maybe if I continue to talk I won't drift back into daydreaming or fall asleep.

"Of course. I couldn't do without my gardener. This morning he mulched the flower beds to keep the weeds out. Can you believe he still digs up plants from his garden and brings them over and plants them in my garden?"

"Is he giving away his plants because he's moving?" asked Verity.

"He's never mentioned moving. He's only sharing his plants with me."

"I hope Theo will be working at the September Tea," said Mary Olivia. "I'm eager to meet him."

"I'll do my best to make sure he's there. Now, if you don't mind, I'd like to tell Verity and Genevieve about helping you organize and declutter your house."

"Sure. It wasn't easy dealing with a hoarder."

"I had to talk Mary Olivia into getting rid of some of her so-called prized possessions such as her high school English essays. She sometimes resisted letting go, but I insisted: one pile for trash, one for recycling, one for giving away, one for keeping. I love to declutter. I try to clean out a drawer or closet a day. It helped get me through last year."

"Chattie's organizational plan made all the difference. I gave away three large bags of clothes to Homes for Domestic Abuse. And I even sent two bags of books to the library.

"My monastery visit helped me put things in perspective. Of course, it's a process. You saw how I got so preoccupied today with those potatoes. Anyway, I've continued this month to organize and simplify. By August you'll see a new me with a new look to my house. But enough about me. I want to know about Rev. Isaiah."

"Papa's living in the past," said Verity. "He talks about his childhood on the farm although we usually can't understand what he's saying."

"That has to be difficult," said Genevieve.

"It is, but the hardest thing for us, in addition to watching him die, is his not recognizing us even when we repeat our names. I know he's 87 and has lived a righteous life and touched countless lives, but he's still our Papa. Last night he said, 'I'm climbing up to Rose.'"

"He's seen a glimpse of heaven," said Mary Olivia.

"I know he has," said Verity, crying. Mary Olivia placed her arm around her friend and whispered words of encouragement. She then brought Verity more tea.

"I didn't mean to break down," Verity said. She blotted her tears with her handkerchief.

I have just thought about a subject we can talk about.

"Yesterday was my wedding anniversary. It made me nostalgic."

"A June wedding. Tell us about it," said Chattie. "I'm a born romantic and love to hear about weddings."

"I could not have asked for a more perfect day for a wedding," said Genevieve, pausing a moment before continuing. "We had a traditional ceremony at our Presbyterian church. It was packed. Since Shipman's parents owned the only furniture store in town, most people knew him." Genevieve sipped some tea. "His mother supervised the wedding. Suzannah Shipman could do wonders with everything she touched. I'll never forget the roses — she had red roses placed all over the church. The garden reception was right here in the backyard. I remember it as if it were yesterday."

Genevieve walked to the edge of the verandah. "To my left, the tents were set up, and tables filled with more food than I had ever seen. To my right were the musicians who played Nat King Cole's 'Unforgettable' and Sam Cooke's 'You Send Me.'"

"What a wedding," said Chattie, joining Genevieve. "And to think we're looking down at the exact place you had your reception."

"Yes," said Genevieve, sitting back down. "It was an emotional day for me."

"Our wedding was small compared to yours," said Mary Olivia. "Liam and I got married in my living room. When my parents passed away, I inherited the house.

"Liam agreed to having my Baptist minister, Dr. Goodson, marry us, but later he insisted we bring up the boys in the Catholic faith. He had a best man, and I had a maid of honor. Our best friends and close relatives attended. It was nice. But…"

"But what?" asked Verity.

Mary Olivia folded her hands and said quietly, "I suspected Liam of messing around with my maid of honor, Catherine — we called her Kitty — although he denied it over and over." Her voice trailed off as if bittersweet memories came to mind. After taking a deep breath, she continued her story.

"After his death, thrice-divorced Kitty called me to express her sympathy. I asked her if my suspicions were true. She freely admitted they had been having an affair for several months up until the night before the wedding. I wish she had apologized, but she didn't. I think she may have actually loved him."

"My word!" declared Chattie.

"Although it hurt at the time, I was glad to know."

"I'm sorry," said Verity. "I attended the wedding and never knew. I should not have asked."

Mary Olivia smiled. "I'm glad you did. I needed to unload my mind about that incident. In fact, I feel relieved now."

The women returned to sipping tea.

No wonder Mary Olivia wanted to get away to a monastery. She endured a lot from Liam. And she's kept it to herself. I can re-

late to her keeping it secret.

"Micah and I got married in Chicago in November," Verity said. "It was a spur-of-the-moment event at a justice of the peace. Micah insisted upon only the two of us being there. Pru and Mercy later told me Papa was disappointed he didn't have the opportunity to marry Temp or me. Temp had eloped with that wild woman Eleanor. We all know how that turned out."

I think Verity may be holding back something. She seldom talks about Micah.

"Our July wedding in my Episcopalian church," said Chattie, "was as perfect as perfect can be. We had a formal reception at the church and then went to a country club where Aunt Boo treated us to a live band. We danced for hours. We were so much in love. I can't remember ever being happier. I wanted to be with him the rest of my life. If only we could have grown old together, but it wasn't meant to be." She began to tear up. "We only had 27 years together, but they were happy years."

"Some people don't get that much happiness in a lifetime," said Mary Olivia.

"You're right. I was fortunate." Chattie slowly sipped her tea.

"Did Roberto have any foibles? Faults?" asked Mary Olivia. "He seems — well — perfect."

"He was a good — and sweet — man. But he wasn't a saint. He annoyed me at times. Especially with his whistling. He whistled so much it got on my nerves. Also, he had to give everything an Italian name. The boys were named after their grandfathers. That was fine with me. After he named our dog Puccini, I called him Poochie. This bothered Roberto because he considered Poochie a shortened name for Puccini. I thought of it as a sweet, intimate name."

"Those are great stories," said Genevieve. "Shipman was a good husband also, but he did annoy me with an expression I could count on when we met new people. He invariably said, 'You can tell I love tall women.' Then he would hug me. He was four inches shorter than me. He realized people noticed our height differences because we often saw people stare."

"Did the staring bother either of you?" asked Verity.

"I didn't get upset because it is a typical response when people see a woman taller than her husband. I don't think it bothered him." Genevieve rested a few moments. "He wasn't an insecure person. I think he tried to put other people at ease, but it did get old hearing him say he loved tall women, meaning, of course, me."

The women laughed.

A good laugh is what we needed after the terrible start of the Tea today.

"How about Micah and Liam?" asked Chattie.

"Drank too much. Had depression," said Verity.

"Drank too much. Ran around," said Mary Olivia. "Let's please talk about something else."

Verity and Mary Olivia looked at each other as if they understood each other's circumstances.

The women resumed sipping their tea.

"Do you ever miss sex?" asked Chattie. She looked from one woman to another.

Chattie certainly changed the subject with a bang. No one has asked that question although Doll talked about her sex life as often as she could.

"Do you?" asked Mary Olivia, looking at Chattie.

"Yes. At times. How about you?"

"God created sex to be a beautiful experience between a husband and wife in love. Liam and I did have a good relationship for several years, but when I found out about his affairs, I lost all interest. If I ever remarry, I would welcome a healthy sex life."

I have never heard Mary Olivia mention remarrying until now.

"Sometimes I withheld love-making from Shipman," Genevieve said regretfully. "I was going through the change, but looking back I know I was wrong — insensitive — to withhold it for as long as I did. Many times since Shipman's death I have lain awake wishing I had been more loving toward him. Many a night I feigned a headache."

Each woman looked at Genevieve.

I can't believe I divulged my experiences. But we are being honest with each other.

"Once I wanted an antique secretary his Aunt Mabel said she would sell to me. Shipman thought I should wait until his spinster aunt died, and I could have it free. I whined and slept in another bedroom for two weeks....One day our store's delivery man brought over the secretary. Shipman had tried to buy it, but Aunt Mabel gave it to me. I denied him sex for two weeks all because of a writing desk."

"I think you're courageous," said Chattie, "to admit such an intimate experience."

"I guess it was what Mary Olivia called 'unloading.' I have

never told anyone these things. It was spontaneous, but I'm glad I shared it." said Genevieve, wiping a tear.

"Our marriage was a rocky one," Verity said. "It's difficult for me to get personal."

"I understand," Genevieve said. "Talking about sex is never easy. At least in my generation. It was even difficult for a husband and wife to discuss it. Now it's in our face so much I miss the good old days." She drank some water before continuing.

"Girls, you might be surprised, but the subject of sex was brought up years ago at the Tea. If only you could have heard Priscilla Wright. Remember, we called her Doll. She once said she and Edmund had a great love life. How could I ever forget when she told us her favorite days were Saturdays and Wednesdays because they had a rendezvous on those days. And those trysts were not always in the bedroom."

"My word!" exclaimed Chattie.

"In fact, the day they made love on the couch was Edmund's last day on this earth. That evening he went for his usual walk. When he didn't return, Doll searched for him, retracing his walking route. She found him dead at the side of the road." Genevieve stopped to get her breath. "The coroner ruled he had stumbled on a rock and fell face down. She told us the story several times, and every time she said, 'At least he died happy. It was a Saturday.' Bert, Stella — you, of course, remember them from my history of the Tea — and I did all we could but laugh out loud the first time we heard her say that, but even a good story gets old. Every time Doll started in about her love life, Bert, who was so embarrassed about Doll's lack of inhibitions, changed the subject."

"I better get back to Papa. Don't forget I'm still having the Tea at my house next month," said Verity. She prepared to leave.

I embarrassed Verity. I wish I hadn't been so explicit.

"That is, unless Papa gets worse. We'll have the Tea on the porch if the weather cooperates. Are you ready to go, Mary Olivia?"

"Ready. We should let Genevieve get back to her novel."

"I was afraid of that," said a smiling Genevieve. "Verity, please keep us updated about Rev. Isaiah's condition."

"I sure will," said Verity, hugging Genevieve and Chattie.

"I must get back to my roses," said Chattie. "Those infernal Japanese beetles. I pick them off every morning and then find they are back again every evening."

"You must be doing a good job. The roses you brought today are beautiful. They will cheer me up for days."

"Good. We all need cheering up."

Genevieve watched as the three walked down the hill. Then she headed to her office deep in thought about the afternoon.

I went on too much about Doll, but I don't think people realize many married women of my generation enjoyed sex. Young unmarried people today think they discovered it.

The Tea was a nice respite. It did me good. Now back to work. Any other rotten vegetables will have to wait. The proofing of my manuscript cannot. I have to mail it to my publisher on Friday. It goes to the printer in August. By fall, I'll have my own book. A dream finally fulfilled.

Next month I should be rested for the Tea. I'm looking forward to seeing Rev. Isaiah.

7
JULY

∽

VERITY

"We can't do great things. We can only do small things with great love."
          Nobel Prize-winning nun Mother Teresa (1910-1997)

Verity stepped onto the front porch to check the temperature on the thermometer her Papa had installed on the porch post many years ago. Sitting down in the porch swing, her mind drifted back to the day before Papa died, a day she would never forget.

∽

"Papa, can you hear me?"

He nodded and gently took her hand. She closed both her hands over his.

She told him that she had something important to tell him before he joined her mother. It was difficult, but she had to because she would never forgive herself if she didn't. She quickly blurted out the fact that she was not a widow and that Micah was not dead. She had left him because he abused her when he got drunk. One night she slipped out of bed, grabbed her packed bag, and left for home. She said she tried her best to stay with Micah.

"You did the ri...right thing," Papa told her slowly.

She replied that she had to confess to him because he was not only her beloved father but also her minister. She knew God had forgiven her, but she still had to let him know.

He told her he knew Micah wasn't dead. He had searched the Chicago obituaries and could not find his name. He whispered, "Knew you had good reason to come home."

He had told Pru and Mercy the first time he met Micah that he was no good. He asked Verity's sisters to lift her up to God and pray that she would see Micah's true side.

She asked her father not to talk any more.

Her last words to him were, "Rest now. I love you."

He looked at her lovingly and then closed his eyes.

After leaving her father, she went to the kitchen to see Pru and Mercy. She felt happy.

"You haven't had this glow since you came home three years ago," said Pru.

"Do you have a beau?" asked Mercy.

"Beau. Me? What can you be thinking? When would I ever have time for a beau? I'm taking care of Daddy. I'm happy, and it's a beautiful day. 'Oh, what a beautiful morning. Oh, what a beautiful day,'" she sang, as she watched Pru and Mercy stare at each other.

When she went back up into Papa's room, she found him in a deep sleep. She and her sisters later learned he was in a coma. It was as if he had been waiting for her confession.

Rev. Isaiah died early the next morning. Verity experienced a deep grief, but also an overwhelming sense of relief that she had finally confessed to him and had heard him say he understood why she had to leave Micah.

Of course, Verity didn't tell her father everything. Some things are too private to tell anyone.

Micah Harris caught her off guard. She should have known no one could measure up to her father's character.

She had three miscarriages. Micah blamed her for his not having sons and carrying on his family name. He was Micah III. He wanted a Micah IV. He started drinking, and when drunk, he would hit her. When sober, he wasn't as mean but didn't understand why she couldn't have his son. His increasingly drunken sprees resulted in rages against her.

Micah was warring against himself — his inability to carry on his father's legacy. He felt he could not measure up to his father's prominence. His father and grandfather, pillars in the African-American community, were crusading newspaper editors. When Micah's father died of a heart attack at age 62, he was greatly mourned in Chicago.

Micah floundered in grief after his father's death. Then for several years he tried to carry on the work of the paper. His father and grandfather had causes. Their work revolved around civil rights. Micah knew social and economic inequities still existed, but he was no crusader. He sold the paper to the assistant editor, who practically stole it from him.

After that, Micah went aimlessly through each day with no clear direction. Then one day his life changed dramatically. He read a story in his former paper about Thomas Jefferson and Sally Hemings' love affair and the children they likely had. Micah quickly pursued an interest that soon became an obsession. Since his father's grandfather had originally come from Virginia, Micah did genealogical research, convinced he was kin to Sally Hemings. Verity was grieving over the loss of their second baby. Micah tried for months to find a family link but always came up empty. His family may have been kin to Sally, but he could never find the connection.

Discouraged, he gave up, became depressed, started drinking and gambling, and lost all of his and Verity's money. With his money from the paper they could have bought a house instead of renting, but it was not to be. After Verity recovered from her third miscarriage and their third eviction from their apartments, she packed and left for Alabama.

A month later Verity received a letter from her cousin Sarah saying Micah didn't blame Verity for leaving. He said he would never bother her. He was still drinking heavily.

∽

Verity glanced at her watch. It was almost time for the girls to arrive. The porch thermometer read 83 degrees.

Good. The temperature and humidity are both low. We can have our Tea on the porch.

Verity had requested Genevieve, Mary Olivia, and Chattie wear bright clothes and hats and be upbeat for Mercy. She had taken her father's death harder than anyone else.

Verity watched as Genevieve slowly parked in front of the house. She greeted her at her car, where Genevieve gave her a long hug and then a sack to carry. After getting Genevieve settled in a comfortable chair in the parlor, Verity opened the sack.

"Peaches. How did you know they're our favorite fruit?"

"I've heard Prudence say she likes to make peach cobblers."

"And she makes the best."

"I'm sure she does."

"Now for your dress. Red looks great on you. And your red hat matches perfectly."

"Thanks for cheering me up. I'm here to cheer you up. But that's my Verity — always thinking of others."

Genevieve thinks I'm perfect. If only she knew.

"You look better than I've seen you in a long time," said Verity.

"I've been getting more rest. The weekend after the June Tea I was exhausted. I slept two straight days. I'm feeling much better now."

Chattie knocked on the door. Verity waved her in.

"How striking you look!" said Verity, hugging her.

"Thank you." Chattie turned around and around playfully in her bright yellow straight skirt with matching sleeveless top and a white hat. "From my favorite consignment shop."

Mary Olivia tiptoed in. "Yellow looks great on you," she said.

"Thanks for the compliment. It feels good to be fashionable."

"You better not wear that 'Wow' outfit around that gardener of yours."

"Stop it, Mary Olivia," said Genevieve. "You're making Chattie blush."

"I don't think I'll be the only one blushing today," countered Chattie. "You could knock a man off his feet with that blue bodice and ruffled skirt. And that blue and white hat. And you've lost weight. You look like you could be a model on a fashion runway."

Turning red, Mary Olivia said, "I guess we're even now."

"Thank you all for cheering me up," said Verity, smiling widely as Mary Olivia gave her a long embrace.

"Speaking of someone looking good, I love your green dress and white hat," said Mary Olivia.

"Thanks. Lime green is a new color for me."

Genevieve told the girls she was glad Verity had asked them to wear hats.

"I had the new hat I wore to the funeral, but I had an excuse to buy another one. This is my year for hats."

"Papa liked women to wear hats. At our church they're a familiar sight, especially on older women. I'm surprised he didn't ask us to all wear hats to the funeral."

"If there had been any more hats at his funeral, we would have knocked each other down," said Genevieve.

Verity laughed. "One of Papa's gifts was discernment. He knew there would be plenty of hats. That's the first time I've laughed since Papa's death two weeks ago."

"Laughter is a good antidote to pain," said Mary Olivia. "Remember what Proverbs 17:22 says, 'A cheerful heart is a good medicine.'"

"I agree. And Papa would want us to be cheerful today. Now let's go to the kitchen."

Verity picked up the sack of peaches. "Pru and Mercy will be joining us today. They're putting the finishing touches on the Tea."

"What delicious looking peaches," said Prudence, taking the sack from Verity. She reached in for a peach, felt it, and then smelled it. "Perfect."

"A present from Genevieve," said Verity.

"Then she gets my biggest hug today," said Prudence, embracing Genevieve. "I can't wait to make a cobbler."

"It's my pleasure to bring some cheer to you girls. We're all going to miss Rev. Isaiah. Last month I never dreamed he would not be here today."

"I don't think we're ever ready to give up those we love," said Chattie. "No matter their age. I sure wasn't ready to give up my Roberto."

"I agree. But Papa was ready to join Mama. He asked us to celebrate his passing — and we certainly did at his funeral," said Verity.

"But it's so hard for me," said Mercy. "I miss him so much."

Genevieve gave Mercy a hug.

"Please try to be cheerful today," pleaded Prudence, looking at Mercy.

"You have a good start with that beautiful red dress," said Genevieve. "And your purple one, Prudence, is stunning."

"Purple is my favorite color," she said, heading to the porch with the rest of the food and reciting, "When I am an old woman I shall wear purple…."

"I'm glad you like mine, Miss Genevieve. And it makes me happy we both wore red," said Mercy.

"Me too."

"Tea time," announced Prudence from the porch.

The women joined her at the same round table they had sat around in March. Two chairs had been added for Prudence and Mercy. A white linen tablecloth covered the table. A red vase containing red, white, and blue gladioluses served as the centerpiece. Blueberry muffins filled up a large white platter. Six white dessert plates and red napkins completed the arrangement.

"What a beautiful table setting," said Genevieve.

After Prudence gave thanks for the food, she poured sweet tea into tall iced tea glasses. Mercy offered muffins to each woman.

They all oohed and aahed over the delicious muffins. Prudence told them blueberry sour cream muffins were Papa's favorite going back to his childhood when his father had grown blueberries on the farm. She baked the muffins in honor of her Papa and said they came from a family recipe.

"What was that poem you were reciting a few minutes ago?" asked Chattie, looking at Prudence.

"It's my favorite poem about growing old. It was written by an English woman named Jenny Joseph. The name of the poem is 'Warning.' The first line of the poem says: 'When I am an old woman I shall wear purple.' Joseph wrote much poetry, but she is known for this poem. Do you know what I find most interesting about the poet?"

"What?" asked Mary Olivia.

"Jenny Joseph hated the color purple."

"That is strange," said Chattie.

"Even if the poet hated the color purple," said Prudence, "I would suggest you Goggle the first line of the poem, read about it, and print it out. It will make you happy when you read it."

"You're using your computer then?" asked Chattie.

"Even though I still do research in the library — old habits die slowly — I do research online also."

"Let's talk about food instead of poetry. What a tradition of food your family has," said Genevieve. "And speaking of food. I don't believe I've ever seen so much fried chicken, fresh vegetables, and desserts than at the meal following the funeral."

"A feast is what we had," said Prudence.

"And Temp was eating," said Mary Olivia.

"He ate plenty," said Prudence. "Temperance stayed here the week before Papa's death. Papa called Temperance the Prodigal Son. He knew he would come home to his father and His Heavenly Father, and he did. Last month on Father's Day he whittled a Bible for Papa. It looked like a book, but he told Papa it was a Bible. Papa was so pleased that he kept the gift next to him in bed. He was holding it when he died. He knew Temperance had come home."

"What a celebration the funeral was," said Genevieve, reaching for another muffin.

"Papa requested a celebration and wanted no one to wear black clothing," said Prudence. "Of course, some wore black, but they were far outnumbered by bright colors — much like we're wearing today."

"I thought the two ministers leading the service spoke from their hearts," said Chattie.

Verity explained how Dr. Thomas and Dr. Robinson had grown up in their church. Rev. Isaiah was proud of them because they both had seminary degrees and successful ministries. He requested that they both speak.

"I'm glad we got there early," said Mary Olivia. "The church was full. Chairs had to be brought in, and people stood in the back."

"It did comfort us that so many people came," said Verity.

"It was my first black funeral and a memorable one," said Genevieve.

"Then I'm sure you found it different," said Prudence. "Our funerals are, as a rule, longer, louder, and more emotional than white funerals."

Verity said that her father had asked that his service not be so drawn out as some funerals were. He was a quiet, dignified preacher. He wasn't always that way. She said as a young preacher he did his share of shouting. But he became more subdued when he got older. She said her mother liked a quieter, what she called "a more reverent, service."

"Papa also didn't want anyone kissing him in the casket or someone loudly talking or screaming around his casket," said Prudence.

"My word!" Chattie shouted.

"I understand your shock. As a preacher, Papa had seen everything. Years ago we were at a funeral, and a son — a short, stocky man — tried to get in the casket with his deceased father. He had to be restrained by three men. Looking back, it was a sad sight — although there was snickering going on with kids and even adults.

"Also, as Papa got older and held funerals, he would get tired of the lingering beside the casket. We four decided not to do that. Of course, some of the older women who had known him all of their lives did linger awhile. I was glad the funeral director motioned them away. We tried to obey Papa's wishes."

Verity explained that Rev. Isaiah had planned every detail of his funeral during the last months of his life — his favorite songs to be played and sung and Scriptures to be read. He asked her to play "Precious Lord Take my Hand" and "It is Well with My Soul" at the beginning of the service.

Prudence added that her father asked Dr. Thomas to read the first 18 verses from St. John. "Papa thought they were the most beautiful in Scripture."

"At the end of the service the congregation's singing of 'Amazing Grace' was awesome," said Genevieve.

Mercy stood and began singing slowly and soulfully. The other women stood and joined in:

Amazing Grace! How sweet the sound,
That saved a wretch like Me!
I once was lost, but now am found,
Was blind, but now I see.

"Last verse," Mercy shouted.

When we've been there ten thousand years,
Bright shining as the sun,
We've no less days to sing God's praise
Than when we first begun.

They remained standing and silent for several minutes.

Their eyes were all closed.

Mercy broke the silence. "Please sit down."

Mary Olivia passed around tissue.

Thank you, God, for this spontaneous deep spiritual experience. My sisters and friends obviously felt the same way.

"Thank you, Mercy. That's my favorite hymn," said Genevieve softly.

"Mine too," added Mercy.

"'Amazing Grace' was Papa's favorite also," said Prudence, drying her eyes. "He loved the story of John Newton's life, how he had abandoned the slave trade, and then wrote the song later. That's why I told the congregation the story behind the song before we sang it."

Verity explained that her father wanted the graveside service to be short because the heat would be sweltering.

She said that the oak tree several yards from the grave had grown a lot since they had buried their mother. Its shade kept mourners out of the sun.

"Papa asked Dr. Thomas to read the familiar words of 1 Corinthians 15," said Prudence.

"When he got to 'Where, O death is your victory? Where, O death, is your sting?' I felt such joy that our lives don't end with death," said Mary Olivia. "And then when we sang 'Victory in Jesus,' I felt Rev. Isaiah's spirit with us."

"M.O., what beautiful words," said Mercy, reaching into her pocket for a handkerchief.

"Papa also specified that Dr. Robinson close with the 23rd Psalm and a prayer," said Verity.

"What a beautiful gesture for the four of you to place a rose on top of the casket," said Genevieve.

"That was my idea," insisted Mercy.

"And a good one," said Verity. "I think Papa's home-going was what he would have wanted."

"One more thing about Papa," Prudence told them. "He believed as many older black folks do that when someone passes, someone will be born."

"A baby is born somewhere in the world every second," said Mercy, scratching her head. "I wish Papa were here to explain that saying to me."

"Rev. Isaiah was certainly the epitome of a Christian," said Chattie.

Verity said her father was a man of great integrity and humility, but he never claimed to be perfect. She said he often talked about his two thorns in the flesh.

"One was Temp's wife. He told us he asked God over and over to not let bad memories of her enter his mind," said Prudence. "Eleanor was a mean, wild woman who broke our sweet brother's heart."

Prudence told them that their father dealt with his other thorn in the flesh for decades. His mother-in-law — their grandmother — intensely disliked him. She was the only person we ever knew who didn't like Papa. Grandma Jessie always blamed him for marrying her beautiful daughter. She fought the marriage, but Mama was in love and determined to marry Papa. Grandma Jessie had plans for her Rose to be a professional singer. All of Mama's life Grandma Jessie — we called her Jezebel behind her back — never let Mama forget she could have been a famous singer if she hadn't become a poor preacher's wife.

"It sounds terrible that we called our own grandmother Jezebel, the meanest woman in the Bible," said Prudence. "But we witnessed her hatred. When she visited, Papa dreaded it. Before her visits, he would pray that finally Grandma would say kind words to Mama. But she got more negative with the years. She ignored Papa as if he weren't there. She had probably vowed when they married never to love Papa and was too vain to break her vow."

"I'm sorry to say she went to church every Sunday," added Verity.

"Going to church doesn't make one a Christian," said Mary Olivia. "We have to make a serious commitment to follow Christ."

"Amen," said Verity. "When Grandma could no longer take care of herself, she moved in with us and took my room. I had to move in with Pru and Mercy. We plotted a strategy to cure Grandma Jesse. We searched the Bible for positive verses to put on her morning tray: 'The fruit of the Spirit is love, joy, peace...,' from Galatians. 'Let us love one another' and 'God is love,' from 1 John. We chose several verses from the love chapter, 1 Corinthians 13 — 'Love is patient'; 'Love is kind.' She never commented on them, but they were never on her tray when we picked it up. After a morning dose of about 20 verses, she recovered enough — she said — to go home. We believed our verses had healed her.

"But we were wrong. As soon as she entered her house, she had a heart attack and died in her foyer. Papa said she left because she knew she was dying and didn't want to die in his house. We'll never know. We hoped our verses made a difference and that she repented of her bad behavior. Mama was sad but said Grandma Jessie never had kind words about anyone. Mama told us early in life she had determined not to be like her mother. And she wasn't. She was the sweetest, most loving mother a child could have. I never heard her say a bad word about anyone."

"I wish I had known your mother," said Genevieve. "Mine died young."

"You would have loved her," said Mercy, tears streaming down her cheeks.

"Now, now," said Genevieve, placing her arm around Mercy.

Verity told them about a letter Papa left them. In it he said he loved them very much and had tried to be a good father. He said the house and contents belonged to the four of them. He insisted they never quarrel about material things. He left them special gifts in his safe deposit box. Pru had the key, so she went to the bank the day after Papa was buried. Temp inherited Papa's pocket watch that had belonged to their grandfather. Pru got their mother's cameo pin. Mercy received love letters Papa and Mama had exchanged while he was in World War II.

Verity showed them her mother's ring she received. Each of her friends examined the diamond ring and called it a treasure.

"I want to show you my letters," said Mercy, jumping up from her chair and running upstairs. She returned with a stack of them.

"What a precious gift your Papa left you," said Mary Olivia. "I know you will read and reread them."

"Papa left *you* the letters, Mercy. They should remain private," said Prudence. "Please take them back to your room."

Pru is right about the letters, but I wish she wouldn't overreact.

Mercy climbed the stairs and returned with tissues. She was soon wiping her tears.

"Your father left a great legacy," said Genevieve. "That was evident from the eulogies at his funeral."

"His eulogies make me wonder what I want people to say about me when I'm gone," said Verity.

"You mean in an eulogy … or an obituary?" asked Genevieve.

"It could be one or both of those or just a remembrance of me," Verity answered.

"You've brought up an interesting idea," said Mary Olivia. "This calls for more tea." She poured each some tea.

They sipped on their tea, seemingly deep in their thoughts.

"Let's write them down," said Prudence. She gave them all a sheet of paper from her quotation journal.

They pondered for awhile and then wrote down their wishes.

Mary Olivia spoke up first, taking time to choose her words carefully: "Her spiritual adventure with Jesus was the most important part of her life. Through Bible study and prayer, she achieved an inner peace that she desires for her children, grandchildren, and friends."

"Profound," Chattie said.

"I can thank Genevieve's challenge for leading me to a closer relationship with the Lord."

"Too kind," said Genevieve, almost in a whisper as if embarrassed. "I guess I'll try my eulogy next. I better write one soon since I'll probably be the next to die."

"Not necessarily," said Chattie. "None of us know what the next moment will bring. I never imagined my Roberto would be killed in his 50s."

"You're right, but I am 77," said Genevieve, pausing briefly to think. "Well, here goes: 'She cared about people. She served on many charity boards, but only because she wanted to help people. She loved God, loved her husband more than he ever knew, and adored her daughter and granddaughter. She treasured her best friends.' I would then have your names listed. Then the last sentence: 'And she found a passion late in life — writing.'"

"Beautiful," said Mercy, wiping away her tears. "It's hard for me to believe I'll be listed in your obituary."

"That will be a long time off," Prudence said.

Chattie spoke next. "My first thoughts are: 'She loved her husband Roberto deeply. She wants her boys to experience that same kind of love. She had a sense of adventure and a passionate love of life. She loved God and His beautiful creation.' Please note in the obituary: 'Because she loved flowers, her sons request friends to pick flowers from their gardens and bring to the graveside service and place them on her grave.'"

"What a novel idea," said Prudence.

"I wish. Before her death my grandmother asked her garden club friends to bring flowers. I've never seen so many. Of course, then I never realized I would be a gardener."

"My eulogy will be brief," said Verity. "'She tried to live up to the meaning of her name — truth. She was true to her family and friends and especially to God.'"

"Before I attempt mine," said Prudence, "I want to mention a sermon Papa preached from 2 Chronicles 21:20 that has always stayed with me. It related the death of King Jehoram, a wicked king. The Scripture said, 'He passed away, to no one's regret.' I think that is one of the saddest verses in Scripture. My prayer is that I make an impact, especially on my family and friends."

"You do," said Mercy. "I don't understand why you told that story of King What's His Name. You're not like him."

"Pru made a valuable point about how we all need to leave a legacy."

"Thanks, Verity," Prudence said, smiling at Mercy. "Here goes: 'She had the best Mama and Papa in the world. She considered it a joy — not a burden — to take care of them. She loved her sisters, brother, and friends. She once knew a great love. She never forgot him and continued to love him until she drew her final breath.'"

The women grew silent as Prudence wiped her tears with her fingers. Verity hugged her sister while Mercy sobbed.

I'm glad I told the girls about Pru's fiancé dying before their wedding day.

"Also, put in my obituary: 'She loved to bake tea cakes, peach cobblers, and sweet potato pies for her family and friends,'" said a still teary Prudence.

"A fitting legacy to a marvelous cook," said Mary Olivia,

who tried her best to smile.

"I don't know what I would want people to remember about me," said Mercy. "Maybe — 'She believed God wants us to enjoy life. She loved to laugh, but she also cried a lot. She believed you have to laugh a lot and allow yourself to cry often to really live.'"

"I guess while we're talking about legacies," Genevieve said, "I should tell you girls you're in my will."

"Miss Genevieve, me in your will?" asked Mercy.

"Yes, you too. I'm leaving my teapots to all of you. I have already written my will to include them for you, but I want each of you to come over to my house as soon as you can and choose a teapot set. Prudence, I would like you to get one of my red ones for your red kitchen. Then please speak up for any others you like by putting your name on the teapot."

"What about your daughter and granddaughter?" asked Prudence. "Surely they'll want your teapots."

"They have already selected one, and years ago they started their own collections. They want my friends to get mine."

"How generous," said Verity.

"Miss Genevieve, can I come over this week and get my teapot?"

"Of course, Mercy, but please call me Genevieve."

"I don't think I can. I've always called you Miss Genevieve, but I do want my teapot."

"You can have first choice as long as you leave Prudence a red one."

"I'll be grateful to get my red one, but I hope I'm in the nursing home before I get another teapot from you."

"Aptly put. We all agree with Prudence, I'm sure," said Mary Olivia. "As long as we're talking about giving things away, my prized possessions are my books. You know I have too many of them. Next month I would like each of you to choose a book from my collection. Prudence, you and Mercy come over any time to look for a book. You'll get first choice."

"I'll be over this week," said Mercy, "after I get my teapot."

Mercy is witty. No wonder she and Genevieve get along so well.

"I'm sharing my plants," said Chattie. "As my perennials expand, I want to dig up any you want."

"Pass-along plants are my favorite," said Prudence.

"I don't know if anybody would want any of the old things in our house," said Verity. "But we do have a collection of crocheted pillows, afghans, doilies, and...."

"Could I have a crocheted doily?" asked Mary Olivia softly.

"Sure, but you must have two of them to put on each arm of your chair," said Verity. "We have plenty that Mama crocheted. In fact, I'm giving each of you two doilies. I'll bring them to the next Tea."

"I did start something," Genevieve said, "with my teapot giveaway.

"By the way, I must apologize for last month's impromptu Tea. I was totally unprepared and completely absorbed with my novel. My announcement in September should help you understand."

"Announcement. Hmm. I can't wait," said Mary Olivia.

"Before we go today, Chattie, I've been curious about how your garden survived the flood last month," inquired Genevieve.

"Only with Theo's help. He came over the morning after the huge rain. The pebbles on the garden pathways had washed out in some places. The mulch was out of the flowerbeds and on the paths. What a mess to clean up. It took him all day."

"Is Theo there much?' asked Mary Olivia.

"He comes over two or three mornings a week."

"You do have a loyal gardener. And loyalty is a good trait. You two must be together a lot."

Chattie blushed.

Verity rescued Chattie by asking Mary Olivia about her August Tea.

"I can't wait for you to see how my house has changed."

"I'm eager to see the transformation," said Chattie.

"No wonder. I could not — would not — have got started without your help and motivation. I'm having the Tea in the sunroom. I wanted to have it under the old pear tree outside the sunroom, but August will be hot."

"Your sunroom will be perfect," said Verity. "I love looking out the windows at the birds and, of course, your horses."

"We will enjoy your room with a view," said Genevieve. "Room with a view. That reminds me of that English movie *Room with a View*. I liked it except for those naked men running around in the woods. That was gratuitous."

"Why was that?" asked Mercy.

"I'll explain later," said Prudence.

"I must be on my way," said Chattie. "I need plenty of rest tonight before garden work tomorrow."

"Off to my beauty sleep," added Genevieve, who grabbed her cane and headed toward the door.

"I'm glad you're getting some rest, Miss Genevieve," said Mercy, helping her down the porch step.

After watching Chattie and Genevieve drive off, Verity joined Mary Olivia and Prudence in the kitchen.

"Verity, you look happy today," said Mary Olivia, "You have a sparkle in your eye I haven't seen for years."

Does Mary Olivia suspect something has happened to make me happy? Even during my mourning for Papa? What would Mary Olivia think about my pretending to be a widow? She would probably understand because of her unhappy marriage. She's the only one I could ever tell. Mercy would worry me to death with incessant questions. Pru would want to do research on the Hemings' family tree. And I would catch her at times looking at me as if to ask 'Why didn't you tell me?' She would definitely be hurt.

"She looks good," added Mercy, who had walked into the room while Mary Olivia was speaking. "The day before Papa died we were teasing her about having a beau."

"Foolish talk. I simply am getting more rest."

I hope Mary Olivia leaves soon. This conversation could get complicated.

"Please continue to rest," said Mary Olivia, embracing her three friends.

They waved to Mary Olivia as she drove off. Prudence and Mercy went inside to clean up. Verity went to the porch swing and sat down to think.

I don't believe I've ever felt such freedom and peace. Finally I'm ready to throw myself into finding my great-grandmother's grave.

How I wish I could tell my family and friends about my leav-

ing Micah. I can't now. Maybe never. I told Papa before he died. And that is what matters.

After living a lie for three years, with my confession to Papa, I'm getting closer to living up to my name.

8
AUGUST

MARY OLIVIA

"Just don't give up trying to do what you really want to do. Where there is love and inspiration, I don't think you can go wrong."
American singer Ella Fitzgerald (1917-1996)

While waiting for the girls to arrive, Mary Olivia sat in her bedroom rocker and reflected about her life-changing weekend at the monastery in April. She had a peace she hadn't experienced in many years. She gave thanks to God every day for His wonderful grace and mercy.

I didn't have to go to a monastery to hear the voice of God. But the visit was exactly what I needed. A perfect haven to reflect, ponder, and begin a deep faith journey with God.

I also made a decision there. I asked God for guidance about whether I should tell the boys about my plans for a divorce and Liam's having a heart attack in a hotel room with a young woman. The answer came when I read two verses, Proverbs 10:12 and 19 — "Love covers over all wrongs," and "he who holds his tongue is wise."

If I ever feel a need to confide in anyone, it would be Verity.

But I see no reason to unload on her. She has enough going on dealing with Rev. Isaiah's death and Temp's problems.

◈

Hearing a car drive up, Mary Olivia looked out the window and saw Chattie's car. To her pleasant surprise, she found her three friends had come together. Chattie and Verity were helping Genevieve out of the car.

As soon as they stepped into the living room, Mary Olivia watched for the surprised looks on their faces. She was not disappointed.

"Wow! Your house looks great," said Verity. "How did you accomplish all of this?"

"Working non-stop all summer," said Mary Olivia, going into a drooped position and then laughing.

They joined her in laughing and hugged her.

"Now sit down on my new leather sofa."

Continuing to look around the room, they chatted about the comfortable sofa and how much they liked the room.

"Remember, Genevieve, in January you said our challenge would help me simplify my life. I didn't understand you then, but I certainly do now. Getting my physical surroundings organized and clear of clutter has been liberating."

"I could never have anticipated where God would take you when I made that statement."

"After Chattie got me started in May with her tips on organizing, the boys and I went through the entire house using her procedure: a stack for keeping, one for giving away, and another for throwing away or recycling. It feels good to rid myself of nonessentials. Stuff.

"Are you ready for a guided tour?"

"I, for one, can't wait," said Chattie. "I want to see for myself how you put my tips to use."

"Let's start here in the living room. We removed all the carpet downstairs and found beautiful oak wood floors. Then we had the floors refinished."

"They look new," said Verity.

"I think so too. We replaced the heavy drapes with white sheers. I bought this burgundy sofa and matching chair. Then I added this patterned rug, sofa pillows, and a floor lamp."

"And the beige walls look so clean and fresh," said Genevieve.

"I'm glad you noticed. The boys and I painted every room in the house."

"It makes me think ... know ... the inside of my house needs painting," said Genevieve. "Could I borrow your painters?"

"I doubt it. I would highly recommend them ... us ... but I don't think they ... we ... want to pick up a paint brush for a long time."

"I sure wouldn't after painting an entire house," said Verity.

"The last person who did our painting was Temp," said Mary Olivia. "Maybe he can paint the next time the house needs it."

"I pray he will," said Verity.

"Without my sons and grandson, I could never have done all of the work in the house. Eric and Blake developed a good work ethic. Eric became a mentor to Blake, guiding him through our work. After he got off work each day, James pitched in at night."

Next Mary Olivia led them to the dining room. She showed them the old mahogany table, chairs, and buffet she had inherited. The boys had cleaned and polished the furniture. The drapes were replaced with white sheers to match those in the living room. She pointed out her new blue placemats and her new Renoir print *Two Sisters (On a Terrace)*.

"I like that print," said Chattie.

"I collect Renoir prints, as you'll see.

"The boys are in the den a lot watching movies and playing games. I bought blue and red containers to store everything from remotes to DVDs to Scrabble. I covered the old couch and chair with new blue and white slipcovers and bought a new rug and a new red beanbag for Blake. I know where to find him now."

"Your house has a simplified charm," said Verity.

"Thanks. But we haven't finished the tour yet," said Mary Olivia, smiling.

"Now to the library. I told the boys I would clean this room, not knowing what a task I had before me.

"First, I took out all the books, cleaned each shelf, and arranged the books by category and author. Histories, biographies, classic novels, poetry, etc.

"Then I parted with many books. I gave away some that were worthwhile reading; but those I found to be fluff, including some Christian books, I threw away. Why give away useless reading?"

"You're to be commended," said Genevieve. "Sometimes

we give away things to people who need them even less than we do."

"An astute observation," said Chattie.

"After the Tea we'll come back here for you to choose your books I promised last month."

"I haven't forgotten your offer," said Verity, smiling broadly.

Verity is upbeat today. Even with the death of Rev. Isaiah, she seems happier than I've seen her since Micah's death.

"I didn't think Mercy was ever going to stop talking about her book on cleaning tips using vinegar and soda," said Verity. "She already has tried one of them. And it worked."

"Which one?"

Verity said that Mercy insisted the kitchen drain wasn't draining properly. Although Pru disagreed, she consented to let Mercy try her cleaning tip. Mercy put a cup of soda in the drain and then a cup of vinegar, let it sit for an hour, and then poured hot water down the drain. Pru was delighted with the clear drain.

"I'm glad Mercy is having fun — and results — with the book," Mary Olivia said.

Verity explained that Pru was fascinated with her book about the 1918 influenza pandemic. "She has learned that between 50 and 100 million people worldwide died in 1918. The figures scared Mercy, who's now concerned an epidemic will kill all of us.

"We've assured her," Verity said, "that God will take care of us."

"Sweet Mercy. I love that girl," said Genevieve, who gently squeezed Verity's hand.

"Now for my bedroom." Mary Oliva led them into a large room painted a pale blue. A dark cherry sleigh bed was the focus of the room. A royal blue duvet with matching pillow shams covered the queen size bed. Near the window next to a rocking chair was a table containing a Bible, journal, and several Christian classics. A lamp, a small candle, and a miniature silver cross also were on the table. A bookshelf against the wall stood next to a large peace plant with two white blooms.

The girls walked around the room trying to take in everything.

"This room evokes calm and peace," said Genevieve.

"It's my retreat. I chose the color blue after reading about its calming effect."

"Another Renoir print," said Chattie, reading the name, *Dancing at Bougival*. "Roberto liked to dance. He would have liked that print."

"I selected it for my room because the color blue is prominent and because, well, it makes me happy."

Verity picked up a cross-stitched verse from the nightstand and read, "'Be still and know that I am God.' Psalm 46:10. Perfect for this room."

"I see only Christian biographies on the shelf," observed Genevieve.

"Yes, biographies have been my favorite reading since the fifth grade when I discovered Clara Barton and George Washington Carver. Now I'm focusing on leaders such as St. Augustine, Jonathan Edwards, John Wesley, Charles Spurgeon, and Sojourner Truth. And I've discovered the mystics: Brother Lawrence, Teresa of Avila, and Julian of Norwich."

"Like Pru, you'll have a lot of stories to share with us," said Verity.

They'll find out later why these books are so valuable to me.

"Even the hostas and caladiums outside your window," said Chattie, "add to the soothing mood of this room."

"I agree. My bedroom is perfect for my studying and contemplation. I get up early and sit in my rocker to study my Bible and pray. Then I walk for 30 minutes and continue to talk to God and enjoy the sunrise. I feel healthier physically and spiritually starting my day with God."

"What book in the Bible are you reading?" asked Verity.

"I'm in Luke now. I started to read through the New Testament after my monastery visit. After researching each book, I then read slowly, meditating upon each chapter."

The girls are curious about the effect the monastery stay had on me, but I don't want to appear to have a holier-than-thou attitude. My friends are Christians. Maybe getting back to the tour will take the spotlight off of me.

"Now for the kitchen.

"You may remember, Chattie, that in April I motioned for you to stay in the dining room while I filled a flower vase with water. I didn't want you to see my messy kitchen. And believe me, the counters were piled high with stuff."

"They sure aren't now," said Chattie.

Mary Olivia explained that she hired a professional painter to paint the dark cabinets white. Then she got new granite countertops and a new tile floor.

"I actually like to cook in my kitchen now."

"No wonder," said Genevieve. "The room is bright and

cheerful."

"I've found a word on the fridge," said Chattie. "'Gormandize: eat greedily; gorge.'"

"The boys and I are learning new words. Of course, you know where I got the idea. Now let's go upstairs. I want you to see the boys' bedrooms — and the new brown carpet."

After peering in three bedrooms, Genevieve said, "Beds made. Everything in its place. Remarkable. My Shipman was neat, but they could have taught him something."

"One wouldn't know two sons and a grandson lived here," added Verity.

"Now after all of our exercise walking through my house, you should be ready for our Tea," said Mary Olivia, as she led them downstairs to the sunroom.

"I sure am," said Genevieve. "But what fun the tour was. It was the first guided home tour of our Tea. But I've taken my share of tours at past Teas. For example, Doll changed her furniture around so much that each time she hosted a Tea her house looked different. But she never gave us a guided tour. We've had a garden tour at Chattie's and now a home tour."

"I can't imagine why we haven't made Genevieve our official historian," said Mary Olivia. "I make a motion that she become our Tea historian."

"I second," said Verity, "and she must stay in that position for years since no one else knows all the minutiae she does."

"Thank you. Thank you," said Genevieve, bowing twice. "I accept your kind invitation." Sitting down in a comfortable yellow and pink chair in the sunroom, she added, "Now I'll have an official reason for boring you with all my stories."

"Entertaining is the correct word," said Chattie.

"I've always enjoyed this room because the windows provide so much light and a beautiful view," said Verity. "And the furniture. It's beautiful. Why didn't you tell us about your new furniture?"

"Oops. The guided home tour is not over. How could I have forgotten this room? Next to my bedroom it's my favorite. I bought all new furniture. A printed sofa and matching chairs, rug, and glass-topped coffee table and end tables. All I lack is a dining table."

"You have turned it into a cozy room," said Genevieve.

"What a view you have of your pear tree, crepe myrtles, marigolds and zinnias," Chattie remarked. "Look. Two cardinals eating birdseed at your bird feeder."

"Like the birds," said Mary Olivia, "I'm getting hungry."

After giving thanks, Mary Olivia announced, "We're celebrating National Peach Month. Please get your iced peach tea and peach muffins and sit on the sofa or chairs."

"I'm glad you chose iced tea for this hot day," said Genevieve after drinking several sips from the clear goblets and then eating a bite of muffin. "So succulent. You know how I love peaches."

"Confession time. I liked Prudence's blueberry muffins so much last month I asked her if I could borrow the recipe and substitute peaches for blueberries. And she gave me three of your peaches, Genevieve."

"I just bragged on my own peaches," laughed Genevieve.

The women joined her in laughing and then quietly ate for several minutes while watching the birds outside.

Either my tour gave us all a good appetite, or we're out of anything to say. That would be a first.

"It's remarkable how much work you've done on your house," said Chattie, reaching for another muffin. "I have to admit I never expected this transformation."

"I liked my stark room at the monastery. It was so unlike my cluttered house. Not that I want only a bed, a table, a lamp, and a plain rug in every room. But I wanted to simplify. Ironically, I have found decluttering my house easy compared with spiritual simplicity. That is, I can't simplify everything around me and not clean out my heart and discard wrong attitudes and habits. God is helping me deal with feelings of cynicism and other sins."

"That goes for all of us," said Chattie. "I'm much too loquacious. I'm living up to my name more and more."

"You're being much too hard on yourself," observed Genevieve.

"But I need — want — to have a quieter spirit."

"That's exactly what I'm asking God to work in me," said Mary Olivia. "The apostle Peter referred to it in 1 Peter 3:4 as a 'gentle and quiet spirit.'

"The monks suggested several books to us. One, *The Practice of the Presence of God,* by Brother Lawrence, is helping me practice the presence of God all through the day."

"What's his secret?" asked Chattie.

"Practicing the presence of God means to have, to quote Brother Lawrence, 'a habitual, silent, and secret conversation of the soul with God.' He says 'to think often on God, by day, by night, in your business, and even in your diversions.'"

"Diversions would mean here at the Tea," said Verity. "Those are beautiful and practical thoughts. Brother Lawrence sounds like the apostle Paul when he says in Acts 17:28, 'For in Him we live and move and have our being.'"

"I'll be glad to share the book," Mary Olivia said.

"I definitely want to read it," said Verity.

"I hope I haven't sounded preachy," said Mary Olivia. "I didn't mean to."

"Everything I've learned from your monastery visit has been enlightening, not preachy," said Genevieve. "And I believe it has even influenced how you look. Your new hair style. Your clothes. And your trimmer figure."

"Thought you would never notice. I had to exercise to get the weight off."

Following her monastery stay, Mary Olivia had removed cobwebs from her exercise bike. Then she started exercising on it about five minutes a day and worked up to 10 minutes three times a day. At dusk each day she began walking one mile a day down her road until she reached two miles a day. Blake helped her lift light weights each day.

"I've lost nine pounds. I've looked frumpy for so long. And I'm tired of being frumpy. I want to be a modern grandmother."

"Frumpy," said Chattie. "Sure don't hear that word much."

"Guess not. But that's the best way I can describe my style. Or lack of it. Frumpy. Not neat. Not in style. Shabby. I was and still am frumpy, but I'm trying to be more classic in my style and neater like you, Verity."

"What a sweet compliment."

"It's true. You've always had a classic style."

"Have you gone back to your church?" asked Chattie.

"Yes. Back to the Baptist church of my youth."

"Baptist? Aren't you Catholic?" asked Chattie. "You're full of surprises."

"I only went to mass sporadically. The boys attended a Catholic school. What a couple we were. Liam, a careless Catholic. Me, a backsliding Baptist. I have gotten involved with missions at my church working at our food pantry twice a week. Eric and Blake attend church with me, and eventually I think James will."

"Isn't it ironic that a Catholic monastery helped you reconnect with God and return to your Baptist faith?" asked Genevieve.

"It makes perfect sense to me. It took a spiritual awakening, or maybe a better word, re-awakening, for me to understand where God wants to use me. I'm going back to my roots but bringing a different spiritual perspective with me."

"Maybe you can do a seminar on contemplative prayer at your church," said Genevieve.

"God may lead me to do that, but He may not. Hopefully, I can help revitalize our prayer ministry. We have prayer warriors I can learn from also.

"But enough about me."

Mary Olivia looked at Chattie and asked, "How's gardening?"

"Well, Theo has been watering a lot since the drought last month."

"Do you hire Theo to water?" Genevieve asked.

"Yes, but also to do other chores. He pulls up weeds, deadheads petunias, and to tell the truth, I often don't know what he's doing. I'm in the house out of the heat. He knows what needs to be done. I couldn't do without him."

Chattie is head over heels in love with him.

"Genevieve, how's your month going?" asked Chattie.

"I'm staying inside reading and resting. Trying to stay out of the dreadful heat. Soon after our last Tea, I welcomed two marvelous guests, Prudence and Mercy." Genevieve caught her breath for a moment. "Prudence brought me a peach cobbler made from peaches I took her last month. I talked them into having dessert with me. It was the best cobbler I've ever eaten.

"After we ate, I had fun watching them select a teapot. Prudence chose a solid red one with a matching sugar bowl and creamer for her kitchen. Mercy inspected every teapot before finally deciding on a dark blue one with a matching sugar bowl and creamer."

"Mercy went on for days about hers," said Verity.

"I love that girl," said Genevieve.

"She looks up to you. I think now that Papa is gone she considers you a mentor."

"Then I must be on my best behavior." Genevieve immediately sat up straight.

They all smiled with her.

"What's Prudence doing?" Chattie asked.

"Besides cooking, she entertains us with lively anecdotes from her library research. Since last month we have learned two little- known details about two famous women. Each concerned a guillotine. Queen Marie Antoinette was executed by the guillotine in 1793 during the French Revolution. A terrible death. Pru said Marie Antoinette had tuberculosis and possibly uterine cancer."

"So she probably would have died soon anyway," said Genevieve.

"That's right. The other story revolved around a First Lady, Elizabeth Monroe, wife of President James Monroe. She went to Paris in 1794 with her husband, who was then U.S. minister to France. When she discovered that General Lafayette's wife was imprisoned and awaiting death by the guillotine, courageous Elizabeth went to the prison to see Mrs. Lafayette. Because of Mrs. Monroe's actions on her behalf, Mrs. Lafayette was set free."

"What interesting tidbits of history!" exclaimed Chattie. "Confession time. I disliked history before joining the Tea."

The women joined Chattie in laughing.

"Mercy and I can't wait for next month's stories. Also, Pru has joined a Scrabble club that meets monthly. It's proved to be good therapy for her grief. You know how she loves words. Well, now she's learning new Scrabble words. Ones Mercy and I learn also. We both may be in need of therapy soon, listening to all the new words she brings home."

The women laughed.

Verity has never been so witty.

"What words has she learned?" asked a smiling Genevieve. "Maybe I can use them in my writing."

"She's only attended one meeting of the Scrabble Club. We learned *Xu*, a monetary unit of Vietnam, and *qat*, a flowering plant which is native to East Africa and the Arabian Peninsula."

"I can't imagine how I could use those two words in an American novel."

The women agreed.

"How's your research going?" asked Chattie, looking at Verity.

"I'll report progress next month about the whereabouts of my great-grandmother's grave."

"You have chosen quite an undertaking," said Genevieve, "and an important one. I look forward to hearing your news."

"What is Mercy doing besides cleaning?" asked Mary Olivia.

"She's going through Papa's clothes. She hopes Temp will take some of them."

"Do you see him often?" asked Genevieve.

"Since Papa died, he stops by about twice a week and eats with us. He's talking more. We think that's a good sign. Of course, we wish he would move in with us and take Papa's old room. Temp told us last week that for years he's been collecting money — pennies, nickels, quarters — he finds on his walks. We had no idea. He has coffee cans full of money. He's going to bring them home for us to see. We told him he should open a bank account. The fact that he told us about his money collection is another sign he's opening up more."

"Give him time," said Mary Olivia. "He'll be acting more and more like the old Temp. God is working in his life."

Eric quietly walked into the sunroom. Mary Olivia's slender son told Verity how much he would miss Rev. Isaiah, who had been a role model to him. Eric's words moved Verity. She dried her eyes with her tissues.

"Did Mom tell you I've enrolled in the community college?"

"I haven't. Why don't you, honey?"

"Well, Mom encouraged me to follow my interests, which are sports and physical training. I've decided to major in physical education and be a teacher in elementary school."

"Good. We need more male teachers," said Verity.

"I agree. I want to get children interested in exercise and fitness while they are young. Miss Genevieve, your challenge to Mom has now touched me, and I thank you for that. I've got to run. Got a date. Good to see each of you."

"Sensible young man." said Chattie.

"It's taken him quite awhile to get his feet on the ground. He's the fencer who's finally decided to get a degree. He's planning to teach fencing at college to help with his costs."

"Sweet young man," said Genevieve. "And, by the way, smart. I read recently fencers are smart. Fencing is not only a physical game but a mental one."

"Interesting. I knew he was smart," said Mary Olivia, "but he's finally applying himself to his studies."

"I don't want any credit for his decision to return to school. But it does excite me." Genevieve stopped for a drink of water. "He said he had a date. Boy, that takes me back a long time. Do you ever think about dating and getting married again? I know I'm too old for dating, but you three are still young."

"Never say never," said Mary Olivia. "It's not uncommon to read about even octogenarians getting married."

"Maybe I've heard too many horror stories," said Genevieve. "Men wanting widows for their money, and some with serious health problems wanting wives to take care of them. Or even worse. Did I ever tell you what happened when Bert dated?"

"I can't remember hearing that story," said Mary Olivia.

"Remember Bert worked at the funeral home and got to know many widowers. About a month after his wife's death, one widower called her up for a date. At first, she couldn't remember him. When he said his name was Pud Wolfe, then she remembered."

"What a strange name," said Chattie.

"I never knew his real name. I heard he was called Puddin' in his childhood because he loved pudding. Then when he got older, his friends shortened it." Genevieve paused to rest. "Anyway, Bert remembered Pud's slight limp, which likely made her more sympathetic toward him. Although reluctant to go out with him, she consented when he offered to take her to a nice restaurant. Bert enjoyed the food but was bored by his incessant talking about his gout."

"King Henry VIII and President William Taft had gout," said Verity. "Trivia from Pru."

"She was glad to leave the restaurant. Then Pud invited her up to his assisted-living apartment to see his late wife's collection of Blue Willow. She declined, of course. He seemed disappointed but drove her back to her garden home. Before she could get out, he grabbed her and tried to kiss ... and ... it's difficult to say ... fondle her."

"My word!" exclaimed Chattie.

"She screamed, and fortunately for her, the car door was unlocked. She ran into her house, locked the door, and watched him drive away. Bert never accepted any more dates from men.

"One other thing. Bert found out later from a friend how Pud got his limp." Genevieve stopped to sip some tea. "When he was married, he had affairs with other women. A husband discovered Pud with his wife. The husband beat Pud so badly that from that time on he walked with a limp."

"This story is a lesson for all of us," said Mary Olivia. "Who knows how many lecherous old men are out there trying to prey on us?"

"Are you making fun of my story about Bert?" asked Genevieve, who looked disappointed.

"No. I just realized I *had* heard the story. It's a good one, though, and worth hearing again."

The women had a good laugh.

"One more thing," continued Genevieve. "Remember a few months ago we were talking about the significance of people's names. Like Theo Root. Well, Pud Wolfe did live up to his name. What a wolf.

"How about you, Verity? Would you consider dating even after my story?"

"Definitely not. Absolutely not interested," she said, shaking her head. "All I can handle now is Pru, Mercy, and Temp."

"Chattie?"

"I wouldn't rule it out, but I don't think I'm ready. Of course, no one has asked me out. I'll make a decision when and if that happens."

"Mary Olivia?"

"I wouldn't mind dating, but I don't anticipate having the

time. I'll be too busy studying."

"Studying?" asked Verity. "You already have two degrees."

"I was saving my announcement for the night's finale," Mary Olivia said. "But here goes," she said, breathing in deeply and letting her breath out. "My first step in my big adventure — I've signed up for a church history course this fall. Next semester I hope to be admitted to seminary. Then…."

"Are you planning to be a minister?" interrupted Genevieve. "At your age?"

"The answer to the first question is 'I hope so.' And, Genevieve, I can thank you for starting me on my spiritual quest. And the answer to the second question is 'I know I'm 61, and when I complete my studies, I'll be retirement age. But that doesn't bother me. God will have a job for me. I may have 20 to 40 years left. None of us know how much time God has for us to accomplish His purposes for our life. I can always be a chaplain in a nursing home — while I'm living there.'"

Chattie laughed. The others smiled.

"Papa would be excited for you," said Verity. "He would be praising the Lord for your decision. And he would think nothing of your age. He would consider you young."

"I think Rev. Isaiah would approve of my goal of becoming an ordained minister. Why not? Women are making great strides today in the ministry. Maybe I will shake up my church although some Baptists do ordain women. I would like to get a Master of Divinity in Church History. I don't know whether I want to preach or teach at a seminary or be a chaplain. Who knows? I may even join the lecture circuit."

"I'm not for sure," stammered Genevieve, "how I feel about

women as senior pastors. But I am happy for your decision. We Presbyterians ordain women as pastors. But that doesn't mean I have to agree with our decisions."

Genevieve's spunk has influenced my life for sure.

Mary Olivia said that God has been dealing with her for some time. It took her going to the monastery to be still and listen and pray about her decision.

"I know God is calling me to the seminary. I know He will reveal His will as I pursue my studies."

"How do your boys feel about your decision?" asked Verity.

"James and Eric want me to be happy. They know I'll have to spend a lot of time studying. I think it will also mature Eric — and Blake — and give them an opportunity to be more responsible.

"My getting the house organized and simplifying my personal life will give me more time for studying."

"I am encouraged by each of you girls," said Genevieve. "I had no idea what impact my challenge would have on your lives. And, Mary Olivia, I apologize questioning you about your plans to be a minister. I was being a hypocrite. Next month I will have an important announcement about my novel."

Chattie told them she was having another Garden Tea.

"I'm looking forward to seeing your beautiful garden again," Verity said.

"It looks quite different than it did in May. Theo and I will be working hard this next month getting it ready."

"I hope Mr. Root will be at the Tea," said Genevieve. "I

want to meet him."

"I've asked him to be there. Who knows? One of you may need a gardener sometime. On a scale of 1 to 10, I give him a 10. You couldn't find anyone who knows more about gardening."

I'm sure of it now. Chattie is interested in Theo. Genevieve's story has got me thinking about Theo's intentions. I don't want Chattie to be taken advantage of or to be emotionally hurt. Even though Liam's behavior was not honorable toward me, I can't be cynical about every man. But as her friend, I have to watch out for Chattie. She's vulnerable. Maybe I'll be able to discern Theo's intentions toward her. I'm praying they're admirable.

Verity thanked Mary Olivia for the Tea and picked up her purse to leave.

"My pleasure," said Mary Olivia, "but you can't go without your books."

"How could we forget our books?" asked Genevieve.

In the library they spent time looking for just the right books.

Sharing my books is such fun. I'm glad I organized them. It makes it easier for them to find ones they like.

"I've found a perfect book," said Genevieve, holding it next to her chest. "Yes, this is the book I want. A history about the settling of the West."

"Biographies of composers," said Verity. "Beethoven. Mozart. Bach. Reading these are going to be fun and educational. I may teach Pru a thing or two."

"I haven't found my book yet. I'm looking for one on flowers," said Chattie, looking through the miscellaneous books.

"Colonial flowers. This looks interesting." Chattie picked up a book with many flowers on the cover. "I'll read it carefully to find out if I have any heirloom flowers in my garden."

The perfect book for Chattie.

"Now for the surprise I promised you last month," said Verity, retrieving six crocheted doilies from her bag and giving each of them two.

"I'll treasure these," said Mary Olivia.

"How exquisite," said Chattie, rubbing her hand over her two doilies.

"I know exactly where I am putting mine. On my end tables in my living room I have pictures of daughter Elizabeth and granddaughter Jessica. Under each frame I will place a doily," said Genevieve.

"I'm placing mine under pictures of my boys," added Chattie. "Now I'm off to my garden. I must get it ready for next month." She grabbed her keys from her purse.

"Don't leave us," said Genevieve. "Verity and I came with you."

"How embarrassing. Gardening may have killed some of my brain cells."

The friends laughed.

"See you next month," Mary Olivia said, as she waved goodbye to the girls.

I surprised them about my plans to be a minister. I know it's a calling from God just as I'm sure Chattie's gardening is.

9
SEPTEMBER

~

CHATTIE

"I'm not afraid of storms, for I'm learning how to sail my ship."
American author Louisa May Alcott (1832-1888)

Chattie placed a pot of yellow chrysanthemums in the center of a green round table on her brick patio. For several minutes she deliberated where to set two other pots. She finally placed them on opposite sides of the patio.

What's the matter with me? Worrying about where to put mums? I know what is wrong, but I don't want to think about it. Today I'm introducing Theo to the girls. I think they will like him, but I'm afraid they will sense my deepening affection for him. I must stop thinking about Theo. Maybe my nerves will settle down if I get my mind back on my flowers.

Walking through her garden, Chattie marveled at the colorful blooms. Yellow lantana. Blue asters. Gold marigolds. White and pink begonias. Yellow cannas. Red coxcombs. Purple and white petunias. Zinnias of many colors.

New garden surprises awaited her each day. A plant emerging from a seed she'd planted. A day lily blooming. Yellow butterflies flitting around zinnias and marigolds. A hummingbird stealing nectar from a purple verbena. She called them her garden "treasures." She stored the moments in her heart as well as in her journal.

"The garden is gorgeous today," she said aloud. "Who would have thought? A hail storm in April. A flash flood in June. A drought in July and August. What a year to begin gardening."

I've gained a new appreciation of perseverance and work well spent. Pulling up weeds, spreading mulch, fertilizing beds, running my hands through the soil. Sure all that work made my back ache and sent me to bed more times than I want to admit. But the time spent in my garden has been a labor of love.

And I've made a new friend. Theo has been with me through all this joy and work. Now I'm getting nervous again thinking about Theo. Back to the garden — and then back to Theo. I must keep my mind on the plants.

She knelt down to smell her favorite herbs — lavender, orange mint, and lemon balm.

I never imagined until I started gardening what different scents I would enjoy.

She remembered one day a week ago breaking off one leaf from each plant and giving them to Theo to smell. He liked the scent of lemon balm so much he took a few cuttings for his garden. He smiled when she teased him she was now sharing her garden with him.

He has the most charming smile. I saw it in my dream last night. But I must not think about that dream. I'm so ashamed. Dreaming about being in love and not with Roberto. My word!

Please, God, forgive me. Please forgive me.

She looked up to see Verity coming toward her.

She didn't hear a car drive up. She hoped Verity hadn't heard her.

∽

"A glorious spectacle." Verity hugged Chattie and then continued to look around the garden. "I've never seen so many flowers blooming in a garden."

Taking her by the arm, Chattie said, "Let's stroll through the garden and talk while we wait for the girls."

"What is that flower? It looks as if it's crying out to be touched."

"That's a coxcomb. The common name for Celosia. Go ahead and touch it. It feels like velvet."

"You're right," said Verity, examining the flower. "Soft like velvet."

"Theo says it's a reseeding annual, which means I should have plants to share next year. That is, if you want them."

"Pru definitely will."

"Let's sit on the bench," said Chattie.

"What a peaceful place. Your garden is an ideal place to pray."

"Feel free to stop by any time to pray. Just remember I may volunteer you to work. Once I start gardening I lose all track of time. I forget everything else because I'm so engrossed in the work. A couple of weeks ago I spent all afternoon dividing clumps of coreopsis and weeding asters. I worked until I could barely see the flowers. Looking up, I saw the full moon behind me. I felt such happiness. I was doing something I loved. I guess what I'm saying is that gardening is therapy to me."

"I can understand that. My tracking down my great-grandmother's grave has been therapy. It has helped me cope with Papa's death. And getting my mind on something constructive and fulfilling a promise to Mama have given my life a renewed purpose."

"A renewed purpose is a good description of what we all are experiencing," said Chattie.

They saw Mary Olivia slowly walking down the stone path, trying to take in everything. She stopped to read one of several stakes Chattie had placed in the garden.

Mary Olivia has an appreciation for living in the moment.

"Sorry I'm late. I stayed after class to talk to Martin, my religion professor. Your garden is even more beautiful than I imagined it would be." She stopped talking to give Chattie an embrace. "I guess you saw me reading one of your quotes: 'Time began in the garden.'"

"Look a few feet to your left, and you'll find another one."

Verity saw the stake also and read a quote by Abraham Lincoln: "'We can complain because rose bushes have thorns, or rejoice because thorn bushes have roses.' Insightful Mr. Lincoln."

"Genevieve is getting out of her car. Excuse me while I greet her."

"I'll sit here with Verity and enjoy your garden," said Mary Olivia.

"You look great, Genevieve. I would even say radiant would be a better description," Chattie said, giving her a big hug.

"Radiant. No one has ever described me that way. If it

means I feel better than I have all year, then it's the right word. And coming out here to your gorgeous garden is helping me more."

"I'm glad you wore your hat. You were smart to do so. It's appropriate today." Chattie slowly led Genevieve down the path.

"Why did you say 'appropriate'"?

"Because of your important — and might I say — much anticipated announcement."

"Oh, yes. My hat might lend a sophisticated air to my revelation. I want to unveil my secret at the end of our Tea."

Chattie and Genevieve joined their two friends at the bench.

"What a superb gardener you are," Genevieve bragged to Chattie. "Your research and hard work have certainly paid off."

"Those are kind words. And it's all your fault."

"I'm happy to take the blame."

"You look refreshed today," said Verity.

"Radiant is how Chattie described me. I'll take both radiant and refreshed."

"You're a class act," said Mary Olivia. "And your blue straw hat is a hit."

"No one mentioned wearing a hat today, but another Garden Tea was my excuse for buying another one."

"Girls, before I introduce you to Theo," said Chattie, "I want to show you two naked ladies that have bloomed. They came from Theo's garden."

"Naked ladies! What a name!" exclaimed Genevieve in an uncharacteristic loud outburst. "I'm sorry. The name jarred me."

"The common name of *Lycoris Radiata*, often referred to as spider lilies. Every woman should have them in her flower beds so she can say she has naked ladies."

The women laughed and talked for several minutes.

"I don't believe we have laughed this much all year," said Chattie.

"I agree," remarked Mary Olivia. "When I get my perennials, I want a naked lady."

"I may need two," said Genevieve, smiling.

Chattie led them to the plants. They all marveled at the clusters of red blooms on leafless stalks.

Verity said that Pru would definitely love one.

"I'll make sure you all get more than one. If you can refrain from thinking — and laughing — about naked ladies, I want you to meet Theo. My word. He's headed this way. Guess he's finished pruning the boxwoods."

"Genevieve, Verity, Mary Olivia, meet Theo Root, the person I owe my garden to."

"Thanks, Chattie, but I work for you. You're the real gardener," he said, taking off his gloves.

"But so much of this garden came from your work and cuttings from your garden."

"I like to share my plants." Turning to the three women, he shook their hands and said, "It's nice meeting each of you."

"Our pleasure. Are you related to the late Elihu Root?" asked Genevieve, still shaking his hand.

"Let me think a minute. My sister has done some work on our family tree. I believe I'm a descendant."

"Not many Roots around. I thought you might be kin. Congratulations. You're descended from a good man. Did you know his father went by Square and his son by Cube?"

"No, I didn't."

I hope Genevieve is finished. Theo, I'm sure, isn't enjoying the attention.

"An honor to meet you, Mr. Root," said Genevieve, "but I need to find a chair now and get off my feet."

Verity walked with Genevieve to the patio.

"Theo, I'll see you tomorrow."

"I'm sorry. I can't come until Friday."

How can I wait three more days to see him?

"Well, I'll walk you to your truck."

"Wait for me. I'm coming too," said Mary Olivia.

How I wish I could be alone with Theo.

"The garden is stunning," said Mary Olivia. "You and Chattie make a great team."

"Thanks. But she's the boss. I'm only her employee."

"You spend a lot of time together. You must enjoy being with each other."

"Gardening is hard work. I like it, though, and the extra money comes in handy. I must go. Nice to meet you," he said, getting into his pickup.

"See you Friday," shouted Chattie, as he quickly drove off.

"Isn't he modest, girls?" asked Chattie, as she and Mary Olivia sat down at the patio table. "I couldn't have done anything without him."

"I'm sure he's a nice man, but he seemed abrupt and defensive," said Genevieve.

"He did act defensive today. And he never has been this way. Maybe he felt uncomfortable around you three. He is used to being around only me.

"Make yourself at home, girls. I'll get the tea and dessert," said Chattie, as she headed for the kitchen.

She hoped her friends hadn't noticed her growing interest in Theo. She propped her elbows on her kitchen counter. That morning she had reread her last journal entry. She had been writing more and more about Theo and expressing too many emotions. Last night she'd had that horrible dream. Theo was passionate in it. He hugged her and kissed her several times. She hadn't seen that side of him while gardening. She must forget that dream, she told herself. She knew it was a sin to have lustful thoughts. Another dream, and she would have to call her rector.

No wonder I had the dream after my venture to Theo's place yesterday. What if he'd seen me driving by his place around dusk wearing a black dress and a black scarf over a black wig and sunglasses? And parking down the street and walking in my disguise by his house to get a glimpse of him. Halfway down the street I did wonder what would happen if he saw me. How could she explain wearing such a garb?

She continued walking until she saw him weeding his flowers — his back toward her. Turning around, she rushed back to her car, her heart pounding all the way.

I thank God Theo didn't see me. And I vow never to drive by his place again.

∽

"You should know by now what decorating motif to expect

from me," said Chattie, returning with tea and dessert.

"That's an easy one. Flowers," said Verity.

"I couldn't resist buying these paper napkins with pictures of yellow mums. I'm using the same dessert plates we had in May. Recently I found some white cups with flowers. And now to unveil more yellow," she said as she uncovered the dessert.

"Lemon squares," said Genevieve. "I haven't eaten them in ages."

"After a silent prayer, we'll eat," said Chattie, bowing her head.

She prayed for her friends, her boys, the food, her garden, and her friendship with Theo.

"Help yourselves. I'll pour our Lady Grey tea. Remember we had it in January at the tea room. Sugar, anyone?"

"None for me. I'm trying to lose more weight," said Mary Olivia.

"I like Lady Grey. Not as much as Earl Grey, but it is good," said Genevieve. After a pause to sip some tea, Genevieve surprised her friends by asking, "Can we agree that Chattie has a boyfriend?"

"Hush," Chattie said, blushing. "We're friends. Good friends who have battled a hail storm, a flash flood, and a drought — all in the garden."

The women laughed.

"Besides, I love Roberto's memory too much to rush into anything."

What is happening to me? Am I in love? Or could it be only infatuation?

"Theo and Chattie are only friends," said Mary Olivia.

Chattie took a deep breath.

I'm relieved Mary Olivia doesn't suspect my feelings for Theo.

"Mary Olivia's right," said Chattie. "We're gardening friends. Later this month we're dividing day lilies from his garden. It's so exciting."

"Is it exciting to be with Theo? Or do you mean watching nature do its thing?" asked a smiling Genevieve.

Chattie blushed again. She knew her friends had guessed her feelings now.

"Genevieve, leave Chattie alone," said Mary Olivia, playfully. "Remember they're just friends."

Is Mary Olivia coming to my rescue or is she being sarcastic?

"I'm sorry," said Genevieve. "I was having fun, but I should not at your expense. I do like Mr. Root. I would like any Root."

They laughed and then continued to sip tea and eat.

"Your lemon squares are rich and flavorful," said Verity. "I've eaten three."

"I admit I ate three also," said Mary Olivia. "And remember I skipped the sugar for my tea."

"Your yellow mums are beautiful," said Verity. "So fitting for a September Tea."

Chattie was glad to think about flowers again. Then she remembered her surprise.

"Yellow flowers always cheer me up. I bought them for a selfish reason, though. I want to get them started in my garden."

"Nothing wrong with that. Remember you're a gardener," said Genevieve. "And we benefit because we enjoy them today and will next fall in your garden."

"How did your plants survive the summer drought?" asked Verity.

"Water. Water. Water. I was out at 6 in the morning and 7 at night watering. I almost fainted when I got my water bill. But I had to keep my flowers alive.

"Over the next two months Theo and I are planting wildflower seeds — cosmos, Shasta daisies, red poppies, bachelor buttons, Black Eyed Susans. ... But enough about my garden. You see what you've done, Genevieve. I fell in love with gardening so much that I bore everyone with my talking."

"You don't bore me. I love a success story, especially one I initiated," giggled Genevieve. Turning to Mary Olivia, she asked, "What's going on with you?"

"Plenty. Last month I told you about signing up for a religion course on church history. Well, we've met for a few weeks now. I absolutely love the class. Martin's a scholar but also a demanding teacher. And a fine gentleman. I respect him a lot."

Now who's interested in a man? And she calls him by his first name.

"Martin is a courageous and inspiring person." Mary Olivia paused a moment. "He has leukemia."

"Leukemia?" questioned Genevieve. "What stage?"

"It's in remission. He seems fine now. And another thing. He's a devout Christian."

"Of course. He *is* in the religion department," asserted Verity.

"That doesn't necessarily mean he's a believer," said Mary Olivia.

"It should."

"I agree, but Martin says religion professors are often agnostic or even worse."

"Atheist?" asked Verity.

"I'm afraid so," said Mary Olivia.

"I'm glad Papa didn't live to find out who's teaching in our religion departments. Pru, Mercy, and I will be adding nonbelieving religion professors to our prayer list."

"Great idea. They have such influence on our young people," said Genevieve.

"Verity," said Mary Olivia, "don't you think it's about time you tell Genevieve and Chattie about our exciting adventure to the cemetery last month?"

"Adventure. It sure was that. Beginning with the heat. We chose the hottest, driest day in August to search for my maternal great-grandmother's grave. Donning straw hats, long sleeves, jeans, and boots, we drove way out in the country down a gravel road to the white man's house. A local genealogist had told me the man could help us. Hearing stories for years that he was a recluse, I assumed he was also a racist. I thought he might even have a gun. Mary Olivia knocked on his door, with me a few feet behind her."

"I was scared also," said Mary Olivia.

"You were my courage. Just like the lion in *The Wizard of Oz*. Anyway, guess what? Mr. Asa Goodnight invited us in after Mary Olivia explained why we were there. He insisted before we talked that we have a large glass of sweet tea. What a welcome treat. It was easy to see he was a born storyteller and that he was jovial — and a good man. He told us that years ago his great-grandfather had given some acreage to a black congregation for a church and cemetery."

"It's always good to find out there were some white Southerners like Mr. Goodnight's ancestry," said Chattie.

"Definitely," said Verity. "But he had Indian ancestors. His great-grandfather was half Cherokee.

"The members met at the church until the early 60s when the building burned down. Some of them believed it was arson; others blamed the wiring of the old church. Mr. Goodnight called the sheriff's office several times. Back then he said the law didn't do much investigating when black churches burned down. He believed it was probably arson, but he finally gave up because he couldn't prove it.

"One day the pastor visited Mr. Goodnight to tell him the members had found a site for another church. Mr. Goodnight said for years people came back for their annual pilgrimage to clean up the cemetery and place flowers on the graves. Then fewer and fewer came. He finally fenced the road in. No one had come for at least 25 years. He kept the cemetery's grass cut for as long as he could.

"Mr. Goodnight hadn't been to the cemetery in many years. Because of his bad heart, he couldn't walk far. But he was determined to help us. He walked with his cane to the woods and pointed across the barbed wire fence to a clearing that long ago had been the road to the church and cemetery. He directed us to continue down the lane until we came to it."

"We were out in the boonies," said Mary Olivia. "It was frightening walking down the shaded lane in the late afternoon."

"It seemed as if we walked for a mile," said Verity, "but it probably wasn't that far. I didn't think I could go any further. We rested awhile and then climbed a hill. At the top I saw it. The cemetery! I can't put into words how I felt when I first saw it. Even if it was overtaken by weeds and thick brush and looked forgotten and forsaken.

"Then we started our search. We walked over the entire cemetery and had almost given up until we found a small marker with my great-grandmother's name etched in the native rock. Her name — Leticia Bell — was barely legible. Overcome by heat and emotions, I sat down on a dirty rock."

"I wish you could have seen Verity," said Mary Olivia. "With tears rolling down her cheeks she repeated over and over: 'I've found the grave of my great-grandmother.' It was a moving experience for me as well. I was also crying."

"It's a trip to the past I'll never forget. Mary Olivia and the boys are going with me next week to start cleaning up the cemetery. Mary Olivia's church members have also volunteered."

Chattie volunteered to help. She said her boys were former scouts who would gladly assist.

I'm more ashamed of myself after listening to Verity's moving story. Slipping around in a black garb trying to get a peek of Theo was a foolish waste of my time and energy.

"Recruit as many people as you can," said Mary Olivia. "But be sure to put on your oldest work pants and wear boots and bring plenty of Deet bug spray. The grass is high, and no telling what we might run into. Ticks. Rattlesnakes."

"Sounds like an adventure to me," said Chattie, smiling.

"I wish I could help, but there's no way I could walk that

far," said Genevieve.

"Moral support is what we want from you," said Verity, hugging Genevieve. "You're the one responsible for taking me on this adventure. You'll never know what it means to me."

"I'm so glad," said Genevieve, wiping tears from her eyes. "And we ... we are still on the adventure. I have an announcement about mine."

Chattie glanced at Verity and Mary Olivia for their reaction. They looked eager about Genevieve's surprise.

Genevieve straightened up after wiping her eyes again and adjusted her hat. She paused a moment and then blurted out: "I'm inviting you to the Booksmith next month. You three will be my special guests at the autographing of my novel."

"Autographing? We didn't even know you had a publisher," said Chattie.

"Remember. I'm good at secrets. I wanted the premier event for my novel to be a surprise. And I wanted my best friends to be there. I hope you girls like my book. You're going to be the first ones to get copies."

"How in the world did you get your novel published so fast?" asked Chattie.

"A good question. It usually takes much longer."

"Could that account for the rotten potatoes?" asked Mary Olivia.

"Well, I guess indirectly. During June, I was busy doing a line-by-line proofing of the book and making changes the editor asked for. It was tedious work."

"I'm glad the potato mystery is finally solved," said Mary Olivia.

"I do apologize for my mess. Looking back, I'm embarrassed. I've always tried to be neat. But Hannah was unavailable to clean. I couldn't back out of the Tea. I'd never failed to have the Tea at my house during my month."

Genevieve paused a moment.

"Now back to the publishing process. My publisher has an imprint called Romance History. One of the authors whose book was to be published in September died suddenly of a heart attack in April." Genevieve stopped to rest.

"The editors then asked me if I could expedite my book so it could substitute for the deceased author's book. I agreed enthusiastically, not knowing all the work involved and how it would almost kill me to finish the manuscript in April and the editing in June. But with God's help, I did it."

"I'm thankful you did," said Verity. "Reading it will be a welcome diversion for me."

"I can't wait to see my book. I feel like a teenager. Do you think I'm being silly?"

"Of course not. You've brought joy to many people for years. It's time you had some fun of your own," said Mary Olivia. "In fact, I hope you become famous."

"Famous. I never thought about being famous although I guess it would be nice to be on the *New York Times* bestseller list," Genevieve smiled. "Thanks for your encouragement. By the way, I'll see the books for the first time before the signing." She paused a moment. "My publisher is sending several boxes right off the press to the bookstore. She's also shipping a box of books to my home. I bought them to give away.

"The autographing will be from 4 to 6 p.m. Then we'll return to my house for a late Tea. Hannah will be there to help me. I've also invited her to the Booksmith. My daughter Elizabeth, of course, will be there."

"Next month's Tea will be special," said Chattie. "But before you three get away from me today, I have a surprise for you!"

"Another surprise?" asked Genevieve. "I thought I was the finale."

"I wanted you to think that. Do you remember at the May Tea when I asked you what your favorite flowers were?" asked Chattie.

"I do because I told you I adore old-fashioned petunias," answered Verity.

"And I remembered your petunias. Now follow me."

Mary Olivia helped Genevieve maneuver her cane down the winding garden path.

Genevieve stopped when she saw a quote on a stake she wanted Mary Olivia to read.

Mary Olivia read the Claude Monet quote: "'I must have flowers, always, and always.' I'm sure, Chattie, you agree with Monet."

Chattie nodded.

They stopped at a fragrant plant for Mary Olivia to read another quote. "'Love is like a beautiful flower which I may not touch, but whose fragrance makes the garden a place of delight just the same.' Helen Keller. Famous Alabamian. Beautiful saying. Like the others, I had never heard it before. Guess that means I'm not a gardener."

"They were new to me also," said Chattie, continuing to

walk. "I chose quotes I liked. And it appears you've liked them too. That makes me happy."

Chattie stopped abruptly. "I made sure none of you ventured this far today."

They gazed upon a colorful flowerbed. Lavender petunias formed the border. Behind them were about two dozen tall Shasta daisies. Three rose bushes with several red roses blooming in front of three hydrangeas in the semi-shade completed the bed.

"Gorgeous!" exclaimed Verity, bending over to have a closer look at the petunias. "And what's this? A metal stake that says 'Verity Petunia.'"

"Go on, Mary Olivia and Genevieve. Find your stake."

"'Mary Olivia Shasta Daisy.' How thoughtful."

"'Genevieve Rose.' What a surprise to have a flower named after me. Just like the Lincoln Rose. You went to a lot of trouble."

"Not at all. In fact, quite the opposite. A labor of love. Every time I walk by your flowers I pray for you. There's not a better place to pray than in the garden. You've probably heard the quote: 'One is nearer God's heart in a garden than anywhere else on earth.' A stake with that quote is somewhere in the garden."

"I can't wait to tell Pru and Mercy about a petunia named after me. Bless you for spending the time to bring us joy."

"My pleasure. I had so much fun preparing this surprise. Come over and enjoy your flowers any time."

"I can't believe this," said Genevieve, walking slowly toward the patio. "A rose named after me. I'm calling Elizabeth when

I get home."

If only they knew what a blessing this is for me. A little step to restore my self-respect after making that ill-conceived trip to Theo's house and having those disgusting dreams.

After receiving long hugs from her three friends, Chattie watched them leave.

"Thank you, God, for bringing these special women into my life," she prayed aloud as she headed toward the garden again. As she cut zinnias for an arrangement, she thought about the October Tea.

We're in for a double treat. Genevieve's book kick-off and a Celebration Tea to follow. What fun we'll have.

10
OCTOBER

GENEVIEVE

> "I've learned from experience that the greater part of our happiness or misery depends on our dispositions and not on our circumstances."
>
> *First Lady Martha Washington (1731-1802)*

Genevieve walked with her cane as quickly as she could into her house, shut the bedroom door, and headed straight for the bathroom.

Splashing her face over and over with water, she tried to wash away the tears. Looking at herself in the mirror, she said aloud: "Annie Genevieve Boswell-Shipman, stop your boo-hooing. Put on your stiff upper lip and face the world. Or as Grandma Lottie used to say, 'Put on your big girl step-ins and deal with it.' Your daddy and grandma taught you to confront anything that came your way. Don't disappoint your daughter Elizabeth or your friends any more than you already have."

Sitting on her vanity chair, Genevieve wiped away tears. "I've blown it tonight," she said, continuing to talk aloud. "Please, Lord, help me compose myself."

"Mama," Elizabeth said softly, as she stepped into the bedroom, "Can I do anything for you?"

Elizabeth is a carbon copy of me. Her height, lean body, and light brown hair do look like pictures of me at her age.

"Baby, I'll be fine," she said, still wiping away tears. "Come on in. I don't know if I have ever told you how wonderful my life has been," she said, drying her face and taking Elizabeth's hands in hers. "But tonight I experienced such disappointment. And … and … it is … difficult for me."

"Mama, it's been a trying night for you, but you're going to be fine. I'm here as well as your three best friends. And Hannah just arrived to help. We're going ahead with a special Tea as soon as you feel better. I'm taking care of everything — that is, with Hannah's help."

"You know I've never skipped my turn having the Tea at my house. Tonight will be no exception. I have to pull myself together. I feel so rejected. And I had looked forward to this autographing all month. We all had."

"Mama, don't be so hard on yourself. You had no idea you wouldn't be the only author at the store."

"I'm crying over spilled milk now, but I'm so disappointed."

"I'll be in the kitchen," her daughter said, blowing her a kiss.

Coming out of the bathroom and taking off her shoes, Genevieve pulled back the thick comforter on her bed. After lying down, she covered up her head with the sheet and a light blanket. Her thoughts went back to the past.

Ever since childhood, I have felt warm and secure with covers over my head. I remember when Mama died I retreated under my covers. I cried and cried until I was cried out, and then Grandma Lottie took me into her bed and held me until I fell asleep. When Daddy died, I escaped to my bed and pulled covers over myself and cried myself to sleep. And when Grandma Lottie died, I went to bed and pulled one of her handmade quilts over my head. I can still smell the slightly musty quilt.

Genevieve closed her eyes and thought back to 3:30 that afternoon when the girls arrived to go to the book signing. She could not have picked a more perfect fall day. Cool and sunny. Her favorite kind of day.

∽

Looking out her bedroom window, she saw the girls dressed in their Sunday best. They were huddled together talking and laughing with Elizabeth. She knew they were waiting for her. Dressed in her robe, she immediately rushed to the front door, opened it a crack, and asked them to quickly come in and help her get dressed.

As they hurriedly gathered in her bedroom, she put on a classic red suit. She thought red would stand out and bring people to her book table. After modeling the new suit, they all gave her their enthusiastic approval. Then she put on a silver heart-shaped pin that they liked. When she suggested a necklace, the four shook their heads.

"If you're going to be on time, we better leave soon," urged Elizabeth.

"One more time. How do I look?"

"Great," they said in unison.

"Time to sell some books then," said Genevieve. She

rushed the women out the door.

Sitting in the front seat with Elizabeth driving, she tried to remain calm but found it difficult.

"I can't believe it. My own novel. What would Shipman think?"

"Daddy would be so proud of you," replied Elizabeth, patting her mother's nervous hands.

"How long will the line be for my autographing? How many people will I know? Will I have enough books?"

"Mom, please don't be anxious."

Arriving at the bookstore, Elizabeth carried in a large easel with a picture of Genevieve and information about her book. She joined the other women at the coffee shop while Genevieve searched for the manager.

She soon found the assistant manager, who paged the manager to come to the customer service desk.

After what seemed an eternity to Genevieve, an attractive young woman appeared.

"May I help you?" she asked.

"I'm Genevieve Boswell-Shipman, author of *Lottie's Love*. I'm here for a book signing from 4 until 6."

"Oh, yes, Ms. Boswell-Shipman," she said. "I've got your table set up. Please follow me."

"Thank you, my dear. I'm so excited. It's my first book and my first signing."

I wonder why the manager doesn't seem more excited. It may be routine work for her. Not for me. I can't wait.

They walked to the middle of the store where three tables were set up.

"I've placed two boxes of your books under the table. If you need more than these 50 books, let me know. As you can see, your table is between our two other authors. You may know the football coach and the deer hunter," she said, before walking away.

"I don't know them personally," Genevieve mumbled. "I assumed I would be the only author here today."

The manager quickly returned. "When your two hours are up, place any books you have left back in the box. I will return to pick them up. My workers will have them on the shelves as soon as possible."

I hope they remember to put them in the historical romance section.

Sitting down at her table, she searched her bag for a lacy beige tablecloth and spread it on the table. She then set out a vase containing blue silk chrysanthemums. Reaching down to the boxes on the floor, she brought out 12 books and placed two stacks of five books on each side of the table and left two in the middle of the table for prospective buyers to look through.

She then reached for another book and briefly clasped it to her chest. She looked at the cover and smiled.

A beautiful young woman between two handsome soldiers. I couldn't ask for a better cover.

She quickly flipped through the book and read her bio on the back cover. For a few minutes she felt a surge of happiness.

Ready for customers, she first met her two fellow writers.

"Hello. I'm Genevieve Boswell-Shipman, author of *Lottie's Love*. Looks like I'll be between you two today."

"Nice to meet you, Ms. ...," said the hunter, shaking her hand.

"Boswell-Shipman."

"Ms. Boswell-Shepherd, I'm Hoyt Wood. My book is about bow hunting in Alabama."

How could he have gotten my name wrong? I should have kept only my married name. Two names must be confusing.

"Glad to meet you," she said as he turned around to autograph a book.

She turned to introduce herself to the coach. "I'm Genevieve Boswell-Shipman, author of *Lottie's Love*."

"A pleasure to meet you," he said, shaking her hand so firmly that her arthritic fingers crackled with his grasp.

She winced. She knew he didn't mean to hurt her. He was used to shaking hands and didn't know about her arthritis.

"I'm Coach Beauregard Johnson. Named after Confederate General Pierre Gustave Tontant-Beauregard. Most people call me Coach. Even my wife would rather call me Coach instead of Beauregard," he said, stressing the first and last syllable. "Excuse me, ma'am, wish I could continue talking, but I better start autographing. My line is already getting way too long."

Soon Elizabeth joined Genevieve and set up the easel near her mother's table. They both watched as the coach's line began curving around the store. The hunter was getting a long line also.

Why was I put between a college coach and a hunter? In Alabama during football season and almost hunting season. How can I possibly compete?

"Elizabeth, I have serious competition. A college coach and

a hunter! I wish I had been scheduled another day."

"Let's be positive. You are going to sell many books. You may get a lot of women who are browsing for just the right book to read. You know that women buy the majority of books. Also, it's time for people to look for Christmas gifts. Yours is a perfect gift."

"That's right. I just don't feel good about this. Look at Coach's line. It's already down the sidewalk, and the line for Mr. Wood is almost out the door. People — including women — seem to be more interested in football or hunting than romance. I've seen some get in both lines for books."

Genevieve occasionally saw Verity, Chattie, Mary Olivia, or Hannah peering through stacks of books to see if she were autographing.

Soon Verity came by and told her they were walking through the store trying to spot potential buyers for her book. If they saw a woman who they thought might be a historical romance reader, they directed her to Genevieve's table.

She thanked Verity. Her friend quickly left.

Elizabeth returned with a story to tell. "Mama, I struck up a conversation with the nicest woman. I said 'Ma'am, have you stopped at the table of the author of *Lottie's Love*?' She said, 'No, I saw her, but I'm only here to buy a book about crocheting.' She then started for the checkout."

"Elizabeth, here comes someone."

"Great. I'll walk around some more."

"Wait. Take one of my books and look at it. Let me know what you think."

A young lady walked up and flipped through Genevieve's

book. "I'm a romance writer too. Can you give me some writing tips?"

"Have a good story idea. Write something every…."

"Do you have a good plot you're not using?" interrupted the woman.

"No. You need to have an original idea you can fall in love with and write about until one day you have a novel. How much have you written?"

"About five pages," she whispered. "I'm getting in the hunter's line. My husband and son will like his book."

When the young woman left, Genevieve blamed herself for not handling the conversation better. She was relatively sure, though, that the lady didn't want to do the work that writing takes. She remembered novelist James Michener saying something like, "Many people who want to be writers don't really want to write. They want to have been published."

Elizabeth appeared again and told Genevieve how much she loved the book. She returned it to her mother and turned around to see another woman approaching the table. She quickly walked away.

"Is yours a children's book?" a middle-aged petite woman asked while staring at the cover.

"No. *Lottie's Love* is a historical romance."

"I have a fantastic idea for a children's book. It's an animal story about a family of bears. Could you help me?"

"I wish I could, but I've never written a children's book. You can go to the reference section here, though, and find some books on how to write one."

"I don't have time to read books. I need some good tips, so

I can turn my great idea into a bestseller and get on a famous t.v. talk show. Guess I'll get in Coach's line. Maybe he'll help."

When Genevieve saw the woman in line to talk to the coach, she reflected on how the woman was looking for a shortcut to fame.

After two hours, Genevieve had signed books for two friends from her church who had seen the small autographing notice in the newspaper. Also, two strangers — two sisters whose fathers were in World War II — eagerly wanted autographed books.

The coach and hunter look exhausted. No wonder. They have sold all their books.

Genevieve quickly packed up the books and left them on the table. She put her tablecloth, vase, and flowers into her bag. Then she searched for her daughter and friends.

The store manager came toward her. Depressed and disappointed, Genevieve didn't want to talk to the woman. She walked as fast as she could past her.

"Thank you for coming today," the manager said, as she watched the author hurry away.

Genevieve found Elizabeth and told her she felt ill and needed to leave immediately. Elizabeth lost no time getting her mother into the car. Genevieve said nothing all the way home. Her daughter didn't see the tears streaming down her cheeks.

∽

Genevieve heard soothing classical music. She assumed the music was Mary Olivia's idea. She wanted to stay in bed and listen to it and go to sleep. She felt so secure in her bed, but she got up. She had to be strong for Elizabeth. She dare not fall apart again.

Looking at herself in the mirror, she straightened her hair and suit. As she opened the door, she met Elizabeth carrying a box.

"Mama, your books were delivered today."

With Elizabeth's help, Genevieve opened the box and lifted out four of her books. Elizabeth slipped out of the room.

Genevieve sat in a chair, opened each book, signed her name, and wrote a personal note to each friend. She decided to give a book to Elizabeth later.

Now she was ready for the Tea.

As Genevieve walked unexpectedly into the den, her friends stood up.

"Stay seated. Please. Please. I've signed a book for each of you. Elizabeth, get Hannah from the kitchen."

Genevieve handed a book to each of her friends.

They all read their personalized notes. Verity was the first to speak up.

"Thank you. I'll treasure this book," she said, placing it near her heart.

"Please tell Prudence and Mercy I will have one for them next month."

"They'll be so excited."

As Chattie and Mary Olivia thanked Genevieve, Hannah appeared, wiping away tears on her apron. Laptop trailed behind her.

"Hannah, I've got an autographed book for you."

"Oh, Miss Genevieve, thank you, First time I've known an author," she said, hugging and clinging to Genevieve. "And to think, people at that bookstore didn't want your book."

"Now, now," she said, gently pushing Hannah away. "I would send one to your mother, but you've told me you read to her."

"It will be fun reading your book aloud to her," she said, returning to the kitchen still sniffling.

"Mary Olivia, I love the music. I figured it was your idea," Genevieve said, sitting down.

"It's one of my favorites. Mozart's *Andante*. I'll turn the music off now."

"Thanks for the lovely piece. You chose exactly what I needed."

"My pleasure," Mary Olivia said just as Hannah appeared with a cake.

"A cake!" exclaimed Elizabeth. "You sure kept that a surprise."

"A gift to my friend."

Genevieve knew Hannah well. She made the cake as a celebration for her book signing.

"What a lifesaver you've been today," said Elizabeth. "I know now what Mama means when she speaks of you in such glowing terms."

"You're embarrassing me," said Hannah, blushing. "It's a blessing for me. And I love to cook. No trouble at all making this apple cake."

"Fresh apple cake. I haven't had one in years. Thank you, Hannah. You always come through for me."

Hannah and Elizabeth poured Earl Grey tea and passed around slices of cake. Genevieve insisted on having only a tiny piece.

"I have no appetite, but I'll try to eat."

Genevieve tried her best to be strong.

Taking a small bite, she said, "It's heavenly. Forgive me, Hannah, for my rudeness. I'll take more."

"Gladly." Hannah gave Genevieve a large piece.

"It's the best homemade apple cake I've ever had," said Mary Olivia.

"I'll second that," said Chattie, taking another bite.

"And I'll third that," added Verity.

"You're embarrassing me again, but I accept the compliments," said Hannah, leaving for the kitchen.

As the women slowly ate and sipped their tea, they waited for Genevieve to get more relaxed.

"Mama, we have some ideas for promoting *Lottie's Love*," said Elizabeth, after finishing her cake. "Would you like to hear them?"

Genevieve nodded.

"I've volunteered to make you brochures," said Chattie. "Roberto and I made many for our cafe."

"And I want to encourage you to become a speaker," said Mary Olivia. "You're a natural storyteller. Church and retirement groups are always looking for speakers. After your speech, you could then sell your books."

"Mama, I can set you up a website."

"I gladly accept all of your help and advice. Best of all, you've cheered me up. It's the writing I enjoy, but I know I have to market the book. The publisher can't do everything. By the way, I already have another book brewing in this old brain."

"That's the best news we've heard," Verity said.

"Mama," Elizabeth said, "I've got some exciting news I want to share."

Genevieve couldn't imagine what news her daughter had.

"I'm going to be a grandmother. You can imagine how happy Jessica and Evan are. I know you are also, Mama." Looking at the other women, Elizabeth said, "My daughter and husband have been trying to start a family for two years."

"Of course, I'm happy," Genevieve said, hugging Elizabeth. "But why did you wait so long to tell me?"

"Because of your book signing. I wanted to wait until we got home."

"I'm going to be a great-grandmother," said Genevieve, smiling and holding Laptop in her lap.

"How far along is Jessica?" asked Verity.

"About 14 weeks," said Elizabeth.

"I know some would say I'm being superstitious or believe in old wives' tales, but remember in July we talked about Papa believing that when someone dies a child is born. Well, Papa died at the end of June. And it appears about that time Jessica got pregnant. I'll have to tell Mercy about the baby. She sure didn't understand Papa's belief. Neither did I. Of course, it could be a coincidence."

"Interesting. I'll have a story to tell my grandchild one day." Turning to the women, Elizabeth said, "I have only one daughter, like Mama did, but my daughter wants several children. You know, Mama, I always wanted a sister."

Genevieve stared at Elizabeth and then began crying uncontrollably. A scared Laptop jumped out of her lap and headed toward the office.

Genevieve could not stop the memories. They were coming too fast.

The girls crowded around her trying to console her. Mary Olivia handed her a box of tissues.

"Mama, what's wrong?"

"I can't tell any ...," said Genevieve, crying again ...,"but I know I must."

She continued to sob. Still crying, she said, "Elizabeth, you ... are not ... my only daughter."

"What do you mean?"

"The baby girl ... only lived a few hours." Genevieve tried her best to compose herself before saying anything else.

"She's buried next to J.D. in a country cemetery outside of town."

"J.D.? Who is he?"

"J.D. was your daddy's best friend. He was my first love. My first husband."

"Mama, you were married before you married Daddy?"

"Briefly." Genevieve wiped her eyes. "But I loved your daddy, my Shipman, deeply. I don't think he ever knew how much."

Everyone in the room, especially Elizabeth, was in shock.

Mary Olivia poured more tea. Genevieve sipped hers for some time. Then she put down her cup and straightened up her drooping shoulders.

"This is going to be difficult for me, but I must tell my story to my best friends and especially to you, Elizabeth.

"*Lottie's Love* is partly autobiographical. It is set in World

War II, whereas my own story took place in 1959. The book, in other words, is my story disguised and fictionalized. Most of all, it's a story of love and redemption."

Genevieve stopped to get her breath.

"J.D. and I eloped when he came home on leave from the army. He was only 18. Two months later he died in a military accident. I'll never forget getting a visit from a major who told me about J.D.'s death. Me a widow at the age of 17."

"Oh, Mama," said Elizabeth, wiping away tears.

"A week after J.D.'s funeral, L.T. returned home from his summer job in Yellowstone. By the way, J.D. and L.T. had called each other by their initials since childhood." Genevieve paused a few moments. "No wonder with names like Julius Demetrius and Lochlear Tobias.

"I've told you girls about how L.T. and I renewed our friendship when he saw me trying on a hat. I'm sure it seemed to some people I was rushing into marriage, but I was pregnant. When I told L.T., he was honored he could raise J.D.'s baby. I've also told you about the beautiful wedding we had two months later. Shipman told me after we married how much J.D. loved me. I did love J.D. and grieved for him for years, but I grew to love Shipman."

Genevieve stopped. "What did I just say?"

"I grew to love Shipman," said Elizabeth.

"Yes. But I'm getting ahead of myself. My baby was born three months after we were married. She was two months premature and lived only a few hours. It was enough time for me to hold her and fall in love with the beautiful tiny baby. I grieved a lot for her and J.D."

The women sat quietly until Elizabeth spoke.

"Mama, I'm sad for you, but I feel a connection to my sister. Did you name her?"

"Of course. Nora. That was J.D.'s grandmother's name."

"Nora. A beautiful name. I … I must see her grave, but I can't go alone."

"I'll go with you," said Verity, clutching Elizabeth's hand. "Everyone here knows I'm having a lot of experience in cemeteries."

"You sure are," said Mary Olivia. "Please tell Genevieve and Elizabeth about the cross you put up at your great-grandmother's grave."

"Are you two all right with my telling the story now?" Verity asked, looking at Genevieve and Elizabeth."

Genevieve nodded.

"Well, Mary Olivia and Chattie came with Pru, Mercy, Temp, and me to the cemetery. We went to commemorate Leticia Bell's life. We took turns hammering the engraved iron cross into the ground. Mary Olivia read the words from Proverbs 31:30 — 'A woman who fears the Lord is to be praised.' Then Pru told us anecdotes handed down from generation to generation about our great-grandmother. She had ten children and lost five of them. Pru said our great-grandmother read her Bible and prayed for two hours each day. She endured many hardships but kept the faith. Pru concluded by reading the engraving on the cross: 'Leticia Bell. Never forgotten'."

"How poignant," said Elizabeth. "I've got goose bumps."

"Me too," said Mary Olivia, "and I was there. Every time I think back to that day, I feel a wellspring of emotion."

"What an extraordinary woman your great-grandmother was," said Genevieve.

"She was," said Verity. "And now tonight, you've found out you'll be a great-grandmother. Like Leticia Bell, you'll be a role model for generations."

"How kind of you. Your story of your great-grandmother has reminded me that my autographing fiasco tonight is insignificant compared to my relationship with my family."

"Well said," observed Chattie. "Tonight has been an emotional one for you — and the rest of us. I have some good news to share. At least I think it is. I'm having my first date with Theo next week."

"Well, I'm not surprised," said Genevieve, wiping her eyes. "I've seen the stars in your eyes for some time."

"Now I'm blushing. Anyway, he asked me out to eat. I guess that's a date. He wants to discuss some things. I'm excited but also scared. I feel like a teenager. I believe he cares for me, but I can't rush into a marriage. But he may not want to marry me. What if he wants an affair? What should I do, Mary Olivia, if he suggests we live together?"

"Quote him the Drop Act which means: Drop him the moment he suggests you move in with him. Also tell him, 'No sex before marriage.' That way you'll know if he's interested in you or only in sex. I personally think you don't have to worry about Theo. After meeting him last month, I think he's a person of integrity. And I'm a pretty good judge of character. Except for Liam, of course."

"I also believe he's a moral person," said Chattie. "But who knows these days? Especially after that story Genevieve told us about Pud, who was a widower."

"I'm excited for you. I agree with both of you," said Genevieve. "Theo seems to be a gentleman."

Who knows? Next month we may have an engagement Tea to plan for Chattie.

"Don't forget the pajama party at my house next month," Verity said. "Be sure to bring your pajamas but don't bring food. We have the menu planned. Hope we surprise you."

More surprises. Tonight my surprise was a shocking one. I'm sure better surprises await us at next month's Tea.

"What fun to look forward to," said Genevieve.

"I hope so. Pru, Mercy, and I are planning an old-fashioned good time."

"Why don't we let Genevieve and Elizabeth," asked Mary Olivia, "have some time together? I don't know about the rest of you, but I'm worn out."

They all agreed it had been a tiring day.

After her three friends left, Genevieve told Elizabeth all she could remember about Nora — that she was beautiful and had tiny feet and lots of dark hair like J.D.'s.

She hugged Elizabeth tightly before her daughter went to bed.

Thinking of the future, she felt her spirits renewed. She sat down on the sofa and closed her eyes and prayed. "Lord, thank you for giving me the strength to tell Elizabeth and my friends about Nora. Thank you for lifting a heavy burden."

My next book. And my first pajama party. At 77! Who would have thought?

11
NOVEMBER

～

VERITY

"Every experience God gives us, every person he puts in our lives, is the perfect preparation for the future that only he can see.... Never be afraid to trust an unknown future to a known God."
Corrie Ten Boom (1892-1983)
World War II Concentration camp survivor, author, and speaker

The last couple of weeks have been difficult, but I no longer have to live a lie.

Verity reflected on how her life had changed.

The brief Chicago obituary stated his name, when he died, where graveside services would be, and what funeral home was in charge. No mention of any survivors. No mention of a wife.

Verity received a note and the obituary from her cousin Sarah at the end of October. Micah Harris died of cirrhosis of the liver. He had never stopped drinking.

She had loved Micah deeply before he started drinking and became abusive and possessive. But he was her husband, and she grieved his passing.

Verity had to be alone to grieve. She told Pru and Mercy

she felt weak and needed rest. She wasn't lying. The news of Micah's death shocked her physically, emotionally, and spiritually. She took her meals in bed while reading her Bible and praying to God, asking His forgiveness again for forsaking Micah. She knew God had forgiven her years ago, but guilt feelings still plagued her. Her only solace was to pray and read Scripture. She claimed Psalms 103:12 — "As far as the east is from the west, so far has He removed our transgressions from us." She repeated the verse until she had memorized it and internalized it.

After three days, I opened my bedroom window and looked outside for a long time. I felt an emotional release not because my grief was over but because I felt alive again. The tall oaks surrounded me, and as their leaves fell, I grabbed one of them, cupped it in my hands, and threw it up as high as I could. Like the leaf, I didn't know where life would be taking me, but I was more prepared for my journey. I felt an inexpressible freedom and liberation. I no longer had to pretend I was a widow.

I catch myself still repeating "I'm a widow" over and over, trying to come to terms with the reality of being one.

∞

A knock at the front door brought Verity back to the present. Getting up from her chair in the parlor, she heard Mercy greeting Chattie, Mary Olivia, and Genevieve. She walked into the foyer, helped Mercy hang up their coats, and embraced each of them.

Mercy led them to an immaculate alcove off the kitchen where tea and sandwiches awaited them at a red table.

"I hope you like mint tea with cream cheese and pineapple

sandwiches," Mercy said.

"It is so cold outside that I'm looking forward to the mint tea," said Genevieve. "And, by the way, I like your blue teapot!"

"Miss Genevieve, you gave it to me." Mercy grinned and poured tea into white cups.

Genevieve and Mercy have fun together.

After Verity offered thanks, they began eating.

"These sandwiches are superb," said Mary Olivia, looking at Mercy. "Cream cheese and pineapple. Great combination."

"I'm glad you like them, M.O."

The women ate and drank their tea and chatted about the cold weather. Their talk was interrupted when Mercy blurted out a question.

"Have any of you ever stayed overnight at an African-American's house before tonight?"

I wish Mercy would keep her thoughts to herself. But that is not Mercy.

"I have," said Mary Olivia, after swallowing a bite of sandwich. "And I've spent the night with Creek Indians also."

"You don't count, M.O., but you're right. We do have Indian blood. How could I forget that? Let me try again: 'Have you stayed overnight at an African-American's house or a Native-American's house?'" Mercy asked, getting louder as she talked. She looked first at Genevieve and then at Chattie.

"I haven't," said Genevieve hesitantly.

"Neither have I," Chattie said. "But, Mercy, it's no big deal to me. You're my friends. I don't see this pajama party as a racial thing."

"Well spoken," said Verity. "Now, Mercy, have you ever

spent the night with three white women?"

"No. I never thought about it like that."

"Subject closed," said Verity. "Let's savor our Tea time together."

"Wait," said Mercy. "I want to spend the night with all of you at one of your houses."

No one spoke.

"Well?"

"You're getting your wish," said Chattie. "I'm inviting all of you to my house next year for a pajama party."

"In fact, I propose we have a pajama party once a year," said Genevieve.

"I second that," added Mary Olivia. "And I suggest November."

"Those in favor, please clap," said Genevieve.

The women clapped, with Mercy clapping the loudest.

"Passed," said Genevieve.

"I can't wait until next year," said Mercy, grinning widely. "Subject closed."

Finally.

"Hold on," said Prudence coming from the kitchen. "I have to vote. I vote yes," she said, clapping her hands.

"Why don't you sit down and have tea with us?" asked Mary Olivia.

"I have only a moment. I must watch the sweet potato pies to make sure they get completely cooked. But first I'll try a cup of Mercy's mint tea."

"You're going to like it," said Verity. "Mercy did a great job with the Tea today."

They watched as Prudence sipped some tea.

"Excellent."

Mercy smiled broadly and gave her sister a big hug.

"When Mercy asked me, if she could prepare the Tea," said Verity, "I didn't hesitate. I needed to be waited on."

"You have felt bad for two weeks," said Prudence.

"Verity, why didn't you let me know?" asked Mary Olivia. "I'm always here for you."

"I needed to be alone and rest. I'm much better now."

If only I could confide in Mary Olivia. She would understand better than anyone, but she has enough going on in her life. Some things can't be shared with anyone but God. It would serve no purpose to tell the girls about Micah's death. They thought he died a few years ago. Now he's really gone. I can't undo the past. With God's help, I have to put it behind me.

"How's work going at the cemetery?" asked Genevieve.

"We've made good progress. In September when Mary Olivia and her church started helping, we counted 110 handmade crosses and headstones. We dug up many old headstones from the section dating from the 1800s. Some were in pieces. We're still in the process of putting together the broken ones. Depressions in the soil indicate more graves. We're relieved that gravestones in the 1900s section are in fairly good shape. It has been therapeutic for me to work around the graves. I know that might sound strange so some people, but I feel I'm making up for all those years of neglect."

"The gravestones are still telling their story," said Prudence. "One said 'Our precious Tullos is now singing with the angels. 1915-1918.' The little girl most likely died during the 1918 influenza epidemic. How sad that gravestone was."

"Another one stated, 'Husband, father, son. Died fighting in a barroom brawl.' We couldn't make out his name or the date," said Verity. "If he were my relative, I would be glad his name wasn't legible.

"My next search will be for the grave of my great-great grandfather whom Grandma Jessie talked about. All I can remember her saying was that he talked in a strange language."

"I appreciate your going to Nora's grave with Elizabeth. It meant a lot to her. Even after all these years, I couldn't go to her grave. It would be too emotional."

Going to Nora's grave was harder than I imagined it would be. It took me back to my three miscarriages. I often wonder what kind of mother I would have been. I'll never know.

"It meant a lot to me also. Your daughter is going to make a wonderful grandmother."

"She is. And I'm getting excited about being a great-grandmother," said Genevieve. "I have bought the most beautiful christening gown. Of course, I first asked my granddaughter if I could. Jessica was delighted. If she has a girl, she's going to name her Nora. That means so much to me.

"The christening gown has to wait awhile, but I've got something for Mercy and Prudence now," Genevieve said, getting out two books from a large bag and giving them to the sisters. "I hope you enjoy *Lottie's Love*."

"I know a real author," said Mercy, holding the book close to her heart. "And she's written my favorite kind of book — a romance."

After hugging Genevieve, Mercy continued, "I'll read every

word of mine, but Pru won't. She'd rather read encyclopedias."

"Thank you so much. I will read *your* book. But Mercy is right. I do find real people and events more fascinating. But your book is based on fact. That's the only type of fiction I read."

"More of us need to be readers like you," said Genevieve.

"I've got a gift also," said Mary Olivia. "I have something for you, Prudence. While sifting through the contents of my house, I came across something I cherish. I want you to have it."

Mary Olivia reached down, lifted a framed photograph from a bag, and gave it to Prudence.

Prudence looked at it and then with her apron wiped away her tears. She reached over and hugged Mary Olivia. "I can't think of a gift I would treasure any more."

"I want to see it," said Mercy, reaching for it.

"Be careful with it," said Prudence, gently handing it to her sister. "It will go on the parlor table with our other family photographs."

"A picture of you and M.O. in front of Grandpapa's house," said Mercy. "Grandmama and Grandpapa and who else is sitting behind you two?"

"My grandparents," said Mary Olivia.

Mercy passed the picture around.

"Where am I?" questioned Mercy.

"You and Verity weren't born," said Prudence.

"I read a quote recently I'll never forget," said Chattie: "'Give away something you treasure. It's a sacrifice that will prove a blessing.'"

"I must write that down right now," said Prudence, getting up to get her journal from the kitchen cabinet. "My journal for quotes is never too far from me. Neither is my journal for new words. Let me see if I can remember the quote: 'Give away something you treasure. It's a ...,'" she said, looking at Chattie for help.

"'Sacrifice that will prove a blessing.'"

"One day this will go on the fridge. Be sure to read our word and quote for this week," Prudence said, getting up with her photograph. "I better check on our pies."

"I'm going to the fridge now," said Chattie.

She wrote down the word and quote and recited the information for her friends. "'Conviviality' means good friendship; fondness for eating and drinking with friends. Appropriate for tonight. The quote for the week is: 'It's the friends you can call up at 4 a.m. that matter.' Marlene Dietrich, American actress."

"I agree with Dietrich. A friend is one that no matter what time of day will come to your aid," said Genevieve.

"You've come up with your own quote," said Verity.

"Well, you know I am a writer." giggled Genevieve.

Genevieve is upbeat. Even after her disappointing book signing last month, she knows how to bounce back. I need to emulate her attitude.

"We have a surprise for you," said Verity.

"Can we take any more surprises?" asked Genevieve, smiling.

"Sure. I can tell you more are coming," said Mary Olivia.

What is Mary Olivia talking about?

"Our surprise is," Verity said, pausing to keep them guessing. "Temp is grilling for us."

"My word! I'm finally meeting Temp. But isn't it too cold for him to grill?" asked Chattie.

"He's used to the cold," said Prudence, who had returned from checking on her pies, "and he insisted on doing this for us."

When they finished the Tea, Temperance knocked at the door. Mercy jumped up to let her tall, slender brother in.

"Temperance, I want you to meet Chattie Milano," said Prudence.

He walked slowly up to Chattie and shook her hand. She closed her hand over his.

Temp is shy. Chattie understands and is trying to make him feel at ease.

"Nice to meet you," said Chattie enthusiastically.

Temperance nodded and backed away timidly. Mary Olivia walked over and hugged him. He returned the hug as soon as he realized who she was.

"I'm ... I'm cooking for ... for ... you all to ... to ... night," Temperance stuttered.

"We're hungry," said Prudence. "Let's tell Temperance how many chicken breasts we want."

Each said one.

"Six chicken breasts plus two for you," said Verity.

"I'll get the ... the grill go ... going," said Temp.

"He stutters," said Verity, after he had gone outside, "but he never did until Eleanor left him. At least he's talking more and stuttering less since Papa died."

The friends chatted while Temperance grilled their chicken.

Then they gathered around the kitchen table and ate chicken along with Prudence's baked potatoes and salad. After eating, each complimented Temperance on the chicken.

Over the objections of Prudence, the women pitched in and helped clean up. While they worked, Temperance went upstairs to bathe. He returned wearing clean clothes and carrying a blanket and a book.

"Sis," he said to Prudence, "I am ... ta ....taking one of Papa's reli ... gious boo ... books."

"Take all you want," said Prudence. "We're keeping Papa's books."

Papa is rejoicing in heaven over Temp's return to God.

Temperance stood around a few minutes fumbling with his book and blanket.

"Do you want to stay and visit?" asked Verity.

"No, bu ... but thanks. I ... I'm going home to ... to read. Bye," he said, waving as he quickly left.

∽

The girls sat down and quietly talked until Mercy abruptly stood up.

"Let's put on our pajamas. I want everyone to see mine."

Without giving her sister an answer, Prudence immediately got up and gestured to them to follow. They went upstairs to Verity's large bedroom, where six comfortable chairs awaited them. One by one each woman got out her pajamas and waited her turn to change.

"I had to buy some," said Genevieve, speaking from the bathroom. "I've always worn gowns. Guess it's my generation. Hope you like mine." She walked out wearing Winnie the Pooh ones. They all clapped.

Mercy laughed. "Wait 'til you see mine, Miss Genevieve."

Soon Mercy came out wearing Eeyore pajamas to the women's laughter and applause.

"My pajamas aren't Pooh ones, but they're over the top for me," said Chattie, modeling her Betty Boop pajamas. The women clapped again.

"I'll be the party pooper," said Mary Olivia, who appeared wearing light blue knit pajamas. "Mine are the monastery style," she said with a serious face.

"I think you should applaud for Mary Olivia and me," said Prudence, who followed Mary Olivia with dark green satin pajamas. The women applauded loudly.

Verity came out smiling with a bright yellow Tweety Bird pair. Mary Olivia whistled, and the others clapped.

"I've never seen those," said Prudence.

"That's because I only bought them yesterday. I wanted some fun ones. All my pajamas are boring."

Same as my life used to be but not anymore.

"Let's play charades," Mercy insisted, not waiting for any more talk about pajamas.

They decided on the categories of books, historical people, movies, flowers, and Biblical names.

Mary Olivia demonstrated the gestures for identifying the five categories and the signs for "sounds like" and then went first. She indicated a book and then put up five fingers.

"Five words," said Chattie.

Mary Olivia nodded. She put up one finger.

"First word," said Prudence.

Mary Olivia then put up one finger.

"Easy," said Mercy. "One."

Mary Olivia nodded. Then she indicated second word and held up 10 fingers 10 times.

"Do that again," insisted Mercy.

Mary Olivia repeated the clue.

"100," said Genevieve.

Mary Olivia nodded and then put up three fingers and demonstrated sounds like and pointed to both of her ears.

"Third word sounds like ears," said Chattie.

Mary Olivia nodded.

Genevieve said, "Years."

Chattie said, "1 and 100 Ears ... *One Hundred Years of Solitude.*"

"Good," said Mary Olivia, sitting down. "I thought I would stump you."

"But you didn't know it's one of my favorite books," said Chattie, smiling. "Nobel Prize winner Gabriel Garcia Marquez. My turn now."

Chattie pretended to sniff a flower and then indicated one word and two syllables.

She indicated first syllable, sounds like, and then pretended to box.

"Sounds like box," said Mary Olivia.

Chattie nodded and then indicated second syllable. She pretended to put something on her hand, being sure to put each finger in the right place.

"Gloves. Box. Gloves. Foxgloves," said Prudence.

"Good. I have one more flower."

She indicated one word with three syllables. Then she held up one finger for the first syllable and indicated sounds like and then waved.

"First syllable sounds like by. Die. Fie. Hi," said Mercy eagerly.

Mercy wants to beat Pru.

Chattie nodded and put up two fingers and indicated sounds like and pointed to her head.

"Second syllable sounds like head. Skull. Brain," said Mary Olivia.

Chattie nodded.

"Hibrain. Hicran. Hydran. Hydrangea," Prudence said.

"You know your flowers," said Chattie, sitting down.

Prudence quickly stood up. She indicated a person and then pretended to place a crown upon her head.

"Crown," said Mercy.

Prudence nodded and pointed to herself.

"Crown and woman. Queen," said Chattie.

Prudence nodded. She put up two fingers, indicated sounds like, and pretended to be sick.

"Queen Sick. Queen Victoria," said Genevieve.

"Good. I have one more." She indicated a book and then five fingers.

"Five words," said Mercy.

Prudence nodded and indicated first word was a little word.

"A," said Genevieve.

Prudence nodded and then put up two fingers and demonstrated a tail.

"A Tail ... *A Tale of Two Cities*," said Genevieve.

"Good," said Prudence, sitting down. "I should have chosen a more difficult book."

"Can I please go next?" pleaded Mercy.

"Take my place," said Genevieve. "I'm too tired to play."

Mercy indicated Biblical name and put up one finger and then three fingers.

"One word. Three syllables," said Genevieve.

Mercy nodded and put up one finger. She indicated sounds like and pointed to herself.

"Sounds like me," said Prudence.

Mercy nodded and indicated second syllable. She lay down on the floor, and they all laughed.

"Me. Lie. Me. Lie," Prudence said over and over. "Elijah."

"You're good, Pru. Can I please go again?"

"Fine with me," volunteered Genevieve.

Mercy indicated a Biblical name. One word. Two syllables. She held up one finger, indicated sounds like, and pointed to herself.

"First syllable sounds like me," said Chattie.

She nodded. Then she pretended to saw.

"Me Saw," said Prudence. "Esau."

"You're too good," said Mercy. "Please ... can I do a book?"

"Go ahead," said Prudence.

Pru is sure she will get this one also.

Mercy put up two fingers.

"Two words," said Chattie.

Mercy nodded. Then she indicated first word, three syllables, and then put up finger for first syllable and indicated sounds like.

Mercy indicated a circle and pretended to knit.

The girls were quiet for awhile until Genevieve finally said, "Yarn."

Mercy nodded.

"I'll go through the alphabet," said Genevieve. "Barn."

Mercy nodded immediately. Then she indicated second syllable was a small word.

"A," said Genevieve. "Barn. A."

Mercy nodded and then waved.

"Barn. A. By," said Genevieve.

Mercy nodded and then indicated second word and sounds like. She pretended to nudge someone.

"Nudge," said Prudence. "Budge. Fudge. Judge."

Mercy shook her head.

"Barn. A. By. Sounds like Nudge," said Prudence. "Barn. A. By. Nudge," said Prudence over and over. "This doesn't make sense."

Mercy started smiling and asked, "Give up?"

After they nodded, Mercy said slowly, "*Barnaby Rudge*."

"Barnaby What?" asked Chattie.

"*Barnaby Rudge.* Charles Dickens, of course," said Mercy.

"I've never heard of that Dickens' novel," said Mary Olivia. "And I read Dickens."

"It's one few people get around to reading," said Prudence.

"If you knew it, then why didn't you get it?" asked Mercy.

"I didn't think of it until you said the title."

"Enough of charades. *Barnaby Rudge* exhausted my brain, but what fun," said Genevieve.

Genevieve spoke up at the right time. Mercy may have con-

tinued questioning Pru thinking she wasn't acquainted with "Barnaby Rudge." Pru knows Dickens' novels. She just had a senior moment.

"How about Twister?" asked Mercy.

"Twister? Are you kidding?" asked Prudence. "We'd all be in the hospital."

The women laughed and agreed with Prudence that they might break bones playing Twister.

"Then how about Scrabble and Checkers?" asked Mercy.

"I hate to be a party pooper, but I'm tired," said Mary Olivia. "Could we sit down and have a word game?"

"Why don't we skip the game part," said Genevieve, "and name our favorite movies, our favorite books, or favorite words."

"Let's do favorite words," said Prudence. "That way I will learn some new words."

"Sure," said Mercy. "Your problem will be which words to choose."

"I like Prudence's recommendation," said Genevieve. "Why don't we name one favorite word, give its meaning, and make a sentence with it?"

"Sounds good. But I'll have to think about words for awhile," said Mercy.

"Let's take a few minutes to collect our thoughts," said Genevieve. "We'll need paper, pens, and a dictionary?"

Mercy quickly found paper and pencils and set down two dictionaries.

The girls looked thoughtful. They took turns thumbing through the dictionaries.

"I'll start," Chattie said after seven or eight minutes. "I have many favorite words; but I narrowed my word down to 'garrulous,' meaning talking too much, usually about trivial things. Garrulous, unfortunately, often describes me. My sentence is: 'The teacher sent Chattie to the office for constantly being garrulous.'"

They laughed except for Prudence, who was busy writing.

"Excellent," said Prudence. "Your word will be on our fridge soon."

"My choice," said Verity, "did appear on the fridge. 'Insouciant.' I love the sound of it and also the meaning — indifferent or free from care. I would like a day of being insouciant."

No wonder I like that word. I'm free of anxiety about pretending to be a widow.

"'Surreptitious' is a word I like to say," said Mercy. "Sister taught us this word also. It means secret," she said, pausing. "If I ever have a boyfriend, I may have a surreptitious meeting with him."

Mercy does surprise me more and more with her wit.

"Not if I can help it," said Prudence, with a disapproving look.

"Words are my hobby, so it's difficult for me to single out one word," said Prudence. "I've chosen 'equanimity,' meaning calmness and composure. My sentence: Prudence endured Mercy's incessant questions with equanimity."

"She's right," said Mercy. "She does have to put up with my questions. But I'll continue to ask them, and she'll continue to practice equa ... or whatever the word."

The women laughed.

"The first word I thought of is 'vicissitudes,'" said Mary Olivia, "because as widows we have encountered them — changes in circumstances or fortunes. The vicissitudes of life make us grow stronger in the Lord."

"How true that statement is," said Genevieve. "I'll use that word in my new novel. Now for my word. I used 'indefatigable' in my first novel. It means tireless and never giving up. You girls have been indefatigable this year in your pursuits."

"You've been indefatigable also," said Verity.

"I think after 'vicissitudes' and 'indefatigable,' it's time to take a break for sweet potato pie," said Prudence, who was putting her journal up.

"I agree," said Chattie. "My brain is worn out."

Prudence brought pie and milk, as well as glasses, plates, and forks, upstairs. As they ate, they agreed it was the best sweet potato pie they had ever tasted.

Now I can tell our family's news. What a relief to think about the future and not dwell upon the past.

"I've been giving some thought for several months about telling you girls about the secret ingredient in Great-Grandmama Ida's Tea Cakes," said Prudence. "I wouldn't tell just anyone, but I felt I built up too much suspense about the secret ingredient. Would you like to know?"

"Only if you want to tell us," said Genevieve. "If it's a family secret, feel free to keep it a secret."

Mary Olivia and Chattie voiced their agreement with Genevieve.

"Well, I'll keep it in the family, at least for now," said Prudence.

Finally I can share.

"I have an announcement," said Verity. "One day I asked Pru if there was something she had always wanted to do. She answered quickly, 'Own my own business.' We all know what a great cook she is. So it was no surprise her dream was to launch a food business. After brainstorming, the three of us concluded an ideal business would be food that would go well with tea. We launched Tea Time Delicacies last week."

"Grand idea," said Genevieve.

"Again, we owe it to you," said Verity. "You've influenced not only our Tea group, but my entire family."

"Papa left us some money, so we'll use it," said Prudence. "He would approve."

"Temp has gotten involved also," said Verity. "He's posting flyers on his daily walks. He walks anyway. Might as well help us."

"And we're taking orders now, " said an eager Mercy. "Miss Genevieve, do you want to or…?"

"Mercy," said Prudence, cutting her off. "The audacity of your asking Genevieve to order."

Mercy bowed her head, feeling embarrassed. "I'm sorry."

"I will be ordering from you soon," said Genevieve, looking at Mercy, who raised her head when she heard Genevieve. "And I will spread the word among my friends. Since Shipman and I were in business for decades, I understand how tough running a business can be."

"See, Pru," said Mercy, "Miss Genevieve is ordering."

I better change the subject. And quickly.

"Tell us about your new novel," Verity said, looking at

Genevieve.

"My second novel is an entirely fictional love story, not based on my life. Remember the book I got at your house in August about the settling of the West?" Genevieve asked Mary Olivia.

"I read the book carefully for background material. Then I started weaving a story about an orphaned girl who left Missouri and headed west with a wagon train. By the way, the vicissitudes of life are going to make her a wealthy wife.

"Girls, this last month I have been happier than I have been for decades. After finally confessing about my first marriage and baby, I feel an indescribable freedom."

They each told Genevieve how happy they were for her.

I wish I could share my joy about being a widow with Genevieve. She would understand. I feel that same freedom.

"You sure have been quiet, M.O.," said Mercy.

"I have, but I might as well start talking. I have an important announcement. Life-changing one. You better prepare yourself. I'm going to shock you."

"Tell us, M.O. Please," begged Mercy, after Mary Olivia paused.

"Girls," she said, taking a deep breath. "I'm getting married."

"Married? Who? When? Why?" asked Verity, pausing after each question.

"You all have heard me talk about my religion professor, Dr. Martin Fairchild. Well, he's asked me to marry him, and I said yes."

"You barely know him. And doesn't he have leukemia?"

asked Prudence.

"Yes, and it's no longer in remission."

"Then why marry him?" asked Verity. "I'm sorry to question you, but, Mary Olivia, your happiness is what I want — we want."

"I know you want what's best for me. Martin told me, 'I know this will sound like a C. S. Lewis story to some people.'" Mary Olivia stopped to explain. "Theologian C.S. Lewis had never married until he was 59 years old. He married a woman with cancer, and she lived only three years. Now back to what Martin said. 'Let them think what they want. I love you. I want to marry you. I need you with me at the end of my life. I know I found you too late, but what little time I have left, I want you to be my wife.'"

"How endearing," said Chattie. "Romantic."

"I thought so also. James and Eric quickly gave me their blessings. They like and respect Martin. Of course, they want me to be happy.

"I have absolutely no reluctance to marry Martin. I love him. I've prayed over it and know it's the right thing to do. And girls, we have so much in common. Theology. History. Opera. Poetry."

But how long will they have to enjoy theology, opera....

"You've covered who and why. Now when and where?" asked Prudence.

"Next month in the hospital. I want all of you there."

Verity grabbed a tissue to wipe her tears. "Of course, we'll be there."

I just hope he lives until the wedding.

"Congratulations. You'll be the only widow from the Tea who remarried," said Genevieve. "Did I ever tell you that Doll almost married again?"

"I don't remember," said Mary Olivia. "Only about her love life."

"She met a charming widower at a senior citizens' group. Kirby Grant claimed he was a descendant of President Grant. Doll loved his stories. She went out with him a few times until one night he asked her about her financial status. She soon discovered he had little money."

"And he was interested in only her money," said Chattie.

"You're right. Not that she was wealthy, but she was comfortable. Doll dropped him fast. She had to put up with his phone calls, but every time he asked her out she would say, 'I prefer not to.' And then she would add, 'Like Bartleby in "Bartleby the Scrivener."' Doll knew lines from many of the classics. Her suitor didn't have a clue Bartleby was a character in a Herman Melville short story. I don't think Doll minded his calling because she got to say 'I prefer not to.' He finally stopped. Doll said he must have been terribly confused over Bartleby."

"That's a funny story," said Mercy. "I may try that with my suitors."

"What suitors?" asked Prudence, who was listening intently to the story.

"You know I have no suitors. But M.O didn't a few months ago."

"Can we host a wedding reception for you after the ceremony?" asked Genevieve.

"I'll talk it over with Martin. If it's all right with him, we'll plan the wedding to coincide with our monthly Tea. Martin has no family. Our only guests will be my boys and grandson and my five best friends."

"I volunteer to coordinate the Tea," said Prudence. "If Martin agrees, then I'll discuss the menu with you."

"I know a fabulous catering business called Tea Time Delicacies that is more than willing to provide the food," added a smiling Mercy.

"Martin and I haven't discussed any type of celebration. He won't mind a small one. In fact, it probably would be a welcome surprise. His life has been a difficult one. His parents died soon after he started college. His only sibling was his autistic brother. Martin visited him regularly at the group home until he died five years ago. During his last year of college Martin became engaged, but his fiancé ran off with an army captain a week before their wedding. Devastated, he vowed to never love again."

"How sad," said Prudence. "I can identify with Martin."

"Teaching and writing kept him busy. Then he met me while his leukemia was in remission. We fell in love. After we had a few dates, he asked me to marry him. I fell in love with him immediately after meeting him. Then he became ill a few weeks ago and entered the hospital. He asked me if I still wanted to marry him. 'Of course,' I said. 'You're going to be fine.' He said, 'I don't think so, Mary O, but I still want to marry you.'"

"I'm so happy for you," said Chattie. "I have some news also."

"You're getting married! I wish we could have a double

wedding, but I don't think Theo would agree to be married in a hospital."

"Oh, no. No. I'm not getting married. I got dumped."

"What?" shouted Mary Olivia, her mouth wide open. She quickly put her hand over her mouth.

"Last month when Theo asked me out to eat, I thought it was for our first date. Well, it was our last one."

"What?" asked Mary Olivia again.

"He told me he's marrying his high school sweetheart."

Poor Chattie.

"Theo and his old sweetheart were reunited in June at a high school reunion. When he found out she was a widow, he asked her out for a date. They dated all summer, and in September Theo asked her to marry him. She accepted."

"That's why Theo was standoffish at your Garden Tea in September," said Mary Olivia. "He knew he was getting married."

"You're right. Now I understand why he acted strange. Theo told me he valued my friendship but that he wouldn't be able to help me any more because he would be moving to Oxford, Mississippi, his wife's home."

"I was in such shock that I remember little of what I said the rest of the night. I remember telling him I was happy for him and wished him...."

"What a jerk," interrupted Genevieve. "And to think that I liked him because he was a Root."

The women laughed.

"I wished him happiness and thanked him for working for me. Then I left. I drove home in a trance. I went to bed and cried until I fell asleep. The next day I cried most of the day. Then I got busy in the garden. My tears fell on the shovel and the leaves of the plants. I'm all cried out now."

"I wish you had called me," said Verity. "I would have brought my hankies, and we could have cried together."

Because of my problems with Micah, I can empathize with Chattie. I know good will come out of my sufferings as well as Chattie's.

Verity said, "The apostle Paul said in Romans 8:28 — 'All things work together for good for those that love God and are called according to His purpose.'"

"I agree, Verity. I felt like such a fool I didn't want anyone to know. I thought I was in love with Theo and he with me."

"You're being much too hard on yourself," said Verity.

"I know now after much reflection I was lonely and jumped to the wrong conclusion about his feelings toward me. He shared his plants with me because he was generous. He considered me only a friend. I was silly to feel otherwise."

"You shouldn't feel that way," said Genevieve.

"Maybe not. But for months I spent so much time gardening with Theo that I got comfortable being with him.

"After I got serious about him, I took off my necklace. I put it back on as soon as I returned from that ill-fated date. Wearing my locket again has helped me heal," Chattie said, removing her necklace from under her pajama top. "I'm fine now. And I'm genuinely happy for you, Mary Olivia."

"Thanks. Who knows? You might find another gardener who's a widower."

"Mmmm. Never thought about that. I definitely will be

looking for another gardener next spring, but I'll find a happily married one this time."

"I may be looking for a man also," blurted out Verity, surprising even herself.

I'm a widow now. I can date.

Prudence and Mercy stared at each other.

"Looking for a man? Why didn't you tell Pru and me?" asked Mercy.

"Because ... after Mary Olivia's experience, I might meet a widower at a cemetery."

"Anything is possible," Genevieve yawned. "Girls, I'm sorry to put a damper on our conviviality. Great word, Prudence. But I must go to bed. It is after midnight. Too much fun and too many bombshells for me tonight. I'm exhausted."

Thank you, Genevieve, for changing the subject. I haven't met anyone I've wanted to date. But my options are open now. I'm a widow. I'm a widow. Maybe if I say it over and over, it will finally become a reality for me.

"Someone please stay up with me," begged Mercy.

"Not I," said Prudence. "Like Genevieve, I'm exhausted."

"You have every right to be," said Genevieve.

"I'm joining you. I have a wedding next month, and I need my beauty sleep," said a giggling Mary Olivia. "That is, if Prudence doesn't keep me up teaching me new words."

"I promise I won't talk about words although I may be asking about the wedding tea menu," she said.

"Mercy, Chattie and I will stay up with you for a minute," said Verity, watching the yawning women as they left the room.

"I don't think I've had this much fun in ages," said Mercy.

Verity hugged her sister. "I had fun too. Playing charades was great fun. And you stumped us with the Dickens' novel."

"That tickled me. And surprised me. But nothing like hearing about M.O.'s wedding. I'm so excited for her. How can I sleep thinking about the wedding?"

"You will. We've all had a long day. Now let's go to bed."

"All right. I'll do my thinking in bed."

"Best place," said Chattie, "for undisturbed thinking and praying."

"I agree," said Verity.

"Good night," said Chattie, as she left to join Genevieve in the guest bedroom down the hall.

Verity lay down next to her sister, whose back was turned toward the wall. She thought about Mary Olivia and Martin's wedding. She couldn't imagine getting married in a hospital.

Like Mercy, I've got a lot of thinking to do. And a lot of praying. Mary Olivia is marrying Martin, who's terminally ill. I must pray persistently for them.

Thank you, God, for restoring my soul. Thank you for my sisters and my friends and the closeness we share. Please give Mary Olivia and Martin strength for the weeks ahead.

I'm a widow. I'm a widow.

She immediately fell asleep.

12
DECEMBER

MARY OLIVIA

"The best and most beautiful things in the world cannot be seen or even touched. They must be felt with the heart."
Deaf and blind author/activist Helen Keller (1880-1968)

"You've got to breathe in or I can't zip you up," insisted Verity.

"I'm holding myself in," said Mary Olivia. "Can you zip me now?"

"Got it. Now your dress is perfect."

"Do you mind if I brush some stray hairs?" asked Chattie.

"Please do. And could you also clasp this pearl necklace for me. It was my grandmother's. My mother passed it down to me. I haven't worn it since I married Liam."

Thank you, God, for Verity and Chattie.

"Everything seems surreal to me," said Mary Olivia. "I am getting married in a hospital to a remarkable man I only met four months ago. I love Martin so much — but he is dying."

The three were in an empty hospital room down the hall from Martin's room. His nurses gladly provided it as a dressing room.

After stepping back to look at Mary Olivia, Chattie said, "You look stunning."

"Martin's favorite color is blue. He insisted I shop for a beautiful blue dress and any accessories I needed. He said over and over that money was no obstacle — that it was his gift to me. For someone who doesn't enjoy shopping, I had a ball. I probably bought the most expensive dress in Birmingham, fortunately on sale.

"Martin's simplicity drew me to him. But for our wedding he wanted me to buy the most exquisite dress I could find. Oh, how he has spoiled me."

"You also chose the most gorgeous one in town," said Chattie. "And your fancy sequined blue heels are a good match."

"You should have seen Martin's eyes when I modeled my dress and shoes. I thought he was going to cry. He probably will today when he sees them."

"He will because it's not only your beautiful dress," said Verity, "but your beautiful soul he sees."

"My precious friend," Mary Olivia said, embracing Verity, "you're much too kind, but on my wedding day I'll treasure that lovely sentiment."

Verity pulled a handkerchief out of her small handbag and wiped her eyes. "I better get used to crying today."

"Me too. I never fail to cry at a wedding. Even my own."

"I'm sure Mercy will cry more than anyone. She always does."

"By the way, where are Mercy and Prudence?" asked Mary Olivia.

"They're sitting in the waiting room with Genevieve. She looks tired," Chattie replied. "Probably because she's working day and night on her second novel."

"But what an inspiration she is," said Verity.

"Amen," answered Mary Olivia.

"Remember the old adage: Something old, something new, something borrowed, something blue. Let's check you out: An old necklace, a new dress and shoes, Verity's borrowed earrings, and lots of blue. You pass inspection," said Chattie, bringing smiles to Verity and Mary Olivia. "No. One more thing. Rose lipstick and a little rose blush."

"I'm glad you two are here." Mary Olivia applied lipstick and blush. "I would probably forget something. Hose. I forgot to put on my hose. And now I've lost them."

"Calm down. Here they are on the floor." Verity handed her the patterned beige hose.

"Thanks for everything," Mary Olivia said as she hugged her friends. "No way I could have made it today without you two. You find the other girls and make sure they're seated before my wedding. Verity, I'll join you soon."

I am thankful Verity is my matron of honor. The hospital has no piano, so she taped our piano pieces. She told me she would rather stand up for me instead of playing a piano.

As the door closed behind them, Mary Olivia reached for Verity's pearl pendant earrings and put them on. Then her mind went back to dates with Martin.

Our first date in September. You were neatly dressed, so unlike Liam, who insisted on wearing rumpled suits to conventions. You seemed confident — unlike Liam, who lacked self-esteem. You were humble unlike Liam, who was a braggart, talking about himself all the time. You were gentle unlike Liam, who was heavy-handed with the boys and me.

I've forgiven Liam, but it's difficult for me not to see the contrasts between you and him.

You insisted on taking the boys out to dinner with us on our second date. They immediately felt at ease with you. Eric told me later, "It's easy to like a good listener and someone who's genuinely interested in you."

Then our third date. What a night! We went to your favorite Italian restaurant. At the end of the meal, you proposed, and I couldn't wait to say yes. Then you showed me the ring, your mother's, that you'll place on my finger today. That night we talked for hours about our plans. You wanted to get married in December. I suggested a Christmas Eve wedding with green wreaths, red bows, and poinsettias as decorations. You loved the idea. Since we both like the mountains, we decided on the Smokies for our honeymoon. But it wasn't to be.

On our next date you suggested we take ballroom dancing lessons. You said it was something you had always wanted to do. I told you I have two left feet, but I sure would try it. You told me a few days ago we never got to take lessons but every night you dance with me in your dreams. When you said that, it was impossible for me to hide my tears.

Then our date during the first week of November. I felt something was not quite right. At dinner you were unusually quiet. Then you told me you had some bad news. I thought you had changed your mind about marriage, but I didn't say anything. Instead, you said you had met with your doctor for tests the day be-

fore, and your leukemia was back. You asked me if I still wanted to marry you. I remember saying, "Marry you. Of course, I want to marry you. I love you. You're going to be fine." I sensed you were concerned about the leukemia when you said, "I don't think so, Mary O, but I still want to marry you."

Martin. Martin. You stole my heart.

Mary Olivia thought about the night before when Martin's face glowed with happiness as they talked about their wedding. Having memorized their vows, they practiced reciting them to each other. It was their private rehearsal time.

Getting on her knees, Mary Olivia repeated Psalm 46:10, "'Be still and know that I am God.'

"Please, God," she said, "still me now."

"Heavenly Father, thank you for your abiding presence. Thank you for bringing Martin into my life. Please give him a deep inner strength for the days ahead. Help me be his loving helpmate. Knowing that you will never leave me nor forsake me, I give you the glory in the name of Jesus. Amen."

∞

As soon as she heard the prelude, Rachmaninov's "Rhapsody on a Theme of Paganini," Mary Olivia left the dressing room.

Rachmaninov. Enchanting.

She met James and Verity at the door to Martin's room. They were both smiling. Verity gave her a hand bouquet of Shasta daisies and then walked to the side of Martin's bed.

When the wedding march began, Mary Olivia entered the room holding on tightly to her son's arm.

What glorious music for the wedding march. Canon in D

Major by Johann Pachelbel. Martin and I can listen to classical music for hours.

Looking around the room at her friends and Blake standing up in her honor, she felt such happiness. When she saw Eric's smile as he stood near Martin's bedside, she experienced joy again. But nothing compared with her happiness when she saw the glow on Martin's face.

James escorted her to Martin's bed, where he lay propped up on pillows. He was dressed in a royal blue house robe.

"Please be seated," Rev. Goodson said. He paused until the guests sat down.

"We are gathered here today in the presence of God and in the company of family and friends to join Martin Fairchild and Mary Olivia McDuff in holy matrimony, which is an honorable and solemn estate and therefore is not to be entered into unadvisedly or lightly, but reverently and soberly. If any persons can show just cause why they may not be lawfully joined together, let them speak now or forever hold their peace," said Rev. Goodson, pausing for a few minutes.

"Who gives this woman to this man?"

"We do," said James and Eric in unison. After Mary Olivia gave her bouquet to Verity, her sons took Mary Olivia's hand and placed it on Martin's. Eric took his seat.

"I have known Mary Olivia many years," said Rev. Goodson, "and have grown to admire Martin these last few weeks. These two special people have a deep love for the Lord and for each other. Therefore, it is with great joy that I marry them."

Rev. Goodson looked down at the groom. "Martin," he said, "do you take Mary Olivia McDuff for your lawful wedded wife, to live in the holy estate of matrimony? Do you promise to love, honor, comfort, and cherish her from this day forward, forsaking all others, keeping only unto her for as long as you both shall live?"

"I do," Martin said, looking lovingly up to Mary Olivia, a tear falling down his cheek.

"Mary Olivia, do you take Martin Fairchild for your lawful wedded husband, to live in the holy estate of matrimony? Do you promise to love, honor, comfort, and cherish him from this day forward, forsaking all others, keeping only unto him for as long as you both shall live?"

"I do," said Mary Olivia, looking down at Martin and wiping away a tear.

"At this time Prudence Williams will read a sonnet," said Rev. Goodson, who sat down near the bed.

Prudence stood up by her chair. "Martin and Mary Olivia have asked me to read one of their favorite sonnets: Sonnet #43: 'How do I love thee? Let me count the ways' from *Sonnets From the Portuguese* by Elizabeth Barrett Browning. I dedicate this beautiful sonnet to them on their wedding day.

Prudence, you're the perfect one to be reading this sonnet. You once had a fiance you deeply loved.

"I love thee with the breath, smiles, tears, of all my life!" Prudence read with emotion.

Mary Olivia tried to concentrate on the reading, but all she could think of was her love for Martin.

Oh, Martin, truer words could never be spoken. I love you with my entire being.

"And, if God choose, I shall but love thee better after

death," Prudence concluded. She sat down and reached for her handkerchief.

Mary Olivia shed tears for the second time of the afternoon, wiping them from her cheek in as discreet a fashion as she could.

Rev. Goodson rose and stated, "Eric will now read a selection from the Bible."

"Mother and Martin, I want to dedicate these verses from 1 Corinthians 13:4-8 to both of you."

"Love is patient, love is kind...."

What a surprise. Eric didn't tell me he was reading one of my favorite passages. I feel another tear down my cheek. I'm so proud of my boys.

"It always protects, always trusts, always hopes, always perseveres. Love never fails," said Eric and sat down.

What a comfort those words are.

Rev. Goodson stood up and looked down at the groom. Martin repeated the vows after Rev. Goodson recited them:

"I, Martin Fairchild, take thee, Mary Olivia McDuff, to be my wedded wife, to have and to hold, from this day forward, for better for worse, for richer for poorer, in sickness and in health, until death do us part."

Rev. Goodson turned to Mary Olivia. She repeated the vows after her minister recited them:

"I, Mary Olivia McDuff, take thee, Martin Fairchild, to be my wedded husband, to have and to hold, from this day forward, for better for worse, for richer for poorer, in sickness and in health, until death do us part."

In sickness. In death.

Rev. Goodson quietly turned to James for the bride's ring. He gave it to Martin.

Martin placed his mother's ring on Mary Olivia's finger. "With this ring I thee wed," he said, looking into her eyes. "Wear it as a symbol of our love and commitment."

James gave the groom's ring to the minister, who handed it to Mary Olivia.

Placing the ring on Martin's finger and looking into his eyes, she said, "With this ring I thee wed. Wear it as a symbol of our love and commitment."

"In so much as Martin Fairchild and Mary Olivia McDuff have consented to live together in holy wedlock, and have witnessed the same before this company, having given and pledged their troth, each to the other, and having declared same by the giving and receiving of a ring, I pronounce them husband and wife. Whoever God has joined together, let no man cast asunder.

"You may now kiss the bride."

Mary Olivia bent down for Martin to kiss her.

"Ladies and gentlemen, it's my pleasure to present to you — Dr. and Mrs. Fairchild."

Everyone clapped. In the background *Canon in D Major* played softly.

James, Eric, and Blake hugged Mary Olivia and Martin. Then the women had their turns.

"Now for the reception," Mercy said. "We've invited your nurses," she said, looking at Martin. "They helped us set everything up."

"Thank you so much for everything."

"My pleasure," she said. She quickly left to help with the reception.

As Mercy served strawberry punch, Prudence watched as guests picked up finger foods Tea Time Delicacies had prepared.

Mary Olivia asked Martin to excuse her for a few minutes to thank Prudence.

"You chose a wonderful menu. Dainty chicken salad sandwiches. Vegetable and fruit platters." She leaned in closer and squeezed Prudence's hand. "And thank you especially for the beautiful wedding cake.

"Can you please help me wheel the cake over for Martin to see?"

"I will not. It's your wedding day. I'll wheel it myself," insisted Prudence. She pushed the cart with the three-tiered vanilla wedding cake to Martin's bed.

This is one day I appreciate being bossed around.

"It's beautiful," said Martin. He wiped a tear with his handkerchief. "Thank you for making it."

"The blessing was mine." Prudence gently clasped her hands on top of Martin's left hand, "May God bless you both."

I've never experienced such agape love as I have today.

Overcome with emotion, Martin wiped both of his eyes. After composing himself, he asked, "Mary O., don't you love the miniature bride and groom on top of the cake?"

"Yes, my dearest. The bride and groom represent our love," she said, giving Martin a kiss on the cheek. "I'll return soon. I promise. We need to get the cake ready for our guests."

Mary Olivia followed Prudence and the cake back to the

serving area. Prudence cut the cake and gave Mary Olivia the first piece before she served the guests.

Mary Oliva found it difficult to eat when Martin couldn't. She knew she must eat for him. He had told her again last night he wanted her to enjoy herself. She knew he could not eat since he had a feeding tube. She knew also that he was content. He reminded her of the apostle Paul when he said in Philippians 4:11, "I have learned to be content whatever the circumstances."

Within ten days after the wedding, Martin's health declined abruptly. With Mary Olivia by his side, he died two days later.

Mary Olivia called Genevieve a few days after Martin's funeral to invite her, Chattie, and Verity to a Christmas Tea.

"Are you sure?" Genevieve asked.

She understood Genevieve's questioning whether she was up to hosting a Tea, but she assured her she would be fine.

"Absolutely. Martin would have wanted me to invite my friends over at Christmas."

The doorbell rang.

"The girls are a little early, but I've been ready for hours," Mary Olivia said in a whisper. She often talked to herself and to Martin.

She opened the door to find the three loaded down with gifts.

"Merry Christmas," the women shouted in unison.

"Merry Christmas to you too. Come on in. Didn't we agree to buy a small gift for each other?"

"We did. A small one monetarily, but that doesn't mean it can't be in a large package," said Genevieve. "And we have gifts to put under the tree for Blake. Three *Hardy Boys* books for his collection."

"How sweet. He'll appreciate those."

"The outside of your house is so festive. Green wreaths with red ribbons hanging on your door and windows," said Chattie.

"Before Martin's leukemia returned, we had chosen red bows, green wreaths, and poinsettias for our Christmas eve wedding. So in memory of his life and his express wish for me to do so, this Christmas I'm decorating with them outside and all through the house."

"Please show us your tree," said Verity, balancing her gift.

"The tree's in the sunroom," she said. "I hope Martin would have liked it."

The three stared at the tree. Then they placed their gifts around it.

They like it.

"I haven't seen such a beautiful old-fashioned tree since I was a kid. The popcorn strings remind me of Grandma Lottie's tree," said Genevieve, leaning on her cane. "I'm sure Martin would have loved it."

"I'm glad you think so. Blake and I had fun making ornaments. We cut angels, bells, and stars out of cardboard and wrapped them in foil and hung them on the tree. We draped several strings of popcorn on the branches and hung candy canes all over the tree. Then we placed a large star at the top. And, as you can see, we placed several red poinsettias around the tree."

They sat down at a new glass-topped table near the tree. A green wreath around a glass candleholder containing a red candle served as a centerpiece. Christmas dessert plates and mugs along with red napkins and red placemats made it a cheerful setting.

After Mary Olivia gave thanks for the food, she said, "I made our family's favorite Christmas bread, Cranberry Orange Walnut Bread. I hope you like it — and our tea. It's a family tradition at Christmas to have Russian Tea. Help yourself to the tea, teapot with hot water, and silverware."

"What a treat," said Chattie.

"This must be difficult for you," said Genevieve. "Martin was buried only a week ago."

"Of course, it's not easy," said Mary Olivia. "How I miss him. But I know how much Martin loved the Christmas season. He wanted to experience another Christmas, but he knew he wouldn't. I may cry today, but you girls understand. After all, we're all widows. In fact, Genevieve and I are twice widowed."

"That's right. It has been a long time since I lost J.D., but it's like yesterday in my mind. And Shipman. Oh, I miss him."

"I know my time at the monastery prepared me for Martin's death." Mary Olivia passed around the bread. "God sent me there to find a serenity I would need now."

"Praise God," said Genevieve.

I've never doubted Genevieve's deep religious convictions, but I've never heard her voice her spiritual emotions until the last several months. What a difference this year has made to all of us.

"How moist this bread is," Verity said. "I like the flavors of cranberries and orange baked together. Pru needs this recipe. And the Russian Tea one."

"You're getting the recipes before you leave today."

They sipped their tea and continued to eat.

"My wedding seems like a dream now."

"It was beautiful and poignant," said Genevieve. "You both were brave."

"Martin was the courageous one. And he continued to be after he went to the Hospice section of the hospital. I stayed by his side except to eat in the cafeteria. Then the boys relieved me. I read him C.S. Lewis, the Gospels, and Philippians, his favorite epistle. I read poetry from Robert Frost, William Wordsworth, William Blake, Sara Teasdale, Elizabeth Barrett Browning, and Robert Browning. In fact, right before he went into a coma, I was reading Sara Teasdale's poem, 'Barter.' I'll never forget the last two lines: 'Spend all you have for loveliness; Buy it and never count the cost.' He squeezed my hand and closed his eyes. He went into a coma and died that night."

"Fitting last words for the love you had for each other," said Verity.

The three women sipped tea while Mary Olivia stood up and walked to the windows, trying to compose herself.

God, I am weak. I need Your strength to make it through this Tea. "God is my refuge and strength. A present help in times of trouble." Thank you for giving me that verse.

She returned to her chair and sipped some tea.

"The graveside service was moving," said Chattie.

"Martin planned everything except for the poem I selected," said Mary Olivia. "I wanted to recite Anne Bradstreet's poem, but I couldn't. I knew I could count on Prudence to read it. And she did with such expression."

"I wasn't familiar with the poem, but it was the most eloquent I've heard of a love between a husband and a wife," said Chattie.

"'To My Dear And Loving Husband' by Anne Bradstreet, a colonial poet, captured a sentiment I wanted expressed:

If ever two were one then surely we.
If ever man were loved by wife, then thee....

"I had read the poem to Martin; he was genuinely touched that I felt that way about him."

"'Do not let your hearts be troubled. Trust in God; trust also in me.' That selection from John 14:1 was a reassuring one," said Genevieve. "I have the passage written down to be read at my memorial service."

"I'm glad Martin chose it. It was — and is — a comforting Scripture to me."

"Our singing 'Nearer, My God to Thee' was poignant," said Verity. "That song is connected to our nation's history. It was sung while the Titanic sank in 1912. And President William McKinley repeated words from the hymn as he lay dying. And the song was played at the burial of President James Garfield who, like McKinley, was also assassinated. Do you know how I learned all of these fascinating facts?"

"Prudence," said Chattie and Genevieve, almost at the same time.

"You're right. After the service, she gave Mercy and me a history of the hymn."

"I'm glad you shared those stories," said Mary Olivia. "They make the hymn more meaningful to me."

"Martin sensed what you needed at his funeral, didn't he?" asked Genevieve.

"He did. And the end of the service was no different. Our saying the Lord's Prayer together was appropriate. Martin and I prayed it together each morning."

"Mercy liked your putting daisies on his casket," said Verity.

"That was Martin's idea. He knew I loved daisies."

"Have you started settling Martin's affairs?" asked Chattie. "Sorry. I should not have asked that question. I had no right to get so personal."

"You're not, because we never talked about his estate. I'm absolutely clueless about it. I'm meeting with Martin's attorney the first of January. Enough about me. I want to know what you three are doing."

"I don't mind telling you what I'm doing because it helps me to be accountable to each of you," Genevieve answered. "Last February when I told you about writing my first novel, I worked harder than ever because I had to finish it. I felt accountable. Now I'm working feverishly on my second novel about an orphan moving west with a family." Genevieve stopped to rest for a few moments. "The young woman named Agatha falls in love with a handsome and ambitious, but poor, young man named Wallace. Agatha is telling the story in flashback about how God worked in her life. She and her husband, amid many adversities, become wealthy. Then they invest their money in worthy causes."

"Sounds like another good historical romance," said Verity.

"No more autographing at a bookstore," said a smiling Genevieve. "The director of our public library has asked me to do a book signing there."

"Great idea," said Chattie.

"How's your garden work going?" asked Genevieve.

Genevieve always knows how to change the subject. She doesn't want to think about the autographing in October.

"I'm raking the flower beds to get ready for spring planting. And winter bulbs will be coming up soon.

"I have some non-garden news. I learned last week my Aunt Chattie died. I was disturbed because the nursing home didn't call me."

"Why didn't they?" asked Verity, looking concerned.

"The staff neglected to see my phone number on her records. When I called last week to talk to her, I found out she had died in her sleep on Tuesday and that the graveside service was on Thursday.

"I know her friends came to the service, but I wish I had known of her death. I would have flown to Wichita immediately."

"I can appreciate your feelings," said Verity. "We have an elderly aunt whom we cherish."

"How's your dessert business going?" asked Mary Olivia, turning to Verity.

"Busier than we ever expected. We're grateful for the holiday orders. Pru and Mercy are enjoying the cooking. It's helping them cope with Papa's not being with us. Temp is distributing flyers. They're bringing in some orders. Pru hopes to teach Temp how to use the internet so he can maintain a website. He's very smart, but he's been solitary for so many years. We have to be patient. We do see more signs, though, that he's slowly coming out of his shell. One day last week he came in with his shoes polished. Before Eleanor left him, he took great pride in his clothes. He may never be completely normal, but we'll never give up on him. We know God hasn't on any of us."

"I'm thankful He hasn't on me," said Mary Olivia.

"Our desserts are in several tea rooms. Even one in Mississippi."

"Your business is going to be successful," said Genevieve.

"Now, Verity, how about your cemetery work?"

"I have some good news. I'm scheduled to speak about the cleanup of old county cemeteries at the first city council meeting in January. I hope the council members will be interested in what I have to say. I know God has called me to be an advocate for the restoration of neglected cemeteries."

"Your work is vitally important. They have to be interested," said Chattie. "Why don't the three of us plan to attend with you?"

"Great idea," said Genevieve.

"I'll give you the date at our January Tea," Verity said. "I want to remind people that preserving our old cemeteries is not only preserving history, but it's something we can do for those who went before us. They sacrificed a lot. We can at least preserve their final resting places. The restoration of our first cemetery should serve as a model for others. God willing, I want to spread my work eventually to other counties."

"What a vision you have," said Genevieve.

"Now I suggest we open our gifts," said Mary Olivia. "I said I would have recipes for each of you. I've put them on top of your gift."

"I'm ready," said Chattie. "My boys have always said that I'm the most curious person about gifts. They love to watch me shake them and turn them over and over."

"Then you get the first gift from me," said Mary Olivia.

"How creative," said Chattie, after receiving her gift. "Recipes for your delicious Cranberry Orange Walnut Bread and Russian Tea.

"Now what could this gift be?" asked Chattie. "It feels like a book. I sure hope so," she said, unwrapping it quickly. "A coffee table book on Southern gardens. My word! I'll treasure it." She hugged Mary Olivia.

"Now for you, Genevieve."

"Mine is a book also." Genevieve slowly removed the paper after getting the recipes. "A book on the Oregon Trail. My heroine will be traveling the Trail. You can not imagine how much this book is going to help me."

"Verity, here's yours."

"Pru will appreciate the recipes." Verity carefully unwrapped her gift. "How fitting. A coffee table book about famous Southern cemeteries."

"Maybe you will find some ideas for landscaping your cemeteries."

"Great idea. I would like to plant more shrubbery and trees

if I get donations and volunteers."

"Now for your gifts," said Genevieve. "I can't wait."

"First, Mary Olivia, one for you and your boys."

"What could this be?" asked Mary Olivia, unwrapping a large Christmas tin. "Cookies. I've never seen so many frosted sugar cookies. Snowmen, Christmas trees, bells, angels, reindeer. And more. Chocolate chip, oatmeal raisin," she said, lifting the layers of waxed paper between different types of cookies. "A perfect gift. I haven't had time to bake cookies. The boys and I thank you so much."

"We got together," said Chattie, "at Genevieve's house and made dozens of cookies this past weekend. And had a lot of fun doing it."

"Now for the next gift," said Genevieve. "Another gift from all of us."

"I was curious about that large, thin package when you came in."

Mary Olivia opened the gift and didn't say anything but stared at it.

"Well, what do you think?" asked Verity. "Do you like it?"

"I can't believe you remembered my love for Renoir prints. This is absolutely beautiful. *Dancing in Town*. What a gorgeous dress the young lady is wearing. Every time I look at this picture, I will think of Martin and his wish to take ballroom dancing lessons. This print has cheered me up so much. It matches the other one in my bedroom, *Dancing at Bougival*."

"I'm glad you liked the gifts," said Genevieve.

"We're leaving now. I'm sure you need some rest. I'm hosting the Tea at my house in January," said Chattie, following

Verity and Genevieve to get their coats. "I know you've always met in January at a tearoom, but I believe we need each other in a cozy home atmosphere next month."

"I agree," said Genevieve, putting on her red jacket. "Why not change our schedule? We're accustomed to change after this past year. I don't even know whose idea the Tea Room was. It might have been Doll's."

"Verity, wait one minute," said Mary Olivia, grabbing three more gifts from under the tree. "These are for your tree. A cookbook for Prudence, a romance for Mercy, and a book of humor for Temp."

"What excellent choices."

Mary Olivia walked them to the door, where she got a big hug from each of them amid many Merry Christmases.

As she closed the door, tears rolled down her cheek.

Thank you, God, for my precious friends.

She returned to the sunroom and sang along with a CD of "Silent Night."

Silent night, holy night, All is calm, all is bright
Round yon virgin mother and child!
Holy Infant so Tender and mild,
Sleep in heavenly peace, Sleep in heavenly peace.

"Martin. Martin," she whispered, sobbing.

13
JANUARY

NEW HORIZONS

"A desire realized is sweet to the soul."

Proverbs 13:19

I've been reflecting about what each of you did last year," said Genevieve, relaxing in a recliner in Chattie's den. "Tell me what you think."

"Mary Olivia: Fulfilled role of mother and grandmother, discovered calling at a monastery, simplified her life, married a soul mate but lost him much too soon, studying to be a minister."

"Pretty good summary," said Mary Olivia. "But don't forget my hosting our first Silent Tea in April."

And with God's help, I am coping with Martin's death.

"How could I forget that? It was a memorable one.

"Now for you, Chattie: Joined our Tea, grieved the loss of her beloved Roberto, spent much of year in her garden, lost her gardener to another woman, became an expert gardener."

"You're good at this."

And I no longer have terrible dreams about Theo.

"Let me catch my breath. Then I will proceed with Verity....

"Now for Verity: Helped sisters as caregiver for her father, grieved passing of father, found great-grandmother's grave, became advocate for cleaning up neglected cemeteries, and helped sisters and brother start a business."

"It was quite a year you summed up. I would add: 'Hosted first pajama party Tea.'"

And I became a widow.

"How could I have forgotten my first pajama party?" asked Genevieve. "That was a highlight of the year. I'm looking forward to the next one this fall."

"I want to echo what Verity so aptly said: 'It was quite a year,'" said Mary Olivia.

"Now how about me?" asked Genevieve. She looked around to see who would take it on.

"Boldly challenged Tea members to pursue a passion," said Chattie. "worked diligently on a novel, endured disappointment at a book signing, experienced restoration after confessing her secret of having a baby girl decades ago, and now writing a second novel — all this, while constantly supporting and encouraging the three of us."

"Kind remarks, but I've been the one who has been blessed this last year. We had a year of change, joy, and sadness. Our adversities, though, have strengthened us."

And my precious Nora is no longer a secret to her sister.

"I'm reminded," said Mary Olivia, "of what the apostle Paul said in Romans 5:3, 'We rejoice in our sufferings, because we know that suffering produces perseverance; perseverance, character; and character, hope.'"

"I am thankful that out of suffering comes hope," said Verity.

I could not have imagined this time last year that I would feel hopeful now about life. It took Micah's dying. Sad, but true.

"I want us to relax and enjoy our Tea today," said Chattie.

"Sounds good to me," said Genevieve, "since I've grabbed the most comfortable recliner I've ever sat in."

"Roberto bragged about that chair. You deserve a rest even though you put us through a lot of hard work last year."

"Did she ever?" added Verity. "My aching shoulders and back tell the story."

"Stay seated and comfortable," said Chattie. "I'm getting the tea and food."

Chattie brought in a shining green teapot and a dessert.

"I appreciate my teapot set, Genevieve."

"My pleasure. We forgot to mention our give-aways last year."

"That's right. I treasure all of my gifts," Chattie said, unwrapping the dessert. "I hope you like my Pumpkin Squares. It's a family recipe we've enjoyed for years.

'I'm serving buffet style from my coffee table. I'll pour English breakfast tea, one we didn't have last year. Help yourself to the squares and napkins. The cream cheese frosting is a little messy."

"I love Januarys. Cold. Time to think. New beginnings," said Mary Olivia, sipping her tea. "The first of the year is a good time to reflect on our goals. Spiritual first. Then all aspects of life. Each day, though, is one of new beginnings for a Christian. I quote Psalm 118:24 each morning: 'This is the day the Lord has made; let us rejoice and be glad in it.'"

"Well put. You're sounding more and more like a minister," Verity said, winking at her friend.

"Speaking of new beginnings, I can't wait until you girls see my new garden home," said Genevieve, wiping frosting off her chin.

"Garden home?" asked Mary Olivia. "Guess this year we're in store for more surprises."

"Why haven't you told us before?" asked Verity.

Genevieve asked for more napkins. "This frosting is what I would call lip-smacking. Great dessert choice, Chattie."

"The pleasure is mine."

"Where was I?" asked Genevieve.

"I had asked why you hadn't told us about your garden home."

"Yes. Because it has been a recent decision. It will be several months ... before I can move. I have to first clean out my house where I have lived for decades. Can I call upon you, Mary Olivia, to give me advice ... about how to rid myself of all the stuff I've accumulated?"

"Simplify. Simplify. Simplify. You saw it in action in my house."

"That's what I'll have to do since my garden home has only two bedrooms."

"What about your beautiful furniture and accessories?" asked Verity.

"After keeping what I need and those having sentimental value, I'll ask Elizabeth and Jessica to choose what they want."

Genevieve paused a moment to drink some water. "Then I would like you girls, including Prudence and Mercy, to pick out anything you want."

"How generous!" exclaimed Verity. "Genevieve, you're truly a kind-hearted friend."

"They are just things. Too many things I don't need or have space for. Maybe you girls will find a few treasures. That way when I'm gone you will remember me."

"You don't have to worry about our forgetting you," said Chattie. "Besides, you're going to be around for a long time."

"My book deadline is June, so I hope you're right. And I've got an idea for a third novel. But now I need your prayers that I can complete this one."

"I'll pray daily that God will give you strength to finish the novel," said Mary Olivia. "I know the power of prayer. So many people prayed for Martin and then for me after his death. I felt the prayers and continue to feel them."

"Of course, I'll pray along with Pru and Mercy," said Verity. "Beginning last January we prayed daily for each of you that God would guide you with your challenge. We'll continue to pray this year."

"I appreciate the prayers," said Genevieve. "Last year I prayed for each of you morning and evening. I should have. I was the one responsible for all of your work."

"I confess my prayer life changed last year," said Chattie. "Before then, I was a selfish pray-er who didn't pray consistently for others — including friends. The year before, I was praying for the boys and primarily for myself for God to help me with my grief. He did. He brought each of you into my life."

"I'll have to admit it wasn't until my monastery visit," said Mary Olivia, "that I started praying daily for you three. My quiet time listening to God has enhanced my intercessory prayer time. Getting closer to God has shown me how much I need to pray for my friends."

"Our friendships have deepened our prayer lives," said Chattie. "Our prayer lives have deepened our friendships. Does that make sense?"

"It sure does," said Verity. "'A friend loves at all times.' Proverbs 17:17. I believe a friend who loves prays. Remember when Job prayed for his friends — those three who gave him a difficult time — God blessed him with 10 children and numerous animals."

"I'm grateful," said Mary Olivia, "to know my closest friends are praying for me as I grieve for Martin."

"Can you tell us about Martin's memorial service?" asked Chattie.

"The college is holding a service the last day of this month. I've worked with the professors in Martin's department to plan the tribute. Verity is playing 'Ode to Joy,' one of his favorite songs. One of the professors will speak about Martin's devotion to his students. Dr. Goodson will read some of Martin's favorite Bible passages. Prudence is singing 'Amazing Grace'. We'll close with the congregation singing 'A Mighty Fortress is Our God.' It will be a simple service but a moving one."

"What a beautiful recognition of Martin's life," said Genevieve.

They each had another Pumpkin Square and silently ate

until Verity remembered to tell them something.

"The city council will meet next Tuesday. Hope you can be there when I plead for the city to get involved in cleaning up our neglected and forgotten cemeteries."

The women agreed they would attend the meeting to support her.

"Thanks so much. Now I must not forget to tell you, Chattie, how much I enjoyed your gardening column in Saturday's paper. Pru clipped it for her garden files."

"I appreciate your encouragement. I thought it appropriate in my first column to share my experience as a gardener these last ten months."

"I was touched that you dedicated it to Roberto," said Mary Olivia.

"Roberto appreciated nature. And he would be proud of my work."

"How did your column come about?" asked Genevieve. "I was surprised but so pleased to see it."

"I was both humbled and surprised when the newspaper editor asked me at the end of December to write a gardening column. I agreed because I fell in love with gardening this last year and want to share what I've learned. The column will revolve around the seasons. Next month I plan to write about forsythias and quinces. In March I am focusing on azaleas. Probably dogwoods in April. It will be a continual learning experience for me as I explore gardening and its history. Who knows? One day I may try to syndicate the column. By the way, can anyone guess who recommended me as a columnist?"

"Girls, in unison, let's answer," Mary Olivia said with her

hands in the air like an orchestra conductor.

"Theo," they shouted.

"Thought you might guess. Theo told the editor I was an expert gardener."

"How sweet of him," Mary Olivia said, drawing out the word *sweet*. "I confess I'm being sarcastic on purpose. I've forgiven Theo. But it's hard to forget how he surprised you out of the blue with his impending marriage."

"It was a surprise, but I jumped to the wrong conclusion about Theo. We had never kissed. I probably was infatuated. By the way, he and his high school sweetheart were married on New Year's Eve. Theo called me a few days ago to tell me to help myself to any plants from his garden. Since his house is still for sale. I plan to dig up some. Does anyone want any plants?

"Pru certainly would," said Verity.

"I may get some. Probably would be good for me," said Mary Olivia.

"I may take a few for a container for my garden home," said Genevieve. "That is, once I get moved."

"Looks like we'll be meeting at my old boyfriend's garden soon," Chattie said. "And we'll be sure to dig up some naked ladies."

They laughed.

"I can at last laugh about Theo. This time a year ago I was happy to finally be laughing after Roberto's death. I could never have guessed the last year would have been so full of heartaches. And joys."

"Remember laughter is good for the soul," said Mary

Olivia. "I've read that experts say we need eight good laughs a day. We're reaching our quota today."

⁂

"Now for my January announcement," said Mary Olivia.

"It can't be as jolting as the November one," Genevieve commented.

"Oh, no. It's a welcome and a humbling one. Martin, of course, left me everything in his will. Quite a windfall. His spartan lifestyle was one thing that drew me to him. It's all such a dream. Our wedding. Then his death. And then this money. I know he planned it this way. Of course, he wanted to marry me, but he also wanted me to be financially secure.

"I want to be a good steward of the money and also make Martin proud."

"You have already," said Verity.

"I'm headed back to the monastery for a weekend whenever I can find an opening. After everything that has happened, I need to go. Martin would approve."

"We both lost our loves — yours to death, mine to another woman. I don't think I can allow myself to get close to another man."

"Come on, Chattie," said Mary Olivia. "Who knows? God may have another gardener for you."

"I better not take another chance on a gardener. Maybe a butcher. Don't need a baker. I had the best baker in the world. I could find a candlestick maker at a colonial village," said a smiling Chattie.

"You remember your nursery rhymes, and you sure are witty today," said Verity. "I think Genevieve's wit has rubbed off on all of us. Mercy even thinks I'm wittier."

"Mercy is the witty one," said Genevieve. "I detected that soon after meeting her."

"Yes, but her wit is a result of her naiveté," said Verity.

"Then more of us should be naive. Too many cynical people in our world today," said Genevieve. "I try to cheer up any cynics I meet."

"And you're good at it," said Mary Olivia. "I've almost forgotten to mention I'm starting a Christian book club next month. We'll meet every two months and will be reading some of the greatest Christian books of all times. We're starting with Augustine's *Confessions*. If you would like to join, let me know. Right now, my son Eric, a professor from Martin's religion department, an attorney from my church, and I are the only ones committed to coming."

"I better limit my clubs to the Tea until I complete writing novels," said Genevieve.

"My gardening column and gardening projects are about all I can handle now," said Chattie.

"I'm planning to attend," Verity said. "Pru may also. It's something Papa would welcome."

"Great. Six potential members. All we need to get started. The book club is something Martin would think a worthwhile endeavor."

"Girls," said Chattie. "I know this is going to seem coincidental coming right after Mary Olivia's announcement. I was the sole beneficiary in Aunt Chattie's will. I'm not receiving a lot of money because Aunt Chattie left most of her property to her church. She stipulated that the church sell her property and buy a home where missionaries can stay while on leave."

"What a great idea," said Mary Olivia. "Sometimes missionaries are home for months."

"Now back to the money I inherited. Like Mary Olivia, I plan to use the money wisely. My vision is to set up a hands-on gardening class for special needs students at the Hope Center."

"Marvelous idea. Children need to know about gardening," said Genevieve. "It was a common activity of our forefathers."

"And Verity, I want to provide trees, shrubs, and flowers at the cemeteries you're cleaning up."

"I'll take you up on that generous offer. Flowers will bring natural beauty to the cemeteries."

"Now to change the subject to something else I want to do with Aunt Chattie's money." Chattie paused a moment.

"I'm inviting you to England with me this summer for a tour of English cottage gardens."

"England? Wow! I've never been out of the country," said Verity. "How generous you are."

"Thanks. But Aunt Chattie is applauding from heaven now. She would think it delightful for me to take my friends to England."

"I'm convinced your Aunt Chattie wouldn't mind your spending her money on a tour," said a smiling Mary Olivia.

"I'm inviting Prudence and Mercy also."

"They will be ecstatic. Especially Mercy. I can hear her now: 'Me go to England? I can't believe it. What do I wear? I'll have to buy new clothes. I may see the Queen.' I can't wait to tell them."

"I'm getting excited planning the trip. I hope to get many ideas for my gardening column. I'll be writing one from England."

"If that doesn't impress your editor, nothing will," said Genevieve.

"Let's spend some time in London," said Mary Olivia. "I've *always* wanted to go to Westminster Abbey. Many famous people are buried there. I want to see Chaucer's and Charles Dickens' and Robert Browning's graves. I know I can spend hours in that famous cathedral."

"Hold on. I thought I had the monopoly on graves," said Verity.

They had a good laugh.

"After our stay in England, let me treat all of you to Martin's ancestral home in Scotland. I'll finance that with the money he left me."

"Sounds absolutely wonderful to me," said Verity.

"I have a surprise I've learned about recently. I have an Irish great-great-grandfather. My mother never talked about her mother's side of the family — the crazy side, she called it. Grandma Jessie said he talked strange. What she didn't know was this strange talk was Irish. Seems there's an Irish plantation owner in my ancestry."

"How interesting. Why don't we go to Scotland and Ireland next summer?" asked Chattie.

"I hope I can make this summer's trip. You know I'll be 78 next month."

"You're in fairly good health," said Mary Olivia. "People much older than you travel all the time."

"And you'll have the five of us with you to help you if you have any problems," said Verity.

"You've convinced me. Something to look forward to when I finish my novel. Our impending trip will make me work harder."

Genevieve paused, as if she were looking for the right words to say.

"I want you girls to know that this staid Presbyterian has grown spiritually this last year due to God and your examples. Mary Olivia, you showed such strong faith during Martin's illness and death. Verity, your family's strength in dealing with your loss was exemplary." Genevieve paused a moment. "And Chattie, your resiliency and joy even while grieving for Roberto as well as your disappointment at love, was inspiring. I want to thank each of you for your impact on my life this last year — and continued influence.

"This last year has surely been an adventure for each of us. Should I issue another challenge for this year?"

"Fine with me. But I'll have no time for a man," said Mary Olivia. "I'll be studying. And still grieving over Martin."

"Sure. Why not? But I'm not interested in another man," said Chattie. "I'll be busy planting flowers and dividing plants for others."

"O.K. with me. Maybe I'll meet a proper gentleman," smiled Verity. "Preferably one who doesn't mind old cemeteries."

APPENDIX

THE HISTORY OF ENGLISH & AMERICAN TEA

Tea time in England dates back to 1662 when Queen Catherine, the wife of Charles II, introduced tea as a social and family habit.

The afternoon Tea as an English institution dates to 1840. The 7th Duchess of Bedford (Anna Maria Stanhope, 1783-1857) is recognized as the creator of afternoon Tea. Because the Duchess had a light noon meal, she was hungry by four o'clock. She started inviting friends for an afternoon meal at five o'clock in her rooms at Belvoir Castle in Leicestershire County, now Rutland County, England. She served tea along with small cakes, bread and butter sandwiches, and other desserts. Her summer practice became so popular that when she returned to London she invited friends to join her for tea. Other social hostesses soon picked up her practice.

In both England and America in the late 1880s, fine hotels began offering tea service in Tea Rooms and Tea Courts.

Today Tea Rooms are found all over America in small towns and large cities. Fine hotels also offer tea services.

HOW TO MAKE A PERFECT CUP OF TEA

Fill a china or earthenware teapot twice, and pour the water (purified water) in a kettle. Bring water to a full, rolling boil.

Bring the teapot to the kettle, and fill it with the boiling water. Put the kettle back on the stove, and bring it back to a full boil.

Let the teapot sit with the hot water in it for 2-3 minutes to warm it up. Then pour out the water.

Add one teaspoon of tea* per cup of tea to the teapot, plus one for the pot. (You can also place the tea in an infusing basket).

Add the boiling water (that has come to a full boil) from the kettle to the teapot, put the lid on, and cover the teapot.

Allow the tea to steep for 3-5 minutes.

Pour the tea into a cup (china is preferable) using a tea strainer.

Have cream, milk, sugar cubes/sweeteners, and lemon slices available for guests.

Enjoy.

*You can also use tea bags. You can skip some steps by having boiling water in your teapot. Then place your tea bag in your cup and pour the hot water over it and let it steep for two to three minutes.

DESSERT RECIPES

CHAPTER 1: JANUARY

Basic Scones or Tessie's Lemon Yogurt Scones
Lady Grey Tea

Basic Scones

2 cups all-purpose flour
1 tbsp. baking powder
¼ tsp. salt
¼ cup sugar
½ stick butter, cut into pieces
1 egg, beaten
¾ cup milk (heavy cream or sour cream can be substituted)

Mix the dry ingredients together in a medium bowl. Cut in the butter with a pastry blender or fork until the mixture resembles course crumbs. Stir in the egg. Gradually add the milk until a thick dough is formed. Turn out the mixture onto a floured board or waxed paper with a heavily floured surface and knead lightly. Roll out the dough to ¾ in. thickness and cut into rounds with a 2 in. cookie cutter.* Place the rounds on a lightly greased baking sheet or on a lightly greased piece of foil placed on a baking sheet. Brush the tops with a little beaten egg or milk. Bake 450 degrees oven for 10-15 minutes until golden brown. Serve warm with jam.

*Or pat the dough into a 1-inch thick round and cut like a pie into 8 pieces. Place them on baking sheet lined with lightly greased foil about 1 inch apart.

Tessie's Lemon Yogurt Scones

2½ cups unbleached all-purpose flour
3/8 cup sugar
1 tbsp. baking powder
Grated zest of 3 lemons
¼ tsp. salt
½ stick cold unsalted butter, cut into pieces
2 large eggs
½ cup heavy cream
3 tbsp. lemon yogurt
1 tsp. lemon juice

Preheat oven to 400 degrees. Line a baking sheet with lightly greased foil. In a medium bowl, combine the flour, sugar, baking powder, lemon zest, and salt. Cut in the butter with a pastry blender or fork until the mixture resembles coarse crumbs. In small bowl, whisk together the eggs, yogurt, lemon juice, and cream. Add to the dry mixture and stir until a sticky dough is formed. Turn out the dough onto a floured surface (waxed paper dusted with plenty of flour is good) and knead with floured fingers and hand about six times. Pat the dough into a 1-inch thick round and cut like a pie into 8 pieces. Place them on the baking sheet about 1 inch apart. Sprinkle the tops with sugar. Bake until golden brown about 15 to 20 minutes. Serve immediately with butter and lemon curd. You can heat the extra scones in the microwave later. Freeze any leftovers in freezer bags.

CHAPTER 2: FEBRUARY

Frosted Heart Sugar Cookies with Easy Frosting
Dipped Strawberries
Italian Cream Cake
Earl Grey Tea

Frosted Heart Sugar Cookies

1½ sticks of butter, softened
¾ cup granulated sugar
1 tsp. vanilla
1 egg
4 tbsps. milk
1 cup all purpose flour
1½ tsp. baking powder
¼ tsp. salt

Cream butter, sugar, and vanilla. Add egg. Beat until light and fluffy. Stir in milk. Sift together dry ingredients. Blend into creamed mixture. Divide dough in half and cover bowl. Chill an hour. On lightly floured surface, roll one half to 1/8 in. thickness. Use cookie cutters to cut into heart shapes. Then repeat with the other half of dough. Bake on greased cookie sheet at 375 about 8-10 minutes. Cool slightly. Remove from pan. Makes 2 dozen. Top with desired frosting.

Easy Frosting

1 cup powdered sugar
2 tbsps. butter, softened

milk

Mix sugar and butter. Add milk (1 tablespoon or more) until you have spreading consistency. Add a drop or two of red food coloring. Frost cookies.

Dipped Strawberries

24-30 ripened washed strawberries
4 cups sweet chocolate chips. (Semi-sweet chocolate or white chocolate can also be used.)

On a low simmer in a double boiler, melt the chocolate chips or microwave them in a microwave-safe bowl. Holding the stem of the strawberry, dip each strawberry, one at a time, into the chocolate. Cool them on a sheet of wax paper until hardened. Dip the same day you serve them.

Italian Cream Cake

2 cups sugar
1½ sticks butter, softened
5 egg yolks
2 cups flour
1 tsp. soda
1 cup buttermilk
1 tsp. vanilla
5 egg whites, stiffly beaten
1 small can flaked coconut, about 1 1/3 cups
½ cup pecans (optional)

Frosting:
1 8 oz. package cream cheese, softened
1 box powdered sugar
½ stick butter, softened
1 tsp. vanilla
¼ cup chopped pecans

Cream butter and sugar; mix well. Add 5 egg yolks one at a time, beating well after each. Combine flour and soda. Add to creamed mixture alternately with buttermilk. Stir in vanilla. Add coconut. Fold in 5 stiffly beaten egg whites into batter. Pour into 3 greased and floured cake pans. Bake at 350 degrees for 25-30 minutes or until cake is done. Cool.

Frosting: Beat cream cheese and butter until smooth. Stir in sugar. Add vanilla and beat until smooth. Spread on cake layers. Sprinkle top with chopped pecans, if desired.

CHAPTER 3: MARCH

Great-Grandmama Ida's Tea Cakes
Lipton Decaf. Tea

Great-Grandmama Ida's Tea Cakes

4 cups flour
2 cups sugar
1½ tsp. baking powder
½ tsp. baking soda
¼ tsp. salt
2 sticks butter, softened

2 eggs
½ cup buttermilk
1 tsp. vanilla
Pinch of nutmeg

Preheat oven to 350 degrees. In a large bowl, mix all ingredients into a firm dough. Roll out on a floured board and use a biscuit cutter or glass tumbler to make circles. Bake on lightly greased cookie sheet 10 to 12 minutes until golden brown. Cool. Freeze any leftovers.

CHAPTER 4: APRIL

Banana Nut Bread
Green Tea

Banana Nut Bread

2½ cups all-purpose flour
3 tsps. baking powder
¼ tsp. salt
1 cup sugar
½ stick soft butter
1 egg, beaten
1 cup mashed ripe bananas (3 small bananas)
1 tbsp. grated orange peel or lemon peel
½ cup milk
½ cup coarsely chopped walnuts or pecans

Preheat oven to 350 degrees. Grease a 9-by-5-by-3 inch loaf pan. Sift flour with baking powder and salt; set aside. In medium bowl, with portable electric mixer or wooden spoon, beat sugar, butter, and egg until smooth. Add bananas, grated orange peel (or lemon peel), and milk, mixing well. Add flour mixture, beating just until smooth. Stir in nuts. Pour batter into prepared pan. Bake about 1 hour, or until cake tester or knife inserted in center comes out clean. Let cool in pan 10 minutes. Remove from pan. Cool completely on wire rack. To serve, cut with bread knife into thin slices.

CHAPTER 5: MAY

Strawberry Cream Cheese Fruit Tarts
White Tea

Strawberry Cream Cheese Fruit Tarts

Quick Crust:
For a quick crust, use frozen pie shells and cut into 2 in. circles and press into muffin tins. Also, crescent rolls can be used. Roll out the dough and seal the perforations and cut out circles. Graham cracker crusts can also be used.

Homemade Crust:
1 stick softened butter
1/3 cup sugar
½ tsp. vanilla
1¼ cup flour
¼ tsp. salt

Cream butter and sugar together until fluffy. Add flour, salt, and vanilla and beat together. Separate into 2-3-inch balls.

Press into muffin tins.

Filling:
8 ounces cream cheese
$\frac{1}{4}$ cup sugar
1 egg
$\frac{1}{2}$ tsp. vanilla flavoring

Beat ingredients together. Place in muffin tins about 2/3 full. Bake at 375 degrees for 12-15 minutes until crust is golden brown. Cool. Top with thinly sliced strawberries.

CHAPTER 6: JUNE

Cucumber Sandwiches
Gingerbread
Earl Grey Tea

Cucumber Sandwiches

$\frac{1}{2}$ seedless cucumber, peeled and very thinly sliced
Salt
Pepper
Vinegar
Whipped cream cheese
Whipped Butter
White, wheat, rye, or oatnut bread

Sprinkle vinegar and salt and pepper on cucumber pieces. Place in colander and drain for at least 20 minutes. Place cucumber slices between layers of paper towels to remove excess moisture. Make sure all moisture is drained before making sandwiches.

Remove crusts of 8 pieces of bread. Butter each of four pieces of bread. Spread whipped cream cheese on each of four slices of bread. Spread cucumber slices on the buttered piece. Then place the bread with whipped cream cheese on top. Repeat for the other three sandwiches. Slightly mash down the sandwiches. Cut into triangles. Watercress leaves and/or alfalfa sprouts can be used on top of the cucumbers if desired.

Gingerbread

1½ cups sifted flour
1 tsp. baking soda
1 tsp. ginger
¼ tsp. salt
3 tbsp. soft butter
½ cup sugar
1 egg
½ cup molasses
¾ cup boiling water

Sift together flour, baking soda, ginger, and salt. Using electric mixer cream butter until light and fluffy. Add sugar gradually. Beat in egg. Blend in molasses. Gradually stir dry ingredients into creamed mixture. Beat thoroughly. Stir in water. Turn into greased and floured 8" square pan. Bake at 350 degrees for 40 minutes. Serve warm. Top with applesauce or whipped cream.

CHAPTER 7: JULY

Blueberry Sour Cream Muffins
Sweet Southern Iced Tea

Blueberry Sour Cream Muffins

1 stick unsalted butter, softened
1 cup light brown sugar, packed
2 large eggs, beaten
½ cup sour cream
1 tsp. vanilla extract
2 cups white flour
2 tsps. baking powder
pinch of salt
1 cup fresh or frozen blueberries

Preheat oven to 375 degrees. Grease muffin pans. Beat butter with sugar until it is light and fluffy. Beat in eggs and sour cream and vanilla. In another bowl, stir together flour, baking powder, and salt. Add dry ingredients to wet and stir just until blended. Fold in blueberries. Don't overmix or muffins will be tough. Spoon the batter into a prepared pan and fill about 2/3 full. Sprinkle some sugar over the muffins and bake for about 20 minutes until lightly browned. Let muffins cool in pan for 5 minutes and then place on a rack.

CHAPTER 8: AUGUST

Peach Sour Cream Muffins
Iced Peach Tea

Peach Sour Cream Muffins

1 stick unsalted butter, softened

1 cup light brown sugar, packed
2 large eggs, beaten
½ cup sour cream
1 tsp. vanilla extract
2 cups white flour
2 tsps. baking powder
pinch of salt
3 large peaches, finely chopped

Preheat oven to 375 degrees. Grease muffin pans. Beat butter with sugar until it is light and fluffy. Beat in eggs and sour cream and vanilla. In another bowl, stir together flour, baking powder, and salt. Add dry ingredients to wet and stir just until blended. Fold in diced peaches. Don't over mix, or muffins will be tough. Spoon the batter into a prepared pan and fill about 2/3 full. Sprinkle some sugar over the muffins and bake for about 20 minutes until lightly browned. Let muffins cool in pan for 5 minutes and then place on a rack.

CHAPTER 9: SEPTEMBER

Lemon Squares
Lady Grey Tea

Lemon Squares

Crust:
1 stick butter, softened
¼ cup powdered sugar
1 cup all-purpose flour

Filling:
2 eggs, well beaten
1 cup sugar
½ tsp. baking powder
1/8 tsp. salt
2 tbsp. lemon juice
1 tsp. finely grated lemon zest from 2 lemons

Crust:
Preheat oven to 325 degrees. Cream butter and powdered sugar together. Gradually add flour, being sure to combine all ingredients well. Press mixture over bottom of ungreased 8 x-8 inch or 9 x 9-in. pan. Bake 20-25 minutes until lightly browned.

Filling:
Beat eggs until well blended. Add sugar, baking powder, salt, lemon juice and grated lemon zest. Beat until light and fluffy for 2-3 minutes. Pour over hot crust. Bake at 350 degrees for 25 to 30 minutes. Sprinkle with powdered sugar, cool, and cut into squares.

CHAPTER 10: OCTOBER

Fresh Apple Cake
Earl Grey Tea

Fresh Apple Cake

2 cups sugar
¾ cup Canola oil
½ cup applesauce

3 eggs
3 cups all-purpose flour
1 tsp. salt
1 tsp. soda
1 tsp. vanilla
2 tsps. ground cinnamon
1 tsp. allspice
3 or 4 apples, peeled and diced
¾ cup chopped pecans

Combine sugar, oil, applesauce, and eggs in large mixing bowl. Beat well. Combine flour, salt and soda; add to sugar mixture and beat well. Stir in vanilla, cinnamon, allspice, apples, and pecans. Batter will be stiff. Spoon batter into a greased bundt pan. Bake at 325 degrees for 45 to 60 minutes. Cake is done when firm to touch. Serve plain or with whipped cream or pour glaze over hot cake.

Optional glaze for apple cake:
1 stick butter
1 cup brown sugar, firmly packed
¼ cup evaporated milk
1 tsp. vanilla flavoring
½ tsp. maple flavoring

Combine all ingredients in heavy saucepan. Bring to a boil and cook, stirring constantly, for 5 minutes. Beat about 1 minute with a spoon. Pour over hot cake.

CHAPTER 11: NOVEMBER

Cream Cheese & Pineapple Sandwiches
Sweet Potato Pies
Mint Tea

Cream Cheese & Pineapple Sandwiches

1 8 oz. pkg. cream cheese, softened
1 8 oz. can crushed pineapple, drained
½ t. vanilla
¼ cup chopped dark red cherries (optional)
10 slices whole wheat or whole grain bread

Mix together cream cheese, pineapple, and vanilla. Stir in cherries. With a sharp knife, trim the crusts of the bread. Then spread the filling on the bread. Cut into desired shapes. Serves five.

Sweet Potato Pies

3½ cups cooked mashed sweet potatoes (4-5 medium potatoes)
1 stick butter, softened
2 cups sugar
4 eggs
½ tsp. nutmeg
½ tsp. allspice
¼ tsp. salt
1 13-oz. can evaporated milk
1 tsp. vanilla

Two 9-in unbaked deep pie shells

Cut potatoes into large pieces. Cook them with jackets on. Cool and remove peelings. Combine potatoes, butter, and sugar in a large bowl, mixing well. Add eggs one at a time, beating well after each addition. Stir in spices, salt, evaporated milk, and vanilla extract. Pour into pie shells. Place on cookie sheet. Bake at 425 degrees for 20 minutes. Reduce temperature to 325 degrees. Bake for 30 to 45 minutes longer or until pie is done (not soft in middle).

CHAPTER 12: DECEMBER

Cranberry Orange Walnut Bread
Russian Tea

Cranberry Orange Walnut Bread

½ cup fresh cranberries, chopped
2 cups all-purpose flour
1 cup sugar
1½ tsps. baking powder
½ tsp. baking soda
¼ tsp. salt
½ cup walnuts, chopped
1 egg
¾ cup milk
¼ cup orange juice
½ stick butter, melted
1 tsp. vanilla flavoring
grated zest of one orange (1 tbsp.)

Preheat oven to 350 degrees. Grease a 9x5x3 in. loaf pan. Wash cranberries and chop well. Combine flour with sugar, baking powder, soda, and salt in large bowl. Stir in cranberries and walnuts. In a small bowl, beat with a whisk — eggs, milk, butter, and vanilla. Make well in center of cranberry mixture. Pour in egg mixture and grated orange zest. Stir just until dry ingredients are moistened. Turn into loaf pan. Bake 55 minutes or until golden brown on top and toothpick inserted in center comes out clean. Cool in pan 10 minutes. Remove from pan; cool on wire rack. Serve thinly sliced.

Russian Tea

2¼ cups orange flavored instant breakfast drink (such as Tang)
1 cup sugar
½ cup instant tea
1 tsp. ground cinnamon
1 tsp. ground cloves

Mix all ingredients together. Store in a covered glass jar. Use 2-3 teaspoons per cup of hot water or mix according to your taste.

CHAPTER 13: JANUARY

Pumpkin Squares with Frosting
English Breakfast Tea

Pumpkin Squares

1 cup sugar
1 cup flour

1 tsp. baking powder
½ tsp. soda
½ tsp. pumpkin pie spice
1 8 oz. can pumpkin (½ of can)
1/8 tsp. salt
¼ tsp. cinnamon
½ cup canola oil
2 eggs
½ cup chopped pecans

Mix dry ingredients together in large bowl. Add ½ cup oil (or substitute 1/4 cup oil and 1/4 cup applesauce) and eggs mixing well. Fold in pumpkin and nuts. Make sure mixture is well blended. Pour into 13" x 9" greased pan. Bake approximately 20 to 25 minutes at 350 degrees. Cool and frost.

Frosting
8 oz. of powdered sugar
4 oz. of cream cheese, softened
½ stick butter
1 tsp. vanilla

Mix together and spread over cooled cake. Cut into squares.

BOOK CLUB QUESTIONS

General Discussion Questions

1. Which of the four widows do you most admire? Why?
2. Which character do you think changed the most in the

novel? Explain.

3. Which minor character was your favorite? Why?

4. Quotations introduced each chapter and were sprinkled throughout the book? Do you have a favorite one? Why do you like it?

5. Tea is served each month at a widow's house. Each setting is different. Which particular one appealed to you the most? Why?

Chapter 1: Chattie

1. What adjective do you think best describes each widow at the end of the first chapter?

Genevieve

Chattie

Verity

Mary Olivia

2. Could you choose a dream/interest and pursue it passionately for a year? Do you have one you would like to embrace now?

Chapter 2: Genevieve

1. *Nothing is ever perfect* is Genevieve's reaction when Chattie comments, "Everything looks so perfect." Did you think Genevieve's thoughts were a foreshadowing, a hint/clue to suggest what will happen later? Did you notice other foreshadowing in the novel? If so, give examples.

2. After the widows find out about Genevieve's throwing herself a birthday party at the Tea, Mary Olivia responds that they

should have brought gifts. Genevieve said, "I didn't want gifts. I don't need more things." What does this comment show about Genevieve's wants/desires at the age of 77?

Chapter 3: Verity

1. *How ironic my name is. One day I hope to live up to it.* When Verity thought this, did you suspect she had secrets? Why?
2. Verity's father, Rev. Isaiah, named his children Verity, Prudence, Mercy, and Temperance. Why did he choose these names? Do you know what your name means? Are you living up to the meaning?

Chapter 4: Mary Olivia

1. Have you ever gone to a monastery to think/meditate/grow closer to God? If not, would you consider going to one? Does one have to go away from home to get close to God?
2. How do you think a vow of silence for a day/days would change your life?

Chapter 5: Chattie

1. Chattie likes one of her late husband's favorite phrases: "Bask in the Moment." What does that phrase mean to you?
2. How did you respond to Chattie's gardener's name — Theodore Root? Have you known people whose professions or demeanors were related to their names?

Chapter 6: Genevieve

1. Genevieve undertook a project that wore her out physically. Have you ever pursued something that was physically exhausting? Why does God want us to rest?
2. Were you surprised about Genevieve's candor about her sex life? Mary Olivia said, "God created sex to be a beautiful experience between a husband and wife in love." How has much of our society rejected this view?

Chapter 7: Verity

1. Did Verity's confession to her father surprise you? Have you ever confessed a secret to someone, and like Verity, experienced "an overwhelming sense of relief"?
2. Rev. Isaiah left a great spiritual legacy to his family. The widows and Prudence and Mercy shared spontaneously about their own legacies. Which one touched you the most? Have you considered what legacy you want to leave to your family and friends?

Chapter 8: Mary Olivia

1. Mary Olivia said that decluttering her house was easier than discarding wrong attitudes such as her cynicism. Do you need to discard bad attitudes in your life?
2. After confiding she was studying to be a minister, Mary Olivia said: "I may have 20-40 years left. None of us know how much time God has for us to accomplish His purposes for our life." Because people are living longer, what implications do

Mary Olivia's statement have for you? (Note: Mary Olivia is 61.)

Chapter 9: Chattie

1. Chattie is disturbed because she is having sinful thoughts and dreams about Theo? Is a widow/woman vulnerable to these thoughts when she works closely with a man? What does the Bible say about lust? (Read Matthew 5:27-28).
2. Chattie showed her three friends a garden bed filled with each of their favorite flowers. She had garden stakes with the flowers named after her friends. What does this labor of love show about Chattie?

Chapter 10: Genevieve

1. In this chapter Genevieve has a disappointing book signing and an emotional breakdown after telling her friends about her baby who died six decades before. Have you ever confided anything to friends that made you emotionally overwhelmed? How did your friends react to your news? How do true friends react?
2. At the end of the chapter, Genevieve thanked God for lifting her heavy burden. How can Jesus help us with our burdens? (Read Matthew 11:30.)

Chapter 11: Verity

1. Verity experienced a sense of freedom after learning of Micah's death. She was finally a "real" widow. Reading the Bible

and prayer helped her with her guilt feelings. She claimed Psalm 103:12. Have guilt feelings ever plagued you? What verses have you claimed?

2. The widows have a fun-filled pajama party at Verity's home. What positive bonding can take place with women when they are in an informal setting?

Chapter 12: Mary Olivia

1. What was your response to Martin and Mary Olivia getting married? Do you think their love was an "agape" type of love? (Refer to Mark 12:30-31 and 1 Corinthians 13:4-8).

2. Why do you think Mary Olivia needed to host a Christmas Tea with her friends so soon after Martin's death? What does it say about the friendship among the widows?

Chapter 13: New Horizons

1. Genevieve said that the women in the past year experienced change, joy, and sadness; but their adversities strengthened them. Mary Olivia then quoted Romans 5:3 — "We rejoice in our sufferings, because we know that suffering produces perseverance; perseverance, character; and character; hope." Have your adversities strengthened you? How?

2. In Proverbs 13:19 we read: "A desire realized is sweet to the soul." After a year pursuing a dream, do you think the four widows can relate to this verse? Why?

Suggestions for book clubs on how to use the book to enhance their meetings:

1. Discuss the book at a tea where the hostess chooses one of the recipes in the appendix to serve.
2. Have members dress up in hats for a formal English Tea.
3. Invite several widows (if you do not have any widows in your club to attend the book club and get their insight into the book.

Made in the USA
San Bernardino,
CA